Naked

Naked

A Novel of Lady Godiva

ELIZA REDGOLD

St. Martin's Griffin ☙ New York

NAKED. Copyright © 2015 by Eliza Redgold. All rights reserved. Printed in the United States of America. For information, address St. Martin's Press, 175 Fifth Avenue, New York, N.Y. 10010.

Designed by Molly Rose Murphy

www.stmartins.com

The Library of Congress Cataloging-in-Publication Data is available upon request.

ISBN 978-1-250-06615-2 (trade paperback)
ISBN 978-1-4668-7366-7 (e-book)

St. Martin's Griffin books may be purchased for educational, business, or promotional use. For information on bulk purchases, please contact the Macmillan Corporate and Premium Sales Department at 1-800-221-7945, extension 5442, or write to specialmarkets@macmillan.com.

First Edition: July 2015

10 9 8 7 6 5 4 3 2 1

For my beloved daughter, Jessica, who has amazing hair.

I waited for the train at Coventry;

I hung with grooms and porters on the bridge,

To watch the three tall spires; and there I shaped

The city's ancient legend into this:

——Tennyson [1842]: *Godiva*

Author's Historical Note

A Love Story to Change History

We all know the legend of Lady Godiva, who famously rode naked through the streets of Coventry, covered only by her long, flowing hair. Or have seen her portrait, even if adorning a box of Belgian chocolates. So the story goes, she begged her husband Lord Leofric of Mercia to lift a high tax on her people, who would starve if forced to pay. He cruelly demanded a forfeit: that Godiva ride naked on horseback through the town. It's something many twenty-first-century women might balk at even for charity—calendar girls aside. There are various happy endings to Godiva's ride: that all the townsfolk of Coventry closed their doors and refused to look upon their liege lady, and that her husband, in remorse, lifted the tax. Other additions to the tale include the famous Peeping Tom (who actually appeared in the sixteenth-century versions of the myth) the only one of the townsfolk who couldn't resist a glance who was struck blind.

Though the legend has lasted for centuries, being revived peri-odically, often during periods of change and liberation in women's lives, there's dispute over exactly what, if anything, Godiva wore on her famous ride, or even if it occurred. Historical fact and a good story don't always go hand in hand. Some historians certainly call it a myth. Yet there's no doubt that Lady Godiva was a real person who lived in eleventh-century Anglo-Saxon Engla-lond. Whatever the facts, she has remained captivating.

Lady Godiva, or Countess *Godgyfu* in the Anglo-Saxon version of her name, spent some of her life in what is now called the British Mid-lands. The area surrounding Coventry is heavily industrialized and bears little resemblance to the largely rural land of her time when it would have been interspersed with villages huddled around common pastureland. Close by, the Forest of Arden would have stretched for many more wooded miles than it does today. As it was to Shake-speare, Arden would have been well known to Godiva.

In my telling of the story I've placed Godiva and Leofric in 1023, at a time not much is known about either of them. Leofric and Godiva's names first appear entwined in records in 1035. Their mar-riage was believed to be some time before.

Anglo-Saxon Engla-lond was a tough time and place for a woman. Constant Danish invasion by those later called Vikings, though the Saxons called them Danes, occurred many times in the tenth and eleventh century. By Godiva's lifetime, the Dane law was the rule in much of East Anglia and the English eastern coast. Records suggest that Godiva was more than equal to the challenges of her day. Her name appears in records as the only female landowner who retained her lands not only against the Danes but also later against the Nor-man invasion of 1066. Her status as a landowner indicates that she inherited her own estate. I have placed Godiva firmly as the heiress and defender of "the Middle Lands." Saxon noblewomen could inherit and govern property and some were certainly warriors. Many were also peace weavers or in old Anglo-Saxon *fripwebba*. These women were known to marry a man from an opposing tribe to establish peace or end war. Queen Wealtheow, Godiva's heroine in *Beowulf*, was such a woman. To be a peace weaver was a mantle of honor worn by any Saxon wife who kept the peace in her home, brave and loyal.

It was also the right of Saxon noblewomen to approve their own husband—upheld by a ruling of King Canute, the Danish king on the throne in England at the time I have set this story. Godiva may well have chosen Leofric. In his lifetime, he was a Saxon hero who fought hard against the Danish invasion. Godiva and Leofric's enemy, Thurkill the Tall, was also a real person who at one stage took control of Mercia during Lord Leofric's lifetime as part of a Danish attempt to quash the mighty Saxons. When and where he died is uncertain. But his name would certainly have been known and was probably a curse to Leofric and Godiva.

I have woven real historical events together with Leofric and Godiva's fictional love story as well as embroidering the legend. However, ancient records suggest their marriage was a strong one, and may indeed have been a love match. By the end of their marriage, Leofric and Godiva together supported monasteries, built abbeys and churches, and aided the poor, with the help of Brother Aefic of Evesham. The original cathedral in Coventry was founded by Godiva and Leofric as a monastic site. Godiva also donated rich garments and jewelry to the city, including bequeathing a valuable silver necklace.

History has been hard on Lord Leofric. In most of the Godiva stories Leofric of Mercia is definitely the villain of the piece, ready to impose heavy taxes and to ignobly allow his wife to carry out her daring ride. Yet by the end of his life, historical documents reveal Lord Leofric was a changed man. My explanation: he fell in love.

My research revealed other interesting facts about Leofric—if facts they be at all. He had three brothers, the elder, Northman, and two younger, Godwin and Edwin. Rumors in the early eleventh century do imply he betrayed his brother Northman and aligned with King Canute but there is limited historical evidence of such a fraternal betrayal. It could easily have been propaganda. As I continued to investigate I became convinced such stories about him were unfounded. Leofric of Mercia was no *huscarl*, though there were many Saxon noblemen who joined King Canute's secret mercenary force. In my view, Leofric of Mercia was not one of them. Was Edmund a *huscarl*? Did he exist? Was there someone else in Peeping Tom's house? We'll never know for sure.

We do know that Leofric and Godiva had a long marriage. They had one son, Elfgar, who became the Earl of Mercia after Leofric's death in 1057. His daughter Eadlgyth—Godiva's granddaughter— had two marriages, the second to Harold II, the King of Engla-lond who was killed in the Norman invasion of 1066 led by William the Conqueror. Godiva's family became not merely Saxon nobility but Saxon royalty.

It's the legend of Lady Godiva herself that has stood the test of time. Rides as penitents like the one Godiva undertook were practiced in that period—though Godiva's nakedness was certainly unique. By all accounts, whether fact or fiction, she was a unique woman. Her courage continues to inspire us, her story to be told, even after a thousand years.

According to the *Domesday Book*, approximately seventy families lived in Coventry in Godiva's lifetime. Today it has 300,000 inhabitants. In Coventry city center is Godiva's Trail: the location of her famous ride. You can walk or ride the marked trail and there are plenty of delights to be found for the Godiva fan. Another Godiva tourist site is medieval Spon Street where Godiva is said to have completed her journey. On the site where she is believed to be at rest with her lord, not far from where she made her famous ride, Godiva's spirit still lingers in the air with Leofric's.

Loyalty. Self-sacrifice. Passion.

True love.

Laid bare.

Eliza Redgold
St. Agnes' Eve, 2014 AD

The woman of a thousand summers back . . .
———Tennyson [1842]: *Godiva*

Naked.

My fingers shook as I unclasped the golden eagles of my belt. Yet it wasn't the lukewarm sun that made me tremble.

The metal belt turned warm in my grasp as I traced my fingers around the eagle's wing.

No. Don't think of it. Don't remember.

But his face came to me, leaning over me, reaching for my body in the rose gold of dawn.

In a splash of silver my keys slipped from the belt, onto the dirt.

Aine picked up the keys, prised the belt from my hands.

So hard to let go.

"Your husband should never have forced you to do this, my lady. It's cruel."

"Hush." My words were swollen, like my eyes, with unshed tears. "He has his reasons and I have mine."

The clasp of my cloak.

My fingers fumbled.

Aine took over as if I were still a child.

The clasp came free.

More silver.

More pain.

The swoop of a swallow's wing from around my shoulders.

My brown cloak.

Gone.

Aine swathed it over her arm.

My red tunic.

A sunset flash over my head.

Gone.

Now only my white shift remained.

The linen drifted between my legs, gentle as fingers.

Only one man's hands had touched me there, just as gentle.

No.

Aine stepped forward, stepped back. "I can't do it, my lady."

"Please. Help me."

In surrender I raised my arms.

My lashes fanned closed.

The scent of lavender.

Soft weave across my face.

The shift fluttered away.

Naked.

I shuddered.

"Courage, my lady," Aine urged. "Let courage clothe you now."

The first chime rang out to strike the midday hour.

Naked

"Let the bells ring. I'm ready to ride."

Ebur whinnied. Leaning close I sought the rough comfort of his mane.

The church bell chimed again.

Aine made a step with her hands.

My braid flew.

Astride.

As I turned toward the main street I began to recall what had led me to this. To this fateful hour. To this naked ride.

"Your hair, my lady!" Aine shouted behind me. "Your hair!"

I

In Coventry:
——Tennyson [1842]: *Godiva*

From the top of the hill I could see it all.

The Middle Lands. The land of my people, the land of my *cyn*, my kin. The land I loved.

Below the town lay, its streets fanned like the bones of a fish, thatched roofs still dappled with late winter snow. Smoke curled from the roof holes, above the cauldrons cooking on the flames, full of hearty *briw*. My stomach rumbled.

Beyond the town, the smaller villages clustered like children at a mother's skirts. Nurtured by the farming land, green and white fields striped here and there with brown. Sheltered by the wildwoods of Arden. Sacred, magic, too far to see. Where I loved to ride.

At one end of the main street our thatched hall loomed, tall and proud within its pickets, the watchtower pointed high. At the other soared the cross of the new church my father had built. A Christ's mass gift for my mother, for the town.

"I won't stop there," he'd vowed. "I'll rebuild our church and our hall, not in wattle and clay, but in stone. Here in the Middle Lands we shall have a fortress, a castle fit for a king and queen, with strong walls and a watchtower that can never be burnt. I'll build in stone, yes, in stone."

"Better to have castles made of wood than made of air, Radulf," My mother had teased.

In reply he'd laughed. "Indeed, Morwen. But dreams must come first."

Dreams must come first.

Leaning forward, I raised my face, as a snowdrop seeks a slant of sun.

I, too, had dreams.

Strong hands clenched my waist.

"What's this?" A voice hissed in my ear. "All alone, without your bodyguard?"

My boots skidded in the mud as I whirled around.

He kissed me.

He'd kissed me before. A friendly peck on the cheek, a brotherly benison on the brow, a playful lingering on the lips.

Not like this.

Hungry. Demanding.

His teeth, sharp, teasing, opened my lips, sucked me in, and sent me spinning. Into the whirlpool of his arms he wrenched me closer.

My hands around his neck. His hands under my cloak. Our bodies pressed together. No space between.

The clean metal smell of his mail-shirt. The water taste of his tongue.

Searching. Devouring.

Out of the vortex. Out of his arms. I managed to twist away.

Dizzy.

"That's what happens when you're out alone without your bodyguard."

Encased in their leather my legs stuttered as I tried to move. I refused to ride in a long shift, sidesaddled. Leather tunic and leggings like a man, brown, tight. Boots to my thighs. Sure of my strength.

But he'd caught me unawares.

"Edmund." I gasped. "You're my bodyguard."

Lightning cracked across his face.

When he'd come to Coventry as a child, so thin, so scared, he'd never smiled. Not for months, as I'd tempted him to play in the courtyard, my wooden sword at my side. Still lean, even now, but tall and strong, a sapling grown. A man.

"A *cniht*, a knight, at last." He'd gone on campaigns with my father. Earned his status. Made me proud. "And now I'm to leave you again. What kind of bodyguard is that?"

"*Cnihts* have to attend the Witan. There'll be other guards here in Coventry."

"But do they know you as I do?" Sleek-footed, he shifted near. "Will they guess where to find you? Up on this hill? Out in the wildwoods?"

He touched the tip of the bow slung on his back. "I'm the only one who can hunt you down."

My stomach eddied.

Still dizzy.

"Godiva. Tell me before I go. You know what I want. Let me speak to your father."

"I'm not ready."

Fist on hilt he drew back, his eyes silver shields.

It wasn't what I expected to say.

It wasn't what he expected to hear.

He turned away, but not before I'd seen disappointment reflected in those grey mirrors. Anger, too.

"Edmund." My fingers on his sword arm. "When you're home from the Witan I'll give you an answer."

Darting away I sped down the hill to where my horse waited. "I'll race you home."

His boots pounded. "You've had a head start. And no acrobatics!"

"Try and catch me!"

On the wind Edmund's voice chased after me. "One day, Godiva."

"Hold still, my lady."

Aine tugged my hair as she began to braid.

"Where were you this afternoon?"

"Up on the hill."

"Alone?"

I shook my head. No need to ask who'd been with me, not for Aine. Small and dark, she'd come with my mother from the west, where many of the old ways still held fast. Herb craft and healing and an uncanny knack of knowing what others were thinking before they spoke. Some of the other servants were wary, giving her a wide berth, muttering about magic. But my parents trusted Aine completely.

An expert twitch. The braid over my shoulder, tied firm with wool.

"There now." She picked up the brown cloak lying on the bed. "All you need is your . . ."

She stumbled.

"Aine!" I grabbed her arms and held her upright. "What is it?"

Her cheeks had paled. "A sight."

"Sit down. Let me get you some water."

Still clutching my cloak she shuddered onto the bench next to the fire.

From the earthenware pitcher I filled a cup and passed it to her. "Tell me what you saw."

After drinking deeply she shook her head. "It's not clear."

"But you saw something."

"Someone. A face," she admitted reluctantly.

"Whose face?"

"It was too quick. All I know is that I'll be glad when your parents have returned from the Witan."

"Should I tell them you've seen something?"

"No need to worry Lady Morwen."

"But if you've had a premonition—"

Aine stood up. With the cloak she mantled my shoulders. "I don't know what it was. I'm all right now. Go."

"You don't want me to stay with you?"

"Go to your parents." With a gentle push I was out the bower door.

Snowflakes dusted my cloak. The wind gnawed and bit. My fur collar muffled against the cold, I raced across the courtyard.

On the bottom step I paused. I'd always loved that moment, just before entering. Outside. Looking in.

Hall-joy tonight.

From within I could hear the talk and laughter. Chinks of light framed the windows, hung from inside with cowhide blankets. At the

8

center of the hall the fire would be glowing, its flame-shadows flickering on the walls. Shield-bronzes gilded, timbers honeyed. Candles ablaze in iron-fist clusters, beacon high on the painted beams. Trestle tables folded out to welcome all.

Soon the mead cups would be full.

Smoke rising from the chimney. Pork roasting on the spit. Even in the open air I could smell it.

I'd been hungry on the hill. Now I was famished.

Through the carved doors.

Safe. Warm.

Snowflakes melted to water drops as I threw back my hood.

On the dais were my parents. Around them thronged the *cnihts,* the most trusted warriors of our bodyguard. Strong men all. Yet none were as imposing as my father, his cloak clasped with the silver sparrow-hawk, amber at the eye. An extraordinary substance, he'd showed me. It could withstand fire.

Beside him, my mother. Gowned in red, garnets banded her hair. Brown-gold. The same shade as my own. Behind her woven tapestries brightened the paneled walls. Scenes of battle, hunting, dancing, feasting. Stitched by her needle.

I'd almost reached them when I spied a flaxen-haired girl standing by the fire.

"Beolinda! I didn't know you were coming."

We embraced tightly.

"My father brought a message. Of course, I begged to come, too."

"Can you stay long?"

"Well, that depends." She scanned the crowd.

"Edmund's not staying in Coventry." I grinned. "He's going to the Witan."

9

She sighed. "He's such a *Saxon*. So blond and tall. But he doesn't notice me."

"I'm sure he notices you." The hourglass shape beneath Beolinda's tunic had attracted many a warrior's attention.

"Not really." She pouted. "He cares only for you." She seemed to have caught Aine's gift of premonition. "Your parents would be pleased."

"Pleased about what?"

"If you married Edmund. He's *cniht* to Lord Radulf now, isn't he, and the best shot in the Middle Lands. Once I saw a marksman split an apple on top of a girl's head." Her smile curved. "I'd let Edmund do that to me."

Edmund made his own arrows. Elm wood. Iron-tipped. That he was the best shot in the Middle Lands sometimes irked. I rarely enjoyed being bested.

But my pure grey gelding, Ebur, had beaten his bay stallion home.

"The Middle Lands will be yours one day, after all," Beolinda said. "You'll need a lord to rule the shire."

"I need no lord, not even Edmund," I retorted.

"Taking my name in vain?"

I spun around.

"That's the second time today you've caught me unawares."

That lightning smile.

Into the vortex.

"Then you should be on your guard." His grey cloak rippled as he took my arm. "I chased you all the way home. Come and eat."

"Hello, Edmund." Lashes fluttered.

His smile flashed. "Hello, Linda."

Another crack.

Beolinda. Struck.

Naked

At the high table she engineered to sit beside him, while I took my usual place next to my mother.

Raising his goblet, my father stood up. "The hawk-eye is mine! To Coventry!"

"To Coventry!"

The responding cry rang to the rafters. Below, the trestle tables were packed with departing warriors and their families. Townsfolk, too, squeezed in.

"Was Radulf hail! Was Morwen hail!"

Knives drummed the wood.

As he sat down, my father gestured to the brown-garbed man at the foot of the table. "Will you say grace, Brother Aefic?"

Bowing his shaved head, the monk intoned the words. The familiar Latin washed over me. *Benedictus, benedicat, per Jesum Christum Dominum Nostrum . . .*

"Amen," my mother murmured.

"What do you expect of the Witan, *Fader*?" I asked when my trencher had been filled, hot pork still crackling from the flames.

"A wise council of lords, I hope, but it's long overdue. In these times we Saxons must stand together, in spite of our differences, or the Danes will soon overrun the whole of Engla-lond."

"The Danes." My mother shook her head. From her ears gold glinted. "They continue to plague us."

Edmund scowled. "And we have their Dane law here."

"If you can call it law," my mother added.

"They mock the Saxon way." Edmund gripped his meat-knife. "Our laws respect our people, whatever their rank. A Saxon will always support another Saxon."

My father exhaled. "The Danes rule by force. Not by justice. They're a ruthless race."

"It's an insult that King Canute, a Dane, is on our English throne. It's wrong they rule us." Edmund's skin had flushed.

How well I understood his anger. In the Angle Lands to the east, Edmund's family had been lost to the Danes. Once he would have inherited landholdings far greater than mine, but now they were gone. My father had fostered him, taking him on as a squire before he became a *cniht*, trained to be skilled with the blade, to defend and uphold the Saxon way.

It had taken time for us to become friends. He'd been wary, I shy. He hadn't wanted to play with a girl. But when I'd routed him with my wooden sword, he'd understood I was a girl to be reckoned with.

"How much Saxon land has fallen now?" Beolinda asked.

My father seized a russet apple from a trencher. Pushing his goblet aside, he placed the red fruit at the center of the table. "Here in the Middle Lands we're safe under Saxon rule."

"Thanks to you, Radulf." My mother patted his arm.

He placed another russet to the left. "To our west, in your homeland, Morwen, the Welsh Lands have resisted Danish invasion."

One russet more set below. "To our south, Wessex remains Saxon."

With a frown he positioned a yellow apple to the right of the central russet. "But to our east, in the Angle Lands, the Danish grip is brutal. Under the Dane law many Saxons are slaves."

Angry muttering among the warriors. Edmund, tight-lipped.

Now my father weighed a yellow apple in one hand, a russet in the other. "But good news has come from the north, from Mercia, where the Danes have so long held sway. I have news of Thurkill the Tall."

I drew in my breath.

Naked

"What good news can be brought of a Dane who has plundered Saxon lands and killed good Saxons? Burning homes, killing livestock, and looting churches?" My mother's usually gentle tone was harsh.

"That he has been defeated."

Cheers went up in the hall.

"Thurkill the Tall has been overthrown in the north by a Saxon Lord. Leofric of Mercia."

Casting the yellow apple aside my father dropped the russet onto the table, above the central one representing the Middle Lands. Transfixed, I watched as the Mercian apple rolled and collided with the one below. They lay, touching each other.

Leofric. The strangest sensation came over me when my father said the name. As if I'd heard it many times before. As if I'd spoken it myself.

"Leofric of Mercia? Who is he?" I asked.

"The new earl. Leofric is young but bold. He led a daring campaign against Thurkill and the Danes to regain the north."

"God be praised!" My mother said. "I've long feared for us."

My father squeezed her ringed fingers. "Fear no more. Although his title has been granted by King Canute the Dane, I'm told the new earl is a good Saxon."

"Will he be at the Witan?" I wondered.

"I expect to meet him. What's said of him impresses me. It's to be hoped that young lords such as Leofric of Mercia will restore the Saxon way. But whether he can stop Thurkill the Tall, and the Danish push for land, we shall see."

"You think the Danish peril is upon the Middle Lands?" Edmund demanded.

"Our lands are small, but our position in the heart of Engla-lond makes us mighty."

Edmund nodded. "At the center is power."

Later, when we were eating an apple pudding flavored with honey, the gleeman took up his place in front of the fire and began to sing.

In a low tone no one else could hear, my mother murmured to me. "This Witan Council is important, Godiva. We won't be gone too long and I want to be with your father. That's how you know the man you love. The days are longer when you're apart."

Her attention moved to Edmund, deep in conversation with my father, Beolinda hanging on his every word. "It's a Saxon noble-woman's right to choose the man she wishes to marry."

Many girls were married much younger than me. I'd been given time.

Now Edmund wanted my answer.

"As heiress to the Middle Lands, you must choose wisely." From her belt my mother took some silver keys. "We'll talk more when I return. We charge the care of Coventry to you while we are gone. Hang these from your belt and let them remind you of your duty to our people."

Cool and heavy. The keys had hung around my mother's waist for as long as I could remember. "I'll wear them, *Moder*. I promise."

For a moment I wondered if I ought to tell her of Aine's fore-knowledge. But she turned away to speak to my father.

The gleeman began to beguile me. When I was small I'd fallen asleep at the table listening to the tale of Beowulf, lulled by its row-ing rhythm. As my mother carried me to the bower I'd awoken from a dream filled with warriors, battling the monster Grendel.

"Were they real?" I'd asked, half asleep, my arms twining her neck.

"Were who real, my sweetheart?"

"Beowulf. The heroes of the past."

Naked

"They're as real as you would have them be, Godiva. As real as love or courage or honor or kindness. Though we can't see these things, they are all that matter."

Her words floated back to me as the gleeman sang.

From down the table, Edmund smiled.

In a flash I knew what my answer would be.

2

The people: therefore, as they loved her well,
——Tennyson [1842]: *Godiva*

"God's greeting, Lady Godiva!"

"Good morning, my lady!"

"God's greeting!" I called.

Once, Edmund had challenged me. I'd claimed to be able to recognize by sound and smell every landmark in Coventry town.

A blindfold around my head, our hands gripped tight.

Out of the hall, down the steps, into the courtyard.

The smell of lanolin and dye. The weaving house.

Baking bread. Roasted meat. The kitchens.

Past the servants' quarters. Past the storerooms.

Mint, rosemary, lavender, rue. The herb garden.

Horse manure. Hay. My nose had wrinkled. The stables.

Through the gates, into the street.

Every step of Coventry, under my feet.

Past the slosh of the water mill.

Raucous shouts, the yeast of *beor* and ale. The tavern.

Curing animal hide. A stench that made me sick. The tanner's.

Past more houses.

The mooing and baaing of cattle and sheep. Wrangling between the shopkeepers and farmers, to get the best price. The market square.

The taste of sawdust on my tongue. The carpenter's shop.

A burst of heat on my cheeks from the blacksmith's anvil. The forge.

Every step of Coventry town. I knew.

We'd laughed as Edmund ripped off the blindfold. Lifted me off my feet.

I laughed again, remembering.

"God's greeting, my lady!" The blacksmith called now, hard at work with his wheezing bellows.

"And to you!" I waved and smiled.

Onward. More houses. At a round, thatched cottage I dipped my head beneath the low doorway. Edmund had hit his forehead on the beam more than once.

"Walburgha?"

Wiping her hands on the homespun tied around her ample waist, she hastened to the door. "Lady Godiva! Come in!"

She bustled to the fire at the center of the room.

"Wilbert! Make way!"

The thin, grey-haired man who sat whittling silently offered me his bench. For years he'd made me toys. Horses, sheep, ducks.

"Thank you." I smiled.

A cough, a shy smile in return.

"Sit down, that's right," said Walburgha. "Now, what can I get you? My bog-myrtle *beor*?"

I'd sampled Walburgha's bog-myrtle *beor* before. My head had ached for a week. "It's early for me, Walburgha."

She beamed. "A honey cake then, the kind you and young Edmund always like so much." She rarely let us past her door without sampling them.

Warm and sweet-smelling. She pressed it on me. As usual, it melted in my mouth.

"Are you sure you're not thirsty, my lady? Be sure to say if you change your mind." Dragging close another bench she settled down on it. "Busy out there on the streets, isn't it, my lady? With market day and all. Why, I can recall this town being not much more than a village. Can't I, Wilbert?"

Wilbert nodded.

"Your father must be pleased with how Coventry has grown. And now he's gone to the Witan! Our own lord!"

Copying Wilbert, I nodded. His main communication with his wife was via gesture.

"And Lady Morwen gone with him!"

"My mother asked me to deliver this to you." From my pocket I retrieved a pottery bottle, safely stopped with wax. It had mandrake in it, to ease bone ache. "Aine made it for you."

Aine's herbal remedies were much in demand, even if the townsfolk were suspicious of her. Beolinda had returned home accompanied by many pots and jars.

"She's been driving me mad," Aine had grumbled in private. "A lotion to remove my freckles. An oil to make me smell sweet. A rinse to brighten my hair. On and on, vain as you please."

I'd chuckled. I'd enjoyed Beolinda's company even if she did only talk about her appearance. And Edmund.

Edmund.

My stomach whirled and rippled. He'd return from the Witan soon and I'd have to give him my answer.

Since Beolinda had left it had been quiet without him, although it had given me time to think.

By contrast, right now it was comforting to just listen to Walburgha's cheerful chatter.

"Your sainted mother!" she exclaimed. "The kindest lady in all of Engla-lond, our Lady Morwen. Always thinking of others, even in her times of trouble. Why, I remember when you were born. How happy our lord and lady were! God's Gift, they named you. What a feast we had! What mead! What mutton!"

Wilbert managed to get a word in. "When will your parents return?"

Cake crumbs caught in my throat. "I expected them last week."

Few families were as close as ours. Like a milking stool we stood strong on three legs. Without them I felt wobbly, uncertain.

Wilbert's brow furrowed.

"Thank you for the cake, Walburgha." I got to my feet. "It was delicious."

"You can have some *beor* next time."

Wilbert touched his brow. "Blessings on you."

Walburgha patted my arm as she showed me out. "Your parents will soon be back. God willing."

"God willing."

At the end of the street I opened the lych-gate, creaking new on its hinges. I hadn't planned it. But my feet made the pilgrimage.

I slipped a veil over my hair. I kept it tucked in my belt, next to my knife. I ought to wear it more, I supposed.

Cool and quiet, inside the church, a splash of holy water on my skin. No one else knelt inside. The curved, clay walls an embrace. Above the carved oak altar soared the painted cross. Its colors depicted gospel scenes, chosen by my mother. Our Lord with children. *Suffer them to come unto me.* Her favorite verse.

Let children come.

My parents had longed for a son.

Years. Hidden tears. I'd vowed to be both son and daughter to them.

The sign of the cross on my forehead, my shoulders, my heart. I prayed, though I couldn't give words to what I prayed for. I could only hope my prayers would be answered.

Some time later I went outside.

I yanked off my veil.

"Oh!"

By the lych-gate lounged a pale-skinned young man.

"God's greeting, my lady."

"To you also, Tomas." I tried to hide my dislike of the town tanner. It wasn't his fault he stank of curing hides. His expression was bland, yet even as a child I'd discerned something shifty in his protuberant eyes. They reminded me of pale green feaberries, that some in the town called gooseberries.

An awkward silence developed as he made no move to step out of my way.

"Will you be holding the *althing*, the shire meeting, my lady?"

"The *althing* will be held next week as usual. If you have any matters to bring, you can bring them to me, just as you do to my father."

The tip of his tongue darted as he licked his lips. "And will we pay you the taxes, too?"

"Of course." I bent my mouth into an unwilling smile. "Whether my father is here or not, the taxes must still be collected." There were many taxes paid in the shire by farmers and townsfolk alike, as well as a market tax. In turn we paid taxes, including a *heregild* to the Danish king on our throne, something my father bitterly resented. They'd been raised time and time again.

"Only asking, my lady." At last he shifted to let me pass by. The smell of hide-cure invaded my nostrils.

As I walked away, his feaberry eyes seemed to burn into my back.

Townsfolk streamed into the hall as the new church bell rang from down the street. Amongst them was Wilbert, his tools in his pocket. Walburgha, too, a hemp kerchief tied under her chin. The innkeeper. The blacksmith, ruddy-cheeked from the forge. Tonsured Brother Aefic, still visiting from the monastery at Evesham. Tomas the tanner, lurking at the rear.

Country folk, too, had come. Farmers, their wives, and their children, from all across the Middle Lands. On foot, in ox-carts.

More than a hundred, I estimated.

Up on the dais I prepared to address the crowd. I'd clothed with care. A clean white shift embroidered at the hem with swirls and circles. A pale blue twill tunic, to shade with my eyes. Sky-colored, my mother called them. Sometimes grey. Sometimes blue. My leather-plaited belt, with my knife and white linen veil square tucked into it. A string of blue wool, tied to fasten my braid. My wolf-collared cloak. And my sword. The treasure my father had given me, with the hawk-eye upon the hilt. Such as he always wore at an *althing*. For justice.

Nerves flickered in my belly. All were quiet as they waited for me to speak.

"Welcome, good people of the shire of the Middle Lands. The *althing* has begun. As was my father's practice to hear your concerns and collect the taxes, so today this is my duty. Be assured that any appeals will be heard fairly. Also be assured that my justice against wrongdoing will be swift."

A scan of the crowd. Walburgha and Wilbert nodded their approval. Surly Tomas lowered his feaberry gaze.

"Who will speak first today?"

"My lady . . ."

Wilbert had just stepped forward when a scuffling came at the door. An oak crash, hard as a fallen tree, it was flung open.

Edmund rushed in, but an Edmund I'd never seen before. Grey-faced, disheveled, travel-stained.

"Godiva."

He came beside me on the dais so quickly I hardly saw him move. A hush fell over the hall.

The scent of metal and sweat came as he reached inside his cloak. Silver and amber.

An extraordinary substance. It can withstand fire.

Into my hand he pressed the sparrow-hawk.

Into my heart.

"Tell me." A harsh caw of pain, such as the black-winged ravens made. Battle birds, callers of omen, bringers of grief. "I must know what happened."

Edmund pushed back his cloak. On his shoulders his metal wings gleamed. Torn through in places, patches of the cloak were dark red. I didn't dare imagine what they must be.

"An ambush."

Blunt words, the blow of an axe. I reeled, my legs hardly able to hold me upright.

In my clenched fist the brooch pin tore at my flesh. My father's body would have had to be cold for it to be taken from him. It had clasped his cloak and his father's before him.

"Who did this? Who killed my parents? Was it the Danes?"

"Thurkill the Tall."

My heart thudded its terrible truth.

The worst of the Danes.

"He caught us unawares."

"My father was never caught unawares by anyone."

"We were outnumbered three to one. The Danes were hiding and heavily armed. We did all we could to fight them off and your father—"

"Yes?" I whispered.

"He died fighting, Godiva, defending your mother."

Pain knifed my gut. As if a blade had found me instead. "My father would have fought to the last to protect his own. And my mother. Did she—did she suffer? She didn't deserve to suffer."

Edmund evaded my eye. "She didn't suffer long."

Was he telling me the truth?

"This loss is immense for the Middle Lands, and for all Englalond." Edmund moved beside me. "Lord Radulf was a fine Saxon and a great warrior. His *wergild* will be great."

The price of a man's *wergild* was equal to his honor. A payment to the family left behind. A Saxon custom the Danes abused. "No amount of money can replace my father."

Shocked townsfolk gathered around us. Wilbert, wiping his nose. Walburgha, flooded with tears.

"I'm sick at heart I couldn't save your parents. As a *cniht* of the Middle Lands, I would have laid down my life for them." Edmund's arm shielded my shoulders. "And for you."

If he'd been lost, too . . . I shuddered, leaning against him. "I know you would have done everything to defend them. All that could have been done."

"And I'll continue to do so, I swear. We'll avenge them, Godiva. Both Lord Radulf and Lady Morwen. You'll have my sword in battle at least."

My pulse began to gallop with fear. "In battle? What do you mean?"

"I bring worse news."

"God's breath! What worse could there be than our lord and lady gone?" Walburgha wiped her cheeks with her kerchief.

"Thurkill the Tall is on his way to Coventry."

3

Light horrors thro' her pulses . . .
——Tennyson [1842]: *Godiva*

"The Danes!"

Cries of horror flew above my head. I raised my hand.

The townsfolk quieted.

"How close?" I demanded.

"Just days away." Edmund's angular face stretched taut. "Thurkill and his men have crushed our eastern borders. They're moving across the Middle Lands, taking the villages, one by one."

More cries to the beams like frightened pigeons. "The Danes!"

"They'll kill us!"

"We'll all be burned in our beds!" Walburgha shrieked.

Wilbert raised his chisel. "We'll fight 'em!"

"We haven't got a chance." Tomas the tanner scoffed. "The town will be cinders."

"The Lord be with us," prayed Brother Aefic.

"We must flee!"

"To where?"

Flight wouldn't save us.

And the Danes would take no more from me.

We charge the care of Coventry to you while we are gone. I'd made my mother a promise in this very hall.

Fight. Save our people.

Shifting away from Edmund, my fingers fumbled as I attached the brooch to my cloak. I stepped up on the dais.

"People of the Middle Lands!" From the pit in my stomach I raised up my breath. "Don't be afraid! By my oath, Coventry will never burn."

The babble dropped, died away. Lids wide. Mouths ajar.

"Good men and women! I am the daughter of Lord Radulf and Lady Morwen." My speech faltered on my mother's name. I heaved another breath. "Terrible is our grief at their murders. I vow to avenge them and all the people of Coventry, against those who took the lives of their lord and lady."

Lifting my cloak, I revealed the shining silver sparrow-hawk. The amber gleamed.

"The hawk-eye is mine! No one will take these lands as long as I live. To arms! Call men who would bring the Middle Lands honor. Summon all those who can come, with whatever weapons they have."

"Get our axe, Wilbert!" Walburgha called shrilly. "Nice and sharp it is, our axe, Lady Godiva."

"We will need your axe. Every weapon will be needed. Go quickly to your homes and families. Make ready!"

Panic. Pushing. Babbling. They began to pour out of the hall.

Talisman—tight, still clutching the brooch, I descended from the dais. Edmund put his fingers on my cheek. I moved away, my shoulders squared.

This was my battle. I had to stand alone.

Fist on hilt, he drew back. "We suffered grave losses, Godiva. Your father had his best warriors with him. There's a chance we may be overcome."

"There's no chance." Such doubt was sacrilege. "Thurkill the Tall will not take Coventry."

"Make way! Make way!"

The tower watchman, puffing for breath, pushed through the crowd and rushed to the dais.

"Lady Godiva! Riders approach!"

"Already?" Surprise flashed across Edmund's face. "That can't be . . ."

The sparrow-hawk released from my furled fingers. "How close?"

"Just beyond the town, my lady."

Too close.

Through the throng of townsfolk, shrieking louder now. Out of the hall.

My cloak, a sail giving speed. Across the courtyard, Edmund on my heels. My sword clanking against my hip.

"Call the warriors!" I shouted to the servants, who scattered across the courtyard like frightened chickens as I pelted past.

Up the ladder. At the top of the tower I leant my chest against the wooden parapet and peered into the distance.

My hand became a shield against the sun. A black shadow appeared, growing larger and larger as each minute passed. The shape drew closer, a spreading swarm across the horizon. I'd have sworn I could hear the drumming of horses' hooves. It was only the sound of my heart pounding as the shadow became more distinct.

"There." Edmund pointed.

"I can see them."

My heartbeat became a gallop.

A glint of gold. A shield struck by the sun.

Drumming hooves in my head.

A single rider broke out in front, hard and fast.

There was only one man it could be.

The wings of a prayer cast over the land. My lips moved.

Spinning around, I scrambled down the ladder and didn't stop until I reached the ground.

To the steps of the hall.

The warriors.

Stalwart. But so few.

The townsfolk. Clustered behind.

Quiet now. Terrified.

Fight. Save our people!

To the front.

Edmund's heavy breathing beside me. I reached for my sword.

The carved silver at the hilt dug into my palm.

A cry from the watchtower. "He's almost at our gates!"

Arched. Wood banded with steel.

"Leave them open," I commanded.

"What for? We can take a single rider from the tower," Edmund spat.

"Others follow behind. Let him come." Murderer. I'd meet him, blade to blade.

Now I could hear it. No longer in my head. Horse hooves came closer. Through the open gates the shadow of a huge animal fell forward onto the ground.

Edmund's arrow. Elm wood. Iron-tipped. At the ready.

"I can take him!"

"No!"

"Stranger!" Even as I cried out, Edmund raised his bow. "Arrows are upon you. Identify yourself!"

If the rider heard he made no sign. Clad in a silver helmet and armored in brown leather, he galloped under the arches, my warning ignored. His great black horse circled the courtyard, raising dust as he halted in front of the steps.

For a moment he didn't move. Nor did I, except to tighten my fingers on the handle of my blade.

He lifted off his helmet.

A pair of piercing eyes met mine.

This is not Thurkill.

The knowledge flashed into my brain. The man in front of me was tall and strong. Many years younger than my father, perhaps thirty years of age, his face a tanned brown. His hair, tawny as an owl wing, fell to the studded collar of his armor, its leather stretched across his shoulders. Carved metal plates barreled his chest.

He spoke. "You are Godiva."

Hawk high I lifted my head. "I am. Who are you? Why have you come to my lands?"

Dirt swirled in the air as his horse hoofed the ground. River deep turned his gaze as he took me in, lingering on the thick braid that fell over my shoulder to brush to my thigh.

"Well?" A flame flickered through me, hotter than fear. A flame I'd never known. "Who are you?"

"I am Leofric. Earl of Mercia."

A Saxon.

Not a Dane.

Beneath the wolf-fur of my cloak collar my tense shoulders dropped.

Beside me Edmund lowered his bow.

"It's true, Godiva. I know his face. He was at the Witan with your father."

Yet I remained sword-ready. "What brings you here, Earl of Mercia?"

He didn't respond. A cursory glance over Edmund and the other warriors. A question of his own.

"Where is Radulf, Lord of the Middle Lands? I must speak to him without delay."

"My father has been killed by Thurkill the Tall." My voice harsh, almost cold. The only way the news could be transmitted, without breaking down. "My mother, too."

He bowed.

"Then I'm too late." He muttered as if to himself.

Too late? What did he mean, too late?

"I met your father at the Witan Council." Raising his head, his deep blue stare submerged mine. "He spoke of you."

Strange trembling started in my limbs. "I ask again. Why have you come?"

A swipe across his forehead. "To warn you."

Edmund thrust forward. "We know Thurkill the Tall approaches."

The black horse hoofed. The earl's stare became cold.

"Thurkill." He spoke the name like a curse. "The worst of the Danes."

I remembered what my father had told me. "He's no friend of yours, I believe, Leofric of Mercia."

"Be assured of that. Thurkill has long been the plague of my homeland. How far is the enemy from Coventry?"

"Days," Edmund said. "No more."

Lord Leofric studied him. "He's close by."

"I'll be ready for him," I said fiercely. "Thurkill the Tall will never take the Middle Lands."

Silence lengthened like a shadow between us.

"Will you give us Saxon hospitality tonight, Lady of Coventry?" he asked at last. "Our journey has been long. My men follow after a hard ride."

I didn't know this man, except by reputation. But my father had spoken well of him.

"You're welcome in this hall, Lord Leofric."

Edmund pulled me aside in a furious whisper. "What are you doing, Godiva?"

My gaze stayed on the Earl of Mercia as he swung down from his horse. "He's a Saxon lord."

Edmund's mouth thinned to a blade. "That doesn't mean you can trust him."

"Try to sleep, my lady."

An open window. A darkling night. A starless sky.

Grief had come like a thief in the shadows, stealing my fighting instinct from me.

In front of my people I'd needed to be brave. But now . . .

Fader . . . Moder . . .

"I can't sleep, Aine. I keep picturing them and what must have happened." Wrapping my arms around my shift, I shivered. Undyed twill, thick-woven. But I remained chilled. "My mother . . ."

This had been her bower.

Her missal on the prayer kneel. Gold and painted pages open. Made by the monks at Evesham, who loved her so well. Her jewel chest on the table. Garnets. Sapphires. Moonstones. On the wall, the flat-pounded silver roundel. Into it her bright reflection would never smile again.

Aine wrapped a lamb's wool shawl over my shift. Red. One of my mother's.

"Hush. I'll make you a cup of herbs to help you sleep. Think on it no more," she urged, as she drew me over to sit by the fire. "You'll go mad. Turn your thoughts away."

With a pestle and mortar she pounded chamomile, valerian, and hyssop, the mother of herbs. In a cauldron over the flickering flames she boiled and stirred.

Soothing fragrance filled the air, but my aching thoughts would not still. Restless, I got up and paced the bower, the rushes crushing beneath my bare feet.

I mustn't think the worst. That way disaster lay. Victory alone must be my aim. But I'd been shocked to discover how few swords and bows were left in our weaponry with the cream of Coventry's warriors gone. We would have to rely on axes, like the sharp one Walburgha had promised, farmers' pitchforks, hastily hewn spears.

Names, faces, axes. I counted. I had only a few fighting men left. But all the men of the Middle Lands would struggle to the death.

Lord Leofric. Earl of Mercia. He slept in our hall tonight with some of his warriors and what remained of my own. The rest of his force camped just outside the town. For the moment, at least, it meant Coventry had some defense. But he would be gone on the morrow.

With anxious fingers I wound the edge of my shawl; its wool blood against my skin. "We haven't got enough men."

Aine came beside me. I could have sworn there was more silver in her hair than yesterday. Lines had deepened on her weathered skin, but her expression remained watchful.

Lifting my fingers one by one, she unwound them from the shawl, closed them on the cup. "Drink."

Unshed tears choked me as I took a sip. It tasted bitter even with the honey Aine had added. "How can I fight Thurkill the Tall and an army of Danes without my parents to guide me?"

In despair, I spilled the cup.

Aine moved with a suddenness that startled me. Her knowing eyes were fierce as she gripped my forearms. "You must be brave, my lady. You've been readied for this since you were born. You are a Saxon, whose women do not give up. Your father, has he not always taught you to keep the Saxon way? You have a duty whatever your own feelings."

"I'm frightened," I whispered, ashamed.

"Do you remember what your mother told you, the stories of heroes, men and women both, warriors in days gone by? She told you those stories for a reason." Aine smoothed my hair. Her face softened. "Remember your mother. Even in her grief when her poor babies died, she thought of the people of Coventry. I saw it time and time again. You need to do the same. You mustn't let your parents or your people down. You are Lady now."

The silver keys.

"I'll do my duty."

My tone as dull as unpolished metal.

"Do more than duty. Show your strength," Aine urged. "Let all know you mean to hold the Middle Lands against Thurkill the Tall. You must show no weakness now."

"No weakness!" I cried. "No weakness! Am I allowed no time to recover from this? Must I disguise my sorrow? In the midst of my grief am I supposed to think of aught else than those I have loved and lost?"

In her quiet way she surveyed me. "That's the spirit, my lady. You shout. Be angry as you ought. Rage against what has happened. Rage. Anger is powerful, it will keep you safe."

Without warning my tears released, gushing down my cheeks, dampening my hair. "Why are they gone? Why? I need them so much!"

She took me in her arms. "There, there. I don't know why, my lady. But gone they are and here you are. And here, God willing, you'll stay."

A knock on the bower door.

My heart leapt like a candle flame.

"Who goes there?" Aine called.

"Leofric of Mercia. I must speak to Lady Godiva alone."

4

Whereat he stared, replying, half-amazed

——Tennyson [1842]: *Godiva*

Aine flung open the bower door, indignant as a ruffled fowl. "Have you no pity? Lady Godiva ought not to be disturbed."

"It's all right, Aine." I clambered to my feet, wiping the telltale trails of tears from my cheeks.

My mother's bower.

Now my own.

Dwarfing it with his size, the Earl of Mercia came inside. His blue stare cast over the wood-paneled room, at the stars painted on the clay ceiling, the gold-glinting tapestries on the walls, the bed puffed with feathers and linen, its oak frame carved with vines and day's eyes, and came to rest on me.

The communication unspoken. The hall would be full of warriors, at rest for the night. His words were for my ears only.

"You may leave us," I said to Aine.

Her cheeks puffed. "My lady . . ."

"You may leave us."

With a huff of disapproval she edged out the door.

Never had I been unattended with a man in the bower before. Not even Edmund. Yet I wasn't afraid.

As he removed his cloak I took the opportunity to study him. Instead of his armor he now wore a brown tunic, the shoulders leather-padded. Even without his battle guise power vibrated around him like the sparks of a blacksmith's anvil. Six feet tall; not the height Thurkill was rumored to be, but enough to tower over me.

Approaching the fire, he met my inquisition with a half-curve of a smile, aware of my scrutiny. His teeth were the strong white of the Saxon.

I stared down at the rushes.

"My sympathy is with you." The words were simple, but as I glanced up I realized they were sincere. His half smile had faded, leaving two deep lines bracketing his mouth.

Pain swayed me but I remained firm-footed.

"Your grief runs deep," he said, as if he'd felt my tremor.

"My grief will know no bounds if I lose the lands of my father to the Dane who murdered him." I lifted my chin to halt a tear-fall. "Tell me. Do you know how many men Thurkill the Tall has with him?"

"They will greatly outnumber yours."

His certainty infuriated me. I yanked my braid over my shoulder. Gripped it firm.

"Men will come from all across the Middle Lands to defend Coventry. They're already traveling, now I have made a call to arms."

"The numbers you can raise won't be enough."

Naked

The cnihts. My father's fierce bodyguard, trained and tested. Skilled with shield, bow, and blade. Gone. Their weapons, too.

Names, faces, axes. I winced. "Many of our warriors have been lost, some of our best, but—"

"The Middle Lands no longer possess the army you need," he interrupted. "You need highly skilled men to beat back the Danes."

This man had fought and conquered. A daring campaign, my father had called it. Leofric of Mercia knew of what he spoke.

"You don't understand the bravery of my men," I insisted. No one must suspect I shared such doubts. Sacrilege. "They won't give up, no matter what the odds."

"They may be brave but Thurkill is ruthless. His sights have long been the Middle Lands. You must know that. Make no mistake, he wants this jewel, and he comes prepared."

Tight as a bit between my teeth, I gritted a vow. "He will not take it."

Lord Leofric dismissed my undertaking. "Let me speak bluntly. We speak that way in Mercia, in the north. I came to make an offer to your father. I'll make you the same."

"And what's that?"

"Mercia's aid."

"The warriors of Mercia to fight alongside the men of the Middle Lands?" My braid loosed. I hadn't expected this. "I thank you, my lord, for the offer of assistance but there's no need."

"If you believe that, you're a fool."

"How dare you!" My words were fire-smoke. We both knew it.

The scent of leather came with him as he shifted closer. "Heed my warning. You can't hold Coventry. Where is Thurkill now? He's with his Danish warriors, invading your border farms and villages.

Women and children scream for pity while we stand here. Men and boys are being struck down as they try to defend their homes. Thurkill will show no mercy. Right now, he's wielding his Dane-axe, the most vicious of them all."

Hadn't I been imagining such hideous scenes, each bruise, every blow? "You're trying to frighten me. I won't be frightened."

"You should be." The earl's gaze raked like a pitchfork over my skin. "Thurkill has a taste for Saxon women."

All at once my shawl seemed flimsy. I shivered. "I won't be taken by Thurkill the Tall, not while a Coventry man stands. They're the most courageous you could find."

"I don't doubt the courage of your men. But Thurkill the Tall has defeated many just as brave."

Another struggle to contain my tears. "Such as my father."

Deep sorrow passed over his face so quickly I thought I'd imagined it. "And my brother."

"Your brother was lost to Thurkill?"

The harsh lines bracketing his mouth deepened to scars. "Mercia was mighty before Thurkill came. Northman, my elder brother, was raised to rule. Now I've been made earl, I've vowed that I will make Mercia strong again, in his memory. Nothing will stop me."

Unexpectedly, I yearned to reach out and smooth the clefts around his mouth. To stroke his hair in the way I stroked my horse's soft mane. I didn't know this man. Yet my instinct was to comfort us both.

"I understand," I said gently, as if I soothed Ebur. "My feelings are the same for the Middle Lands."

"Then you must accept Mercia's aid." On restless feet, he shifted away. "It was agreed at the Witan Council that Saxon lords must unite."

If my plait were hemp it would have frayed. I fretted it again. Could I trust him? It was always a risk allying with another lord, even a fellow Saxon. My father rarely entered into alliances with others, Saxon or no, except under the auspices of the Witan Council.

But my father wasn't here.

"Lord Leofric." Swallowing my apprehension I released my braid and offered my hand. "Let us combine our forces for the Saxon honor of both our families and our lands."

Firm and dry, his grasp closed over mine, his skin calloused with hard riding. Huge. Fingers long and powerful. At release they trailed hot across my palm.

My breath came fast. "Then we're agreed?"

"There's no time to waste. Tomorrow I must talk with your best warriors and plan our attack. Who is your father's sheriff? Who will lead your men into battle, with your father gone?"

Along with my shawl, I gathered my dignity around me. "I will."

His boots stirred the rushes, as impatient as a horse pawing the ground. "You misunderstand me. Not who will lead them as their lady, but who will take up arms."

"You misunderstand *me*. I will lead the battle against Thurkill the Tall."

Amazement flared in his eyes. "You're no more than a girl!"

"Girl or not, I mean to fight." Seizing my sword, I raised it high above us. The shawl slipped from my shoulders, pooled red at my feet. "I'll face Thurkill the Tall with my own sword. I'll not cower and hide indoors until the battle is over. In the fray I'll fight for my own lands. I have no brothers, Lord Leofric. I was raised a warrior."

Both son and daughter. I'd vowed to be.

Hilt-handed, he'd instantly moved away from the exposed blade. "Girls don't fight in Mercia."

"You're not in Mercia now."

"So I see." He let go his hilt. But he stayed back, surveying me. "In Mercia, men wield weapons while women weave."

It was an old Saxon saying. One I disliked.

"I can weave and I can also wield a weapon." I swished my blade. "Can you do both?"

A fleeting grin creased his cheek. "No."

"My mother taught me to weave and my father taught me to fight." I lowered the sword point to the floor. The flat of the blade caught the firelight. "I ask nothing of my people I don't ask of myself."

He rubbed the golden night-stubble on his jaw. "I know not of another noblewoman who fights."

"Why, there was one of your own countrywomen. Don't you know the tales of the brave and the true? There's a legend of a great lady of Mercia who was a warrior, too. Didn't your ancestress Aethelflaed build great fortresses, and do battle herself against the Danes?"

"Who told you of Aethelflaed?" he demanded.

"My mother. She raised me on stories of such noblewomen, that in turn I should become one of them."

"Aethelflaed was my kinswoman, though it was a hundred years ago that lady of Mercia lived."

"The spirit of such women doesn't die." I gulped. "Nor will my mother's spirit as long as I can fight and defend my lands."

"Have you fought before?"

"Not yet." I pushed down the bile of panic.

"You could be lost in battle. What then of Coventry, of the land of your father and the spirit of your mother? Have you thought of that?"

I traced the carved hilt of my sword. "My lands and my people are as dear to me as my life."

My heart thumped as he studied me. "I don't believe I can sway you."

I remained silent.

Finally he bowed. "So be it. It's not my resolve to weaken yours."

The hilt loosened in my perspiring hand. Sudden exhaustion sapped my bones.

He frowned. "The hour is late. Will you bid me leave?"

At my nod of consent Leofric of Mercia grabbed his cloak and stalked from the bower.

My fingers shook as I laid down my sword.

5

So the Powers, who wait
On noble deeds . . .
——Tennyson [1842]: *Godiva*

"You're making a mistake, Godiva!" Edmund thumped his fist down on the high table.

He'd found me alone in the hall, poring feverishly over a parchment map, trying to work out the best plan of defense.

Think. I'd told myself feverishly. What would my father do? Finger on map I'd traced the town of Coventry. It had grown so big. Surely it would be a tempting prize for Thurkill the Tall. I would focus on the town, I'd decided, trying to ignore the nausea that roiled my stomach at the thought of the Danes, already brutalizing our outlying villages. Burning homes, killing livestock, looting churches.

No matter how my heart ached it would be impossible to defend them all.

Thurkill mustn't reach the fertile farming land that circled Coventry, painted verdant green on the map. We would need food, to hold out against the Danes. If it came to the worst, I would fight him to the edge of the shire, into the wildwoods. Into Arden.

Rolling up the parchment, I stayed calm as I faced Edmund. "A mistake? What do you mean?"

"What do you think I mean? You can't trust the Earl of Mercia!" His skin had reddened, right up to the roots of his pale hair. I'd never seen him so angry.

"Why not? I don't understand. He's a Saxon like us, at the Witan with my father. We must accept Lord Leofric's offer. If Coventry falls, the Middle Lands are lost."

Edmund shook his head. "There are things you don't know."

"Then tell me."

"We don't need Mercian men. That's all you need to know. We can fight the Danes without them."

"How can you say that? You know it's not true. If we're to defeat Thurkill once and for all, we need to take the earl's aid."

"You mustn't join forces with Leofric of Mercia. I won't let you!"

"What do you mean, let me?" I snapped. Edmund had no right to tell me what to do.

"You should have consulted me. I should be acting as Sheriff of Coventry, of the whole shire. It's what your father always promised as well as . . ."

"My father made you no promises!" I knew what he was going to say. It had been implied what would come if Edmund and I . . .

He swirled me into his arms.

"Godiva." His lips on my hair, my forehead, my cheeks. "Don't try to do this without me. I know how you're feeling. I'm the only one who understands you."

Comfort. Relief. Familiar. I leaned into him.

"With your parents gone, it's even more urgent. We have to talk. What I asked you before I went to the Witan..."

Out of his arms. I yanked away.

My chest heaved. "Not now, Edmund."

He deserved an answer, but there was no time. Not with Thurkill at our borders.

His elbows. Sharp wings. "You used to confide in me. Why are you shutting me out?"

"I'm not shutting you out. But these are my lands to defend. This is my decision and mine alone." I grabbed a jagged breath. "We mustn't fight between ourselves. We must fight alongside Mercia if we're to save the Middle Lands."

"Godiva, you've got to listen to me! This is a mistake."

A tremor of doubt. Edmund wouldn't be the only person to question my decision to take Mercia's offer of aid.

My feet planted in my boots.

"Please, Edmund," I whispered as the hall door opened. "Don't be angry. I need you."

His grey eyes narrowed. "Just don't say I didn't warn you."

The Earl of Mercia joined us on the dais. For a moment he paused, surveying Edmund and me where we stood together in front of my parents' chairs.

Edmund moved closer to my side until we were touching. His energy sparked through me.

Lord Leofric halted on the other side of the table.

As they entered the hall, I studied the half a dozen men coming in behind him, the warriors of his personal bodyguard. Almost as tall and strong as he, with the same rough-hewn features, yet none of them had the burnished metal of his hair. Some of my guardsmen came, too. But they were not the best fighting men. They had been lost.

When Lord Leofric spoke, his deep rumble seemed to gather the group. "We are warriors of different lands: men of Coventry and men of Mercia, but we come together as Saxons. To win this fight against the Danes, there must be no nay sayers among us. Are all here agreed to join together on this?" His gaze roved over each man at the table.

"It is agreed by us, the warriors of Mercia, Lord Leofric." A huge man named Acwell put his closed fist to his chest.

"By all of us." Another Mercian warrior made the same gesture.

"And by the *cnihts* of the Middle Lands." Edmund sounded reluctant.

Leofric darted him a glance. "We can have no slow sword."

Edmund's hand rushed to his hilt. "You insult me, Mercian."

Concealed by the table-edge my hand stayed his. "My warriors are with me, Lord Leofric."

"No men will fight as bravely as the men of Coventry will fight for the honor of our dead lord and for Godiva," Edmund said tightly, but beneath my fingers his fist uncurled.

"That's as well, for we have no time to waste." Leofric's tone was abrupt as he leaned toward me. "Thurkill must not reach the town of Coventry."

I nodded.

Leofric rubbed his jaw. Clean-shaven now. The night-stubble gone. "It's my aim to ensure we bring Thurkill out on to open ground, where he's weakest. What I know of the Dane is that he prefers to avoid open battle. Lying in ambush, as he did for your father, is his preference. In Mercia, we spent one full summer trying to draw him out, like a fox from a hole. But when we met him, in full combat, we won the day."

"Thurkill is a coward at heart," I said bitterly.

"You speak the truth," Leofric replied. "He prefers to come by stealth and gain advantage that way. But we won't give him that opportunity, not this time."

"We don't have to force him out. We could beat him at his own game. We could hide and lie in wait," Edmund objected.

Leofric swung on him. "That's how you would fight?"

"It's how Thurkill beat Lord Radulf."

Leofric exhaled with disgust. "It's not the Saxon way."

It was hard to ignore the tension between the two men, staring at each other with increasing dislike.

"Tell us more of your plan, Lord Leofric," I requested hastily.

"Thurkill will be expecting us to stay and defend the town, not to emerge from it. To succeed, there must be no skulking or hiding. We shall have an advantage ourselves if we find a place to meet him. An open plain, flat and wide."

In my mind, I scanned the area that surrounded Coventry. "There is such a place, not far from the town. It's to the east. You know the place, don't you, Edmund?" I smiled at him as I unrolled the parchment and found the position on the map.

"Yes." Edmund gave me no answering grin.

His expression inscrutable, Leofric glanced again from me to Edmund, before turning to study the point I marked with my finger. For a second his finger brushed mine.

His life force blasted. A different vigor from Edmund's but just as powerful. Strong. Earthed. Grounded.

A connection kindled between us. I snatched my fingers from the table.

If he noticed he made no sign.

"This is a good place," he said, studying the map. "We must choose the ground carefully."

"And then make our battle plan?" I asked.

He showed a glimmer of surprise. "You know of battle plans as well as knowing how to fight?"

Once again he'd underestimated me. "I studied battle craft in full with my father. He didn't think it useful to wield a sword if I didn't know tactic and strategy."

Trying to imagine what my father would have planned, I pondered. "We lost so many warriors in the ambush. But we still have enough strong men for a shield wall."

"The youngest and strongest men must go at the front," Leofric agreed. "You don't need only to use your men, warriors of Mercia will stand shield, too."

"We'll be grateful. The stronger our wall, the better it will be for those behind, who will be more lightly armed." Names. Faces. Axes. As I considered my forces I frowned anew. "Many men have come to fight. They're willing but they're not trained, and their weapons vary. Some will only have stones and catapults."

"Then we must certainly strengthen your wall. Do you still intend to fight?"

Why did he ask again? There was no way I would revoke my sword. "I do."

"I'll defend you, Godiva." From Edmund hostility speared toward Leofric. "Only *cnihts* of the Middle Lands should be your bodyguard."

"Only you remain," Lord Leofric said quietly.

Edmund's jaw clenched. "I'm enough."

"My own sword will defend me," I broke in. "This is my battle."

I've sworn Thurkill won't take my lands and if I die defending them I won't have died in vain."

"No Saxon blood will be spilt in vain if the Danes are stopped. The whole way of Saxon life is at risk if we don't face our foe," Leofric said. "Are we agreed, then?"

Running my fingers up and down my plait I sensed the earl's awareness of my habitual gesture. "Agreed."

"Then Coventry will be safe," he said.

As if I had drunk the heated cow's milk Aine used to pour me as a child before I went to sleep, a sense of reassurance spread through my limbs.

Yet I knew the chance of victory.

Slight.

Night had fallen like a black mantle. I glanced around the quiet hall. The trestle tables had been unfolded, laid flat against the walls, and only the high table on the dais remained. Both warriors of Mercia and Coventry had spread out their cloaks on hides and blankets to rest before the battle that would come at daybreak. Some were talking quietly. Others were playing tic-tac-toe, but most were already sleeping, their weapons lying beside them. Leofric's men appeared to be a powerful force, strong, tested. All his warriors had the same toughness.

The flames of the central fire were burning low. I knew I should go to the bower, and try to sleep, too. Instead, I wrapped my cloak even more tightly and drew myself closer to the flames.

A guard crept over. "All is prepared for the morning, Lady Godiva. The men will be ready at dawn. There are scouts watching in case Thurkill tries to take the town tonight, but all is quiet so far."

"Thank you. Get some sleep now."

"Yes, my lady." He found a space not too far from the fire near some of the other Coventry warriors. Edmund wasn't among them. I'd searched for him.

The Earl of Mercia was seated to one side of the fire. Like me, he'd not yet sought sleep. His expression was in shadow, but I could make out his strong profile.

Was I right to trust him?

"You should sleep, Lady." He spoke low, but his deep tone reached me across the flames. "We ride out at dawn. There's nothing more to be done tonight. Why do you not go to your bower?"

"I'd prefer to be here with the men for a while. And I'm not sure that I could sleep."

"It's often that way the night before battle."

Restless, I got to my feet. "Will you have some ale with me?"

At his nod I moved to the high table, where I'd ordered bread, cheese, and ale to be left out for the men. I could sense the earl's surmise all the while. Unsteadily, I poured ale into two tankards and returned to the fireplace to offer one.

Avoided touching him.

"How old are you?" he asked, as I took a frothy sip of ale.

"I will be twenty years of age this autumn." My birthday was just before All Hallows. It had always been celebrated in the town.

"You're not yet twenty? That's young to fight."

Edmund was a few years older than me and he'd been fighting for years. Again I peered around the dim-lit hall, wondering where he could be. I wanted him beside me on this battle eve.

"How old were you, my lord, when you first fought in battle?" I asked Lord Leofric.

"Younger than you," he conceded. "But not as small."

I bristled. I wasn't small for a woman. "When my father taught me to fight he showed me how to move my body to defend myself, how to wait and spot the best opportunity to attack my opponents. It's not about brute force, he believed. 'Don't let your smaller size deter you from victory. Skill and intelligence can be just as powerful.' That's what he said."

The memory was now bittersweet.

Leofric nodded. "There's something in that. Are you an archer as well?"

"Sword-craft is what I prefer. Edmund always won in bow-craft. He's the finest shot in the Middle Lands. But I once bested him in a sword fight." I grinned. "He didn't like that much."

"If you were taught by Lord Radulf then you'll fight well. Your father was a strong warrior, I know."

"On my sixteenth birthday he gave me my sword and my set of armor. It's light yet strong."

"Light yet strong." The earl's voice seemed to brush my skin. As I stared into the fire I could only hope he assumed the warmth stealing into my cheeks came from its heat.

I changed the subject. "Will you tell me more of Mercia, Lord Leofric?"

"What would you know of my homeland?"

"I know that you have towns of great size. I've heard of Chester."

"There's also Derby and Nottingham. Yes, our towns are growing apace at last. When Thurkill had control of Mercia he stripped it of all its wealth. Mercia was once powerful in this isle. But we fared badly when the Danes came. We were too much of a threat. They sought to crush us."

"But you won your lands again."

"Not without cost. My three brothers and I were outlaws for years."

"You have other brothers?"

"Two younger. Edwin and Godwin." He brooded into the fire. "They are still in the north or what's left of it. Thurkill left our coffers bare. I've had to raise our taxes. But my people understand. Mercia must be rebuilt. I'm determined on it."

"I believe you'll do it." How could I believe otherwise with his tone edged with metal, his profile carved as if from fierce rock?

"Are you afraid of facing open battle?" he asked abruptly.

"Yes." Impossible to lie. "I'm afraid. But courage is going on whether you're afraid or not, isn't it? It isn't courage if you don't feel afraid. Courage is what we need at our worst not our best. That's what my father taught me."

"That's true. When you have courage you have no choice but to go forward, to do what needs to be done, no matter how difficult."

"You know courage, I think, Lord Leofric."

Again he stared into the flickering fire as if scrying them, and then at me. "It's been called upon for me to show courage. But like all men, I didn't know I possessed it until the moment for requiring it had passed. Courage is only known after the battle is won."

I shivered. "I hope I'll know it."

Standing up, he lifted his tankard and drained the ale. "I'll leave you now. I can't stay indoors."

"You're going outside? Into the cold?"

"When we were outlaws, I began to prefer sleeping in the open air. It's almost too warm in here." His mouth curved slightly as he glanced at my cheeks. "Do you not find it so?"

My blush deepened.

"Sleep well, battle maid. At dawn we'll be ready. And have faith. I don't think your courage will fail you now."

6

She sent a herald forth,
And bade him cry, with sound of trumpet
——Tennyson [1842]: *Godiva*

The morning dawned cold and bright. The scent of grass in the air too soft a perfume for the day ahead. On the mud-trod plain outside Coventry our warriors were gathered.

Uneasily I shifted on Ebur's saddle. My armor was light, as armor went, as I'd told Lord Leofric, but the weight still lay heavy on my shoulders.

My grip went to my braid as it often did when I was nervous. But my hair wasn't in its usual thick rope. Instead, my fingers touched the metal of my helmet.

Earlier, Aine had tied my hair back. "It must be firmly fastened." With skillful fingers, she'd twisted it into a braided coil and secured it with a string of wool. "There. That will fit below your helmet, and it won't come loose, whatever happens."

Whatever happens. Aine's words rang in my ears as I stared across the vast field at a terrifying spectacle.

The Danes. So many more than the Saxons. Panic overwhelmed me at the sight of the solid wall of men, most on foot, a few of them on horseback. How could we defeat them once their shields were up, their axes high, their catapults, heaving with stones, at the ready? I could hear their jeering and hooting, calling out curses and threats. They'd found out we were coming to meet them on this open stretch of grassy land. I didn't know how.

Had I led us into a trap? I darted a peek over my shoulder. We had men for our own shield wall, tall, strong men, many of them young and bold. Once their shields were raised, the edges touched. Surely they would form a defense too hard for the Danes to break.

Behind the shield warriors were the townspeople, men I had known my whole life. Wilbert, shifting his axe from hand to hand, his expression firm. The blacksmith, the inn keeper, no doubt wishing himself on the mead-bench instead; the butcher, the miller and his two sons, a farmer, carrying only a hoe . . . all of them had come. Closer to me were the warriors who were now my bodyguard, Edmund leading them. They were mounted too, but later, when the horns blew and the battle began, we would join the men on foot.

When the battle began.

Courage, I told myself. *Courage.*

I hadn't known it would feel like this. I hadn't known fear would sour in my mouth, that my stomach would churn, my palms dampen inside my leather gloves, or my legs turn so weak I could barely hold on to Ebur's sides with my clenched, leather-clad thighs. It was fortunate I hadn't been able to break my fast that morning, though Aine had tried to make me eat. There was no way I could keep anything in my roiling belly.

No! I refused to give in! Fear was the point at which weakness could enter, like a pottery bowl made poorly, or a thread loose in the loom, leaving a bowl to break, a garment to unravel. Fear would not enter into my soul, just as no Dane would trample the soil of my lands. No Danish blade would take the lives of the women and children of Coventry, huddled in their homes now, praying that the men of the Middle Lands, and the men of Mercia, too, would hold off Thurkill the Tall.

The men of Mercia. I cast a sidelong glance at their leader, mounted beside me. His jaw was set hard as he stared straight ahead, coolly surveying Thurkill's troops. His leather armor, battle-scarred, spread across his vast chest, his helmet low over his brow. He held himself taut, at the ready. His black horse, the magnificent animal on whose back I'd first seen him, hoofed the ground into clods of mud, seeming as eager to begin battle as his master.

"It's not too late for you to retreat to your hall," the earl said, low. "I can lead the battle."

"I must do this." I took a deep breath, as if I could draw courage in like air. "It's just . . . there are so many of them."

"Numbers don't decide the victor, just as size does not." He glanced at my armor, shaped to fit me with its carved metal breastplate, the leather tight on my body. "If we have the will, the battle will be ours. Surely your father taught you that."

I nodded. I knew.

"Do you wish to try to truce with Thurkill?" he asked me next.

"You go to truce with him?" Edmund, mounted on his bay stallion on my other side, broke into our conversation. War-shirted. The silver wings of the *cnihts* of the Middle Lands swept his shoulders.

Attached to both men's saddles were the rounded shields of the Saxons. Edmund's leather-wheeled, the metal at the center shiny and smooth. On Lord Leofric's a double-headed eagle was carved. The largest of the hawks. I, too, carried a shield. An oval shape upon which the proud sparrow-hawk flew, amber-eyed.

Leofric's glance at Edmund was a dismissal. "To try for peace first is our trusted way. I've sworn to it since I became earl. If there's a chance of saving Saxon blood we should take it."

Edmund snorted. "We should just go straight into battle!"

"What do you say, Lady of Coventry?"

First I studied one, then the other. Edmund's face had reddened again. Leofric's appeared emotionless.

"Not a single life should be lost, if it can be saved before battle begins," I said at last.

Edmund flashed silver fury. I knew how angry he was with me. In his view my decisions were ill-judged. Dangerous. Foolish.

With barely a yank of the rein Leofric rotated his horse. "Come with me, Lady."

Wind whipped my cheeks as we galloped across the plain. On the surly faces of the Danes I witnessed amazement that we should ride over to them. The jeering quieted. Mutters at the sight of Leofric. No one dared catcall as we pulled up our horses in front of a man on horseback.

Thurkill the Tall.

Trepidation turned to rage, burning on my tongue. My hand ached for my sword. Scream, swear, kill. I hadn't known I had it inside me, this boiling cauldron of fury.

"Will you truce, Dane?" Leofric threw down the words.

Silence as Thurkill slowly removed his helmet.

My gasp choked me. The ugliest man I'd ever seen, with a vast dome shaved to the scalp, his skin pitted and yellow, fight-scarred. His beard dirt brown, his eyes perturbed me most: small and cruel, as though they delighted in causing pain. Barreled in leather armor, the shoulders padded and iron-studded, his massive body had oxen-strength. His stare held the cunning of vermin.

Tucking his helmet under his arm he gave a mocking bow. "The Earl of Mercia. You're far from your lands."

"And you're far from yours." Leofric's tone remained even. "Too far."

Thurkill grimaced. Twisted his massive head. It seemed as if maggots crawled over my skin. "This must be the new Lady of Coventry."

"Because you killed my father who was lord," I burst out.

"A bold maid!" Thurkill sneered. "Ah yes. I remember your father and your pretty mother, too. A bold one like you."

Fury boiled in my gullet. Fury and fear. I gulped them down.

My mother. Suffering. At the mercy of this brutal monster.

"You'll pay for what you did to my parents, Thurkill."

"*Nidstang.*" A Danish curse. Foul to the ear. "Save your threats. The whole of the Middle Lands are mine for the taking with only a maid to defend them."

"Do you not see me before you, Dane? Lady Godiva is not alone."

A leer at Leofric. "Is that so?"

"I'm not here for a day's ride. The warriors of Mercia will stand beside the men of the Middle Lands until you are defeated, as you were in the north."

Strength surged through me at Leofric's words. I'd been unsure of my decision to let his warriors fight alongside my men. In front of Thurkill the Tall, I could only feel relief to have the Mercian lord beside me.

"You challenge me?"

Leofric shrugged. Never would I have guessed he was in the presence of the man who had killed his brother Northman, he remained so calm.

Thurkill grunted. "Did you think I'd quake in my boots at the sight of you here, Saxon? Even with your warriors, this will be sport before we ride on. Oh, I'll take your challenge for what it's worth. The Middle Lands are almost mine. There's nothing you can do to stop me taking the rest and the fine town of Coventry, too."

"I've stopped you before," Leofric said. "I stopped you in Mercia."

"Mercia." Thurkill spat. "There's nothing left in Mercia."

Leofric's leather glove tightened on his reins. From his few words by the fire I knew what pain Thurkill's plunder of his homeland had wreaked in Lord Leofric. I more than knew it. To my amazement it ripped through me so keenly that if I hadn't been on Ebur's solid back I would have swayed.

Yet when he spoke the earl was steady. So steady I shivered. "Mercia will rise again under my command, greater than ever before. You haven't defeated me."

"You'll rue coming here, Mercian. You should have stayed in the north."

"I'll defend all Saxon lands."

Thurkill cursed again. "Saxons. Fine words you have but that's all. I'll soon be done with you. You waste your sword, Earl of Mercia. There's little worth taking here." He ran his thick tongue over his lips as he ogled me. "Or perhaps I'm wrong. Should we share the spoils?"

As I opened my mouth, Leofric threw me a glance of warning.

"Come, Thurkill." His tone was now almost bored. "Enough of this. Will you do battle today or can this be settled now?"

A mocking laugh. "Settled? The great Earl of Mercia? Retreating? Oh, you Saxons. Always talk when what's needed is action."

"My sword is ready for battle." Leofric spoke through gritted teeth. "But we both have men who will die this day. Will you truce?"

Thurkill glanced at his warriors and guffawed. Copying their leader they did the same. "This skirmish will only give me pleasure. When I've finished, the Middle Lands will belong to the Danes."

"I'll not give you the chance to retreat again."

"You'll be the one to retreat before this day is done."

"Then we fight."

"Will you rally the men?" Leofric asked, as we rode across the plain once more. Behind us the Danes had started up a war-chant, banging their drums. In time with the beat my pulse began to race.

"Me?"

"Put the courage of Coventry into their hearts." I caught the river blue of his glance. "They'll fight all the stronger for you."

His tone made my pulse beat even faster. I gave a quick nod of assent as we turned our horses to address our men.

So many. I could barely see them all.

The herald stepped forth. The horn pealed its brazen note.

"Saxons!" Lord Leofric cried.

The men gave a rousing cheer in response.

"Men of Coventry, Men of Mercia, we are Saxons all!"

More cheers rang out.

Leofric sent me a nod of encouragement.

"Good men!" My voice came out in a mouse squeak.

I couldn't let them down.

Leaning over I ran my hand along Ebur's neck. I'd plaited his long mane for battle in many braids as tight as my own.

Ebur's ears pricked back as I whispered the words. Not Saxon words, nor Latin, nor Aine's or my mother's Welsh, nor even a language I knew. An ancient whisper, an old language from far back in time, it came to my lips on a breath of wind.

The noble pact between human and horse.

Ebur's great head bowed and whinnied.

Releasing my feet from the stirrups, in a heave I was up on my knees and standing on the saddle.

Beside me I heard Leofric's fast intake of breath.

A cheer rang out.

"Good Saxons!"

Now I could see our forces, right to the rearguard, and they could see me. My legs locked strong and sure, Ebur rock-steady beneath me. To my relief, this time my words carried on the wind.

"We've come together to defeat a common foe, the Danish invaders. We will not let them spread their claws further into Englalond's heart. This peril shall not cross the borders of the Middle Lands. Fight, today, to halt them in their path. Fight, today, to keep them from our homes, our goods, and our families. Fight, today, for Saxon lands and for the Saxon way!"

A deafening roar in reply.

"For the Saxons!" a man called out.

"For Lady Godiva!" Wilbert cried.

"For Lord Leofric!" Acwell, the Mercian warrior, shouted.

I slipped back into the saddle.

Edmund flashed me a smile. No longer angry.

Cheers rang as I sensed our men's battle courage building. The Saxon drummers started as I rode with Leofric and Edmund to the rear.

Lord Leofric took his place beside me. "Ready?"

With a shaking hand I lifted my sword. "Ready."

7

Made war upon each other . . .
——Tennyson [1842]: *Godiva*

"Shields up!" Leofric roared.

My heart pounded faster than the battle drums as the men on the front line hoisted their arms, their backs set as firm as the round shields they held aloft.

Surely such a wall of resolve would not break.

Then the stones came. Flung across the plain from massive catapults, they dashed across the sky, some small and sharp, some as big as boulders. Men began to fall like cut trees.

An anguished cry came from a man crumpled to the ground directly in front of me. Instinctively I let go Ebur's reins to scramble down.

A glove clamped on my arm.

"Stay," Leofric snapped. "If you go in now, your warriors will follow. Let the catapults do their worst."

"But he's hurt!"

"There'll be many more hurt before this day is done."

Rock after rock heaved back and forth, each a thud in my stomach. There must have been at least three of theirs to each of ours. Horror-struck I watched our shield wall begin to give way, gaping holes forming like jagged teeth. As one man fell another stepped forward to mend the breach, but our ranks were thinning at a hideous rate.

"How long will it hold?" Panic made my tone fretful. At least it disguised my terror.

Leofric threw me a brief glance. "As long as their courage."

Courage had a scent, I learned, as I watched men collapse to their knees as the stones struck them down, only to haul themselves upright again. It rises, like yeast from new baked bread. Fear has a smell too, sour as cream gone bad in the churn. Both hung in the air above the battleground.

The yeast of courage I needed now. I breathed it in as the stones kept coming.

"Look out, Godiva!" Edmund shouted. A far-flung stone almost grazed the side of my helmet as it whizzed by. In time I ducked. Like relentless rain they pounded on, each strike a thud in my heart.

Too soon it rang out, the call I feared. "The shield wall has fallen! The Danes are through!"

"Now!" Leofric lifted his leather-clad fist like a flag.

With a roar, the foot-warriors surged into the fray.

The sign of the cross. My legs were weak as I slipped from Ebur's back and sent her with a slap across the flanks to a serving boy. Too young to fight, he stood with mouth agape.

My own mouth had dried to sawdust. The Danes pelted across the plain as hard and fast as their stones. Our shield wall became a

wall of men no longer, but a heaving mass of fighting, struggling bodies, of grunts and curses, and the thud of blade against shield.

The metal clanged in my ears as I stood there. I didn't know
what to do.

"Stay behind me, Godiva!" Edmund, shield-high and helmeted,
thrust himself in front of me.

His words brought me to myself. I didn't want to stay in the rear.
"I came to fight, Edmund! Don't try to stop me!"

Lifting my shield high, I dodged him and charged forward. My
sword struck out, my aim uncertain.

Steady. Steady.

A shield edge caught me in the small of my spine and I whirled
around, my sword at the ready. But it was one of our own men, a
farmer I recognized from a nearby village. His eyes were glazed with
an expression I hadn't seen before, something between excitement and
repulsion. Battle fever, I remembered my father called it. As if propelled by it the farmer pushed past without recognizing me, his lady.

When I turned back I could barely move. On four sides men
fought hand to hand, blade to blade. Edmund disappeared as
men closed in. The stench of sweat and blood filled my nostrils.

I could still see Leofric, taller than most. Like me he was now on
foot. As I glanced toward him he swung his sword in mighty side-
sweep, bringing down two Danes in a single blow.

He would stay near me, I knew. How did I know? When he didn't
even turn my way, as he slashed his way to the front? I can only say
that the air between us wasn't air, but something thicker, denser, an
invisible rope that bound me to him as surely as if it had been tied
around my waist.

Then I saw it. Wilbert crouched on the ground, the axe that Walburgha had been so proud of, cleft in two. Horror drained his face

as a Danish warrior loomed over him, ready to strike. With a dreadful air of resignation, Wilbert covered his grey head with his arms.

"No!" Aloft I raised my sword, shoved my way through the shouting mass of men and leapt in front of Wilbert. My helmet slipped off with a clunk, but I paid no heed. No time to retrieve it.

My sword cut into the arm of the Dane.

Snarling he drew back, blood dripping from the wound I'd made. His thick lips formed a sneer as he sized me up. I gulped, beating down my instinct to turn and run. This was no ordinary warrior, his carved axe and heavy armor told my sinking heart. This was a warrior of Thurkill's bodyguard; his most skilled and brutal men, trained not just to kill but to kill without mercy.

My sword met the slice of his axe just in time. We went to it, blade to blade. My father's teaching reverberated as I fought. A strange calmness overtook me as I made nimble steps, thrusting and turning. Forward, back, in, out. I could have been in the courtyard of Coventry hall, so steady my weapon became.

Wilbert clambered to his feet and staggered out of the way. Part of me sighed with relief. He would be safe now. The other part of my brain stayed on my opponent, now using my sword, now parrying his axe, now keeping my shield high.

Never had I fought a man as menacing as this, even though he was injured. Built like a bullock, he doubled my size.

Size does not decide the victor. It wasn't my father I heard, I registered briefly with surprise, but the Earl of Mercia. The power of the words surged through my veins, spurring me on. Forward, back, in, out.

Too soon I began to tire. My muscles ached, the blade hung in my fist. No matter how hard I tried, each thrust I made became weaker, its aim less sure. He knew it, the Dane who fought me. It registered with malice in his leer when in a misstep I dropped my shield. Boots sliding in the mud the grassy plain had become, I tried to retrieve it before staggering up to face him again.

The warrior snatched his advantage. I had no chance. Giving up on my shield, I darted aside, but before I'd fully righted myself, his axe slit open my leather sleeve, and cut into my skin.

Pain sliced hot and hard. Then it became no more than a prick of a needle, as with all the courage left in me I hoisted my sword. At least he'd only caught my shield-arm. My other hand still defiantly clutched my sword.

Harder and harder our combat became. My fatigue became dizziness, dizziness a kind of drunken dance as my sword kept moving.

Forward, backward, in, out. Then I noticed. I rubbed my free hand across my face. Could my opponent be starting to tire, too? Was it possible? He'd been hurt by my sword cut, and from fighting others before me, I suspected, as he began to lumber like a wounded ox.

Size does not decide the victor, the voice urged me again. Swiftly I shifted my feet into the special dodge move my father had taught me, to take advantage of my small size. Darting forward, I brought my blade upward between the Danish warrior's legs, and struck.

With a roar of agony he crashed to the ground.

Leaving him there, I rushed to Wilbert. "Are you hurt? Let me get you to safety!"

His skin was as grey as his hair. "Save yourself, my lady!"

"No, Wilbert! Come on!"

Wincing as the movement tore the wound on my arm wider, I hauled him up. I had to get him out of the fray. A man his age should have stayed at home, not fought in open battle.

"Come with me, Wilbert! Think of Walburgha! She'll refuse to forgive me if anything happens to you!"

"She—won't—forgive—me—my lady, if you come to harm."
His lips were white-edged, speech an effort. "Leave me here, I beg
you."

"Come!"

I'd yanked him to his feet and laid his arm across my shoulders
when I heard Lord Leofric shout my name.

"Godiva! Behind you!"

"Godiva!" Leofric's bellow of warning came again. Letting go of
Wilbert I spun on my heel and gasped with fear, the sour milk of it
filling my mouth, coating my tongue. Bearing down on me with a
vengeance, his brutal axe held aloft, was the Danish warrior I thought
I'd felled.

I tried to move but my feet refused to respond. Nor would my
arms. As my brain sent desperate messages to raise my sword, it
slipped between my fingers.

With a cry that sounded like outrage, Leofric vaulted between us
and brought down the man's shield with a crunching blow. His sword
clashed with fire as if striking an anvil, as it met the Dane's axe.

My shaking hands flew to my mouth to catch my escaping
breath. The courage inside me collapsed as—transfixed with dread—I
watched the warrior who had tried to kill me try to kill Leofric,
Lord of Mercia.

But he'd met his death-match. Leofric's sword arced through the
air and split open the Dane's head.

Stumbling away I clutched my belly, retching. Nothing came.

Leofric's gloved thrust wrenched me out of the mass of heaving
bodies and hauled me down behind the safety of a catapult frame.
"Godiva."

He crouched beside me. His breath battle-heavy, his face streaked
with dirt and blood.

The sounds of the swords and shields stilled to a hum.

"You're wounded," he said.

The fight had made me shake. Nothing compared to what his nearness now made. He lifted my arm, peeling the sleeve to where the Dane had slashed his axe. I bit my tongue as the leather pulled on my torn flesh. He tore off his glove. His bare hand. Gentler than I ever imagined, he traced the lip-shaped wound.

"It's not too deep."

He kept hold of my arm. Impossible to pull away as he gripped me with an expression I couldn't fathom.

"Godiva!" Edmund raced over, ducked behind the frame. Panting, he pushed his helmet from his sweating brow. "What happened? Are you all right?"

Leofric dropped my arm and turned on him with a face so furious I quailed.

"No thanks to you!" He shouted before I could speak. "You're her bodyguard! A *cniht*! What were you thinking to leave her like that?"

Edmund's jaw clenched.

"It wasn't Edmund's fault!" I cried. "It was mine. He tried to keep in front of me but I ran to help Wilbert."

"Your bodyguard should defend you no matter what happens. It's his Saxon charge."

"Godiva, forgive me." Edmund's voice was hoarse against the clashing blades. "I looked and you were gone."

"You ought never to have let her out of your sight," Leofric said, taut-lipped.

He seemed to speak to himself as much as to Edmund.

"Take her to safety," he ordered next. "She must fight no more."

"No! I . . ."

"Lord Leofric!" A Mercian warrior rushed up. "Thurkill has fled!"

Leofric seized the man by his tunic. "What?"

"He's vanished, my lord! He's fled to the woods and his men are following him!"

He spoke the truth. Amazed, we watched as the Danes remaining in the field surged like a swarm of bees into the thick woods on the opposite side of the plain.

Bewilderment broke out amid our men in a babble of calls and jeers. "They're running away!"

Acwell, the strongest of Leofric's bodyguard, cried out, "Thurkill is injured!"

"Did you see Thurkill hit?" Edmund demanded.

Leofric scowled. "If I'd seen him injured he'd be dead by now."

"You'd kill a man lying hurt?" The question tumbled from my lips before I could stop it.

"As you should have done just now." The tenderness he'd shown me when he'd tended my wound vanished. "If you'd finished the job properly you wouldn't have needed my aid."

His words jabbed like spikes. "It's dishonorable to kill a man who lies defenseless!"

"Death is a greater dishonor." Without another word he stalked away.

"Victory for Godiva!" Edmund waved his sword toward the sky. In the distance I spotted ravens swooping in. "The Danes retreat! The battle has been won for Coventry!"

He flung his arms around me.

"The Danes retreat!" Whoops and yells rang out as another cry went up. "The Saxons! The Saxons!" Men of the Middle Lands and Mercia alike embraced each other. With relief I saw that Wilbert, hoisted, cheering between two Coventry men, seemed to have recovered from his fright.

Too numb to join the cheers, I clambered up from behind the catapult frame and stared.

Victory had come at a cruel cost. Sorrow flapped its black wings over the torn field where the killed and wounded lay in blood and mud. Choking on my tears, I registered familiar faces that would never smile again. The youngest of the miller's sons. A farmer, still clutching his hoe.

Leaving Edmund, I hurried over to where a Saxon lay fallen, struggling to stay alive.

Blood gushed from a deep gash across his chest as I knelt down beside him. Aine, with her salves and herbs, might be able to save him, as she had done for many Coventry men before.

"My lady," he gasped.

A death rattle. I recognized it. There'd be no saving him. I took his bloodstained hand in mine. "Don't try to speak."

Still, he struggled on. "The Danes, my lady. The Danes."

"Defeated." As I said a prayer over him his face relaxed into repose. *"Requiescat in pace.* Rest in peace." A sign of the cross.

Drawing on all my remaining energy I stood up and forced myself to address the men. "Saxons! Tend to our wounded. Bury the vanquished. Bring all those who are hurt to Coventry and come, too, those who have fought for honor this day, from Mercia and from the Middle Lands. We shall feast tonight!"

At my bidding, the Saxons started to lift our dead and injured men. Even undertaking this somber task, their overall mood remained jubilant. To speak of feasting at such a time was not in my nature, but my father had once told me it cured battle fever. The men continued to clap each other on the shoulders, with nods and cheers.

A sole man didn't cheer. Lord Leofric stood apart. Sword gripped, he stared across at the retreating Danes and shook his head.

8

Then fled she to her inmost bower . . .
——Tennyson [1842]: *Godiva*

"You're quiet, Lord Leofric."

The Earl of Mercia stared at me, his expression brooding. Dressed in a dark tunic and cloak, his armor gone, he sat to my right at the high table but appeared to take no joy in the celebrations.

Below us, the long trestles brimmed with warriors and towns-folk. Up to two hundred could eat in the hall and there must have been close to that number tonight. Extra benches had been laid out, not for just the returning warriors, but for their relieved wives and families.

The sounds of mirth and merriment mingled with the smoke of the roast boar rotating on the spit above the main fire. Serving boys ran back and forth filling bowls with pottages of peas and barley, whole fish cooked in embers, baked eel, and platters of carrots, parsnips, and beans, herbed with thyme and dill. Each table held loaves of fresh round bread, pats of pale gold butter, hens' eggs, and round cheeses as well as clay jugs of ale and mead.

Leofric's throat contracted as he took a gulp of ale. "We celebrate too soon."

Edmund was seated on my other side. "Thurkill has retreated."

Leofric stared into his goblet. "For now."

"I'm counting the days until that man is out of the Middle Lands and in distant Mercia." Edmund breathed in my ear.

"Lord Leofric saved us," I murmured, not wanting him to hear. Edmund's constant complaining had begun to wear on my nerves like the throbbing of my wound. "We needed his forces today. Without the Mercians, I've no doubt Thurkill would have been victorious."

Edmund scowled but he couldn't deny it.

Beneath the bandage my arm twanged as I reached for the sparrow-hawk brooch attached to the breast of my tunic. Aine had clipped on the brooch after tending to the wound on my arm, anointing it with an herbal salve.

"Why you have to put yourself in danger I don't know." She tutted as if I were a child who'd tumbled in a bramble bush.

"You know why."

I'd winced as she cleansed the ripped skin. If my men fought, I fought. What they had to bear, I bore. Their pain was my pain. Accompanied by Brother Aefic, I'd attended to the dying before going exhausted to my own bower.

Aine had made no answer as she'd released my hair from the tight battle coils and set to with a brush, turning my hair to soft waves of bronze that rippled down my back. Even though I'd lost my helmet, her neat handiwork hadn't come loose.

Now the unruly strands tumbled over my shoulders, waving over my waist to curl just above my thighs. Pushing it from my forehead I rose to my feet. My tiredness had passed. The feasting cure for battle fever worked for fatigue, too.

"Friends! Warriors!" I called from the high table. "*Was hail!*"

"*Was hail!*" Horns and tankards were lifted in reply. Walburgha's cheeks were red, Wilbert, scrubbed and appearing no worse for wear, beside her.

"This great day we have avenged the death of my parents, Lord Radulf and Lady Morwen." My fingers tightened on the stem of my goblet. I still found it hard to say their names. "We have fought to defend the Middle Lands from the Danes. We have kept the honor of Coventry!"

"Aye! Coventry!" The cry went up amidst the rattling of wooden trenchers and the drumming of feet. The candles, jugs, and platters on the long tables juddered.

"We of Coventry are grateful to the men of Mercia who fought so bravely with us, and to their lord." Lord Leofric discomfited me with a sardonic smile before lifting his cup in reply. I faltered for a moment before continuing the toast. "Thurkill the Tall, the Danish terror, has been defeated! He will plague us no more!"

Now the cheers were fit to lift the rafters. "Mercia! Mercia! Coventry! Coventry!"

Seeking silence, I held up my goblet. "Lives have been lost, but they have not been lost in vain." At this, many faces saddened. Like me, some had come to celebrate Coventry's victory without the company of those they loved. My heart ached but I had to continue. Spirits needed to remain high. It would numb my people's pain until they could face their grief. "We will not forget the fallen, but rejoice in our great victory: Saxons all!"

Amidst more cheering and drumming of feet, I'd just taken my seat again when Walburgha, clearly merry on mead, came up to the high table.

"My lady! The Mercians say they are greater tellers of riddles than the people of the Middle Lands!"

"Is that right, Walburgha?" I chuckled.

"What a thing to say!" Her hands on her hips, Walburgha puffed out her red cheeks. "My Wilbert is the greatest riddler there is."

To my surprise Lord Leofric leaned toward her with a glimmer of a grin. "Perhaps there should be a challenge from the riddlers of Coventry to the riddlers of Mercia."

"That's it!" Walburgha cried. "A riddling challenge! Will you allow it, my lady?"

"Don't allow it, Godiva," Edmund muttered. "Don't get too friendly with the Mercians."

"It's all right." I smiled at Walburgha. "I'll allow a riddling challenge."

It would lighten some mournful hearts in the hall, I hoped. I stole a glance at Lord Leofric. There seemed no chance of lightening his mood, but perhaps he too imagined it would lift those of his men.

It didn't lift Edmund's. Tight-lipped he left the hall, a pitcher of water spilling on the table as he got up. It dripped onto my tunic. I wanted to run after him. But I couldn't leave.

Bustling to the edge of the dais, Walburgha cried out so loud that even amidst all the hubbub she could be heard.

"Hear me, good folk! There's to be a riddling challenge between Mercia and the Middle Lands!"

Applause and laughter broke out up and down the hall.

Walburgha beckoned to her husband. "Come now, Wilbert!"

Emptying his tankard at a gulp, Wilbert came forward to the

sounds of cheers as he climbed the steps to the dais. He appeared slightly sheepish, but in strong accents he began to recite with comical gestures:

"I am a wondrous creature, a joy to women,
a help to neighbors; I harm none
of the city-dwellers, except for my killer.
My base is steep and high, I stand in a bed,
shaggy somewhere beneath. Sometimes ventures
the very beautiful daughter of a churl,
a maid proud in mind, so that she grabs hold of me,
rubs me to redness, ravages my head,
forces me into a fastness. Immediately she feels
my meeting, the one who confines me,
the curly-locked woman. Wet will be that eye."

Wilbert guffawed. "So what's the answer to the riddle? What am I, Mercians?"

In a huddle, the Mercian warriors consulted each other, laughing.

"Don't you know the answer?" The Coventry blacksmith called out after a few minutes.

Appearing shamefaced, the Mercians shook their heads.

"Why, it's an onion!" Wilbert shouted triumphantly.

"They don't know their onions!" Walburgha shrieked. "They didn't guess aright! Coventry has won this round!"

More good-natured laughter rang through the hall.

"Bring your best riddler forward, you Northern knaves!" Wilbert called.

After more discussion and laughter between the Mercian warriors, a man with long hair and the thickest arms I'd ever seen came forward. "I'll riddle for Mercia," he cried.

He leapt up, and taking his place on the dais next to Wilbert, intoned loudly:

"A young man came walking, to where he knew she
was standing in the corner, he stepped up from far away,
the hardy retainer, raised his own
garment up with his hands, thrust under her girdle
something stiff as she stood,
worked his will; they both quivered.
The noble one hastened, at times his able
servant was useful, but he tired
after a while, though stronger than her before,
weary of that work. There began to grow
under her girdle what good people often
adore in their core and acquire with coins."

Great roars of hilarity ensued as the Mercian riddler finished. I'd been unable to retain a giggle of my own. The man's gestures had been even more comical than Wilbert's.

"What say you, folk of Coventry?" the Mercian riddler called. "Do you know the answer?"

"'Course we do!" Walburgha shouted instantly. "Just give us a minute."

"But the answer's easy." Wilbert broke in. "It's a butter churn!"

With obvious reluctance the Mercian riddler nodded. Uproar broke out among the townsfolk of Coventry.

"We've won the challenge!" Walburgha beamed with delight. She waved a scolding finger at the Mercian riddler. "You'll have to pay the price!"

"What's the price?" he asked, taken aback.

"We should make you take a penitent's ride through the streets for the shame of such poor riddling!"

From the high table I thought it fit to intervene. "That's a bit harsh, Walburgha!"

Wilbert seized a jug of ale. Froth foamed as he thrust it toward the Mercian. "Drink this then! It will improve your riddling!"

To the sounds of counting and more laughter the Mercian riddler swigged the ale.

"The penitent's ride?" Leofric enquired.

"Do you not know of it? It's a new Christian custom. For penance, those who would take shame upon themselves walk or ride through the streets in only their shift."

He raised a brow. "In only their shift?"

My cheeks must have colored scarlet. The saucy riddles hadn't made the heat rise to my face but to my consternation the merest lift of Lord Leofric's eyebrow did. Seeking refuge in my goblet of ale I judged it safer not to reply.

As he leaned toward me again my heart quickened.

"How is your arm?"

I remembered his gentleness when he'd touched me on the battle-field. "It's better. Aine has put some herbal salve on it. It will soon be healed, I'm sure."

"You're in no pain?"

A tendril of hair fell over my shoulder as I shook my head. I didn't know what gripped me, but it wasn't pain. "No."

"Make sure you get some rest." He stood, making my body aware of the height and strength of his, before he bowed. "It grows late. I'll bid you good night . . . Godiva."

With a swirl of his cloak he left the hall.

The night air blew cool as I lifted my face to the dark sky. Soon spring would arrive, but still a chill wind blew across from the eastern coast. Only a few stars could be seen through the clouds, but I could make out the moon in the bright shape of a crescent.

My skin remained warm long after Lord Leofric left the noisy hall. My appetite gone, I'd toyed with some barley pudding and apples, but my energy had diminished and my wound begun to ache. Soon I, too, made my excuses, though most of the revelers remained behind. The sounds of their laughter and a song being struck up to the ripple of harp strings echoed behind me as I made my way across the empty courtyard to my bower.

My weakened arm twanged. Aine had wanted to suspend it in a rope sling, but I hadn't wanted to. Now I wished I had. It would take weeks for the deep cut to be fully healed, and then I would need to build the muscles up again. Again the memory came to me of how tenderly Leofric had touched me when he realized I'd been hurt. Again, that strange swooping sensation in my belly and a weakness in my knees. It must be battle weariness and fatigue, the effects of too much ale. In the morning I would be myself again.

Outside my bower I stopped and glanced into the darkness. For a moment, I had the strangest sensation of being watched. Yet I could see no one. Usually there would be a few men clustered in the courtyard, playing dice or sitting around a small fire. Tonight, all were in the hall.

The bower door stood ajar. Pausing on the ball of my foot, I skimmed another wary peek over my shoulder. It must be the remnants of the day's fighting, I explained my disquiet to myself, but all my senses remained on alert. The door creaked as I eased it open with two fingers. Puzzled, I craned my neck and peered in, my palm resting on the wood, my body poised, still half outside. The room lay in darkness. No candles were lit, and only a shaft of the crescent moon shone through the window, splashing onto the rushes.

Why was the bower empty? Aine had waited to help me to bed since I was a small child, no matter how late I stayed in the hall, or how many times I told her I could tend to myself. Even the fireplace appeared to be cold.

The hairs on my neck stood up as I sought my sword but came up empty. Uncloaked, unarmed, I'd gone to feast.

A tentative tiptoe forward. Another. "Aine?"

The cold metal of a blade slammed flat against my neck as he came up behind me before I could scream. "Don't move."

My pulse thumped out a terrified tattoo. I could barely swallow with the metal pressed into my skin. Somehow I found words.

"What do you want?" In shame I heard my strangled note of fear.

"What do I want?" He laughed; the same terrible mocking laugh I'd heard him make before the battle had begun. "I want the Middle Lands. Then today I saw something else I wanted."

Yanking my hair, Thurkill the Tall wrenched me closer, so close I smelt his foul breath. "You."

9

And all the low wind hardly breathed for fear . . .
——Tennyson [1842]: *Godiva*

Scream. Kick. Run. Spit. Fight.

A putrid rag stuffed in my mouth.

The point of Thurkill's knife jagged on my neck. His other hand a bolt around my wrists as he pushed me through the bower doorway. Across the courtyard. Toward the gates.

No guards nearby. No Edmund at my side. No one to help me. Draped by darkness, no one to see me either.

The rising bile of terror scorched my gullet as we passed through the unattended gates.

My people. Feasting in the hall, unaware of my danger.

No blame attached to them. It was I who should have expected another attack.

Lord Leofric's grim face flashed into my mind. The Earl of

Mercia had suspected something amiss in Thurkill's sudden retreat. Why hadn't I listened to him?

My mind screamed out. *Help me!*

In the shadows beyond the gates, Thurkill's horse was tethered to a tree stump. He dragged me toward it.

He was going to take me away from Coventry.

Don't let him take you.

Part of my numb brain registered. I had to seize a chance for escape, before he abducted me to another place. Where all help would be gone.

Think. Quickly.

He'd have to release his hold on me to unfasten his horse. My body tensed, ready to spring free.

But Thurkill had recognized the opportunity, too. His grip became a deadlock.

"Untie it!" he grunted, indicating the knotted rope with a jerk.

I shook my head.

He slapped me across the face.

"Untie it!"

Fumbling for time. Too soon the knot came free.

Thurkill's blade pressed harder against my neck. Grabbing the rope, he shifted the knife to aim straight at my heart and bound my hands with it.

A lamb to slaughter.

Mounted. The blade still against my neck, Thurkill forced me onto the saddle. In a loud rip my tunic tore down the middle, between my legs. Heaving himself behind me, his belly pressed into my buttocks. The butcher stench of him.

A brutal kick against the horse's side. Into the darkness.

Don't let him take you.

The reins. Out of reach.

The ground. Better to fall from a galloping horse than be taken by Thurkill the Tall.

His muttered curse as I wriggled. He clamped his hold. We rode on.

Rain began to pummel my clothes, my skin.

To fight down the fear coming up in my mouth I focused on where we were going. Driving rain lashed my cheeks as I flung my head from side to side, scanning for landmarks—a lone farm, tall trees, a clump of bushes—anything I could make out in the dark. The Middle Lands were like the back of my hand, every hill, every valley scored on my skin. He was traveling east, a knoll to our right indicated, as the horse's hooves thundered along. Was he taking me to the Angle Lands?

Another slap across my face.

Onward. An hour passed; another. My sliding survey. Still searching the darkness.

Farther and farther. Away from Coventry.

As he pulled to a sudden stop my neck snapped in pain. The horse pawed. Dimly I distinguished a wooden hut in front of us. It appeared to be deserted.

Thurkill dismounted and wrenched me down. Cramped, sore. Yet as I slid off I seized another chance to wrench free from his grasp.

My weight tumbled into him.

A kick. Only my leather shoes. The strips of my wet, torn tunic strangling my legs. Feeble. No boots.

He guffawed.

Another kick. More force.

A better aim.

"Nidstang." He cursed.

Grabbing me by my hair he began to haul me toward the hut.

Don't let him take you inside.

"Aagh!" My scream escaped now, shrill and desperate, forcing the rag from my mouth. A noise I didn't know I could make.

His fist came up.

Then it came down.

The smell of smoke woke me as if Aine had lit the morning fire.

But I was not in my bower. I sensed it before my lashes flew open. Hooves kicked inside my brain. Bursts of red light. Pain shot like forge sparks from where I'd been struck by Thurkill's fist on the side of my forehead. How long I'd been unconscious, I didn't know. Minutes. Hours. My body stiff. Chilled. Damp. From under the door a draught curled around my legs.

The wind howled.

Coughing, I choked. The rag stuffed in my mouth. Tied firmer this time. Instinctively I reached to pull out the foul-tasting piece of linen but my hands were still roped. So too were my legs, now tight-fastened at my ankles.

Bound and gagged. Slay-ready.

Twisting my neck brought another blast of pain as I scanned my new location. I lay on a pile of rags on a dirt floor inside the hut. The single-room dwelling appeared disused. No furniture, not even a stool. Parts of the thatched roof were missing, jagged teeth, the straw singed and black. At the center of the floor, a circle of pebbles, a small fire burned.

A hovel.

Abandoned.

Get away!

Like a worm I lifted my body, ready to move any way I could.

And froze.

Naked

Men's voices filtered in from outside.

Every nerve of my body strained as I tried to hear.

Only two, as far as I could make out. Not a gang of warriors. One was Thurkill—I recognized that guttural tone. The other was slightly muffled, as though wrapped in a cloak.

They were arguing. They spoke in Danish—that much I could discern. I spoke but a little of the language, but some of it was similar to my own. Only a few words were distinct, the rest lost to the shriek of the wind.

Soon the argument stopped.

A set of footsteps sounded, as though a man was walking away. A horse neighed.

Hooves clattered away.

Dread gagged me as much as the rag in my mouth as the other steps came back toward the hut.

Thurkill kicked open the door.

Before I slammed my lids shut I saw his arms full of wood, his boots coated with mud and grass. His massive Dane-axe strapped to his belt, his dagger on the other hip. I slammed my lids shut to pretend I remained unconscious as his boots clumped across the floor. My heart pounded as through my lashes I watched him load the fire with fuel, the flames licking high.

From inside his cloak he brought a hare, hanging limp. With a gluttonous thrust of his knife he skinned it and tossed it on the flames.

Minutes passed. Long, painful minutes. He sat sideways to me, sucking his teeth, watching the animal burn.

Don't breathe in. Don't breathe out.

But the smell of smoldering flesh made me want to retch.

My stifled choke betrayed me.

His massive back stiffened.

Brute slow. He hauled to his feet.

A piece of wood scorched from the fire.

Holding the flaming torch aloft he thudded over to where I lay.

Firelight buffed his bald dome as he leaned in.

My eyelids widened in revulsion. Even gagged, my lips drew back.

"Welcome, Saxon lady," he jeered.

Gross-tongued, he licked a drop of saliva from the scar at the edge of his mouth.

"About time you woke up. It's not the same if I can't see your face. Such a pretty face."

I flinched.

Smirking, he fingered the sparrow-hawk brooch pinned to my tunic. "I've seen this before."

With one hand he ripped it down my front.

"I'm going to make you struggle."

Another claw. Another rip. My shift. Woven so fine.

"I want it to last."

Spittle on my skin. Dripped between my breasts.

"I'll make you beg like a bitch, just as I did your mother."

My mother. I choked. The last sight she'd seen had been this killer's leer. *But she would never have begged.*

"I'm going to do to you what I did to her. I made your father watch."

Moder. Fader.

Help me.

The flaming piece of wood jerked higher. Fire-lit him. A swamp-thing from hell.

Thick fingers became talons. Stroked my hair.

Reached for my bared breast. Caught the nipple. Dug.

No fear. No fear. I would show no fear.

84

But to my shame I heard my muffled sob. Fear forced out by repulsion, grief, and anger at my mother's fate. Now mine.

The kind of fear that gutted courage, destroying hope in its wake.

"There's no one to hear you," he sneered. "We're all alone, at last."

A voice came from the doorway.

"Wrong again, Thurkill."

10

Was clash'd and hammer'd ...
—————Tennyson [1842]: *Godiva*

Thurkill the Tall hurled me aside and spun on his heel.

My stifled gasp as I fell on my elbow. My heart leapt of hope.

The burning torch still aloft, Thurkill gave a mock bow. "Lord Leofric. I expected you, though not quite so soon."

Thurkill's words sank my heart to my stomach, a pebble dive, wrong-skimmed. Stifled by the rag in my mouth, I gasped.

A trap.

If Leofric cared he made no sign. He moved in from the shadows and pushed back his hood.

His hair. Rough glinting in the firelight.

His eyes. River darkness.

The door creaked and slammed shut as he sauntered into the broken-down hovel with a dismissive glance, barely looking my way.

Yet as on the battlefield, the air between us was not air, but something thicker, denser. An invisible rope that bound me to him as surely as if it had been tied around my waist.

"So predictable, you Saxons," Thurkill sneered, "with your famous code of honor. What you said before the battle got me thinking. Why should I waste my men on the battlefield, when I can keep the maid of Coventry hostage and get exactly what I want—and more?"

So he'd planned to keep me alive. Shudders overcame me.

Thurkill's hostage.

Better off dead.

"What's this, Thurkill? A change of strategy? You're taking hostages now? You destroyed my cities in Mercia. Left all for dead."

Thurkill smirked. "Merely to break the Saxon spirit."

"Impossible."

"*Nidstang.*" Thurkill cursed. "Enough of this talk. I'll trade the maid for the Middle Lands."

"Bad trade," Leofric said, in the flat tone I now knew to be so dangerous. Did Thurkill also know Leofric was at his most deadly when he sounded calm? I feared he did for he spat on the ground, so close to Leofric I flinched.

"Was it? You've come for her. Now I can kill you in single combat."

Leofric shrugged. "What difference does it make if I'm killed? Another good Saxon will step up to take my place."

"Come now." Thurkill's mocking laugh. "We're both leaders, you and I. We understand power. Not all men will follow another man as they follow us."

"You flatter me." Leofric sounded anything but flattered. "But I have brothers to take my place."

"Younger brothers," Thurkill corrected. "They're not leaders such as you—or your elder brother Northman."

"Don't speak my brother's name."

Thurkill raised a brow. "No? Don't speak the name—*Northman?*"

The silver of Leofric's sword flashed out from beneath his cloak as fast as a falling star.

With a roar Thurkill lunged, brandishing his torch.

Struggling for breath I watched them fight, cursing the ropes that bound me. Now I knew why Thurkill the Tall was feared across land and sea. His size, yes, his brute force, these were his advantages, but they were not his true strength. His strength lay in his being the size of a bear with the cunning of a fox.

Every move, every slash of the blade and swish of the battle-torch gripped me, flaming and spitting sparks, until it seemed I fought Thurkill, too.

In. Out. Back. Forth.

Blow for blow, my hand held Leofric's sword. Each move he made, I made with him as he dodged and parried, his feet quick, his arm quicker. But Thurkill was quick, too, quicker than a man his size should be.

In a sharp sideways slice, Leofric knocked the torch from Thurkill's fist. Sparks flew as it rolled on the ground toward where I lay. Immediately Leofric lowered his sword, his gaze following the torch's fiery path.

Slamming down my bound feet, I surged my body toward the torch with all my might and kicked loose dirt onto the flame.

When I looked up, I realized what Leofric's glance toward me had cost him.

Thurkill had reached for his axe and his dagger, too. He'd dropped the torch near me as a distraction. On purpose.

Against the gag in my mouth I tried to cry out, strangled by the foul rag. My neck jerked, my lids wide. Leofric must have read my warning. Instantly he regained his focus. He jumped aside, and with a soul-curdling yell Thurkill raised his axe and slashed it across Leofric's shoulder.

Leofric made no sound, but as the blood gushed from his sword arm he stumbled, his face white with pain. His blade sank, point resting in the hovel dirt.

Thurkill had control now and he knew it. Choking on my fear, my bound limbs stiffened as Thurkill circled and crouched, weapons in both hands, his whole, huge body a taunt.

"This axe killed your brother." Thurkill spoke almost conversationally, sending a hell chill down my spine. "I watched him die. *Northman.*"

Leofric's sword stayed down. His head lowered.

Time stilled.

My heart. A stutter beat.

Thurkill lifted his axe. As if in slow motion I watched it come down in a gruesome sickle sweep.

Leofric's sword flew as he leapt across the room and plunged it straight into Thurkill's chest.

"I warned you." Leofric thrust the blade deeper. *"Don't speak my brother's name."*

Thurkill crashed to his knees, his weapons clattering to the ground. Shock rounded his mouth as a death grunt came from it, a squeal like a wild boar killed in the woods.

Cowering with terror I slammed my eyelids shut until the hideous sound stopped.

When I opened them again, Leofric was leaning on his sword, breathing heavily. He'd finished Thurkill off to make that revolting noise end.

The sword clanged as he threw it down and knelt beside me.

Pulling his cloak from his shoulders he covered my body, hiding my bared breasts. He tore the rag from my mouth.

"Godiva. Did he—hurt you?"

"No," My tongue, numb and sore, didn't seem to work properly in my dry mouth. I could still taste the rag. "You came in time."

"Here." Swiftly Leofric knelt to loosen the ropes that bound me. I rubbed the chafing red marks around my wrists and ankles.

Hauling myself upright I pulled the cloak close, the rough wool scratching my bared skin. It smelled of lye, blood, and sweat. I couldn't stop shaking.

"You're Dane-axe cut," I said hoarsely.

Still kneeling, he shrugged my concern away.

Hard-mouthed he leaned over and ran his finger over my bruise. "He did this to you."

The touch of his fingertips made me quiver. I could only nod. Fury flared in his eyes before he drew away.

"How did you find me?" My voice was still rough.

"I told you. I prefer to sleep in the open air. I suspected there was more to come from Thurkill the Tall. I found your nurse tied up, but she's come to no harm," he added rapidly, at my start of panic.

He'd guarded my bower.

"On my horse I followed hard, but I nearly lost you in the darkness. Then I saw Thurkill's horse." Firelight glinted on his hair as he leant back on his haunches and surveyed the hut with a frown. The hare was charred to black bones. "This doesn't make sense. It's curious that Thurkill was alone."

"But he wasn't alone. I heard another man outside the hut just before you got here. They were arguing."

His shoulders stiffened. "Did you recognize who it was?"

Naked

"No." I winced. My neck was sore. I rubbed it. "The other voice was muffled."

"Could you hear what they said?"

"Not really. They spoke in Danish. I only recognized a word or two." I rubbed my muscles. "They kept saying something that sounded like *huscarl.*"

"*Huscarl?*" he demanded. "You heard the word *huscarl?* Are you sure?"

"I think so." Another nod. Another wince.

"Did they mention Canute?"

"King Canute? No, I don't think so."

In a stride he was at the door, threw it open. Stared out, as if daring someone to come. The cold air swirled inside.

"Whoever it was, there's no one out there now. Come."

He held out his hand.

And stumbled.

Ignoring his outstretched hand I clambered to my feet. "Your cut. It's bad."

Pain etched his mouth. "A scrape."

"Let me see," I insisted.

Blood seeped from the leather vest, turned his sleeve scarlet. Thurkill's axe had gone in at Leofric's shoulder, deep into the muscle, almost into his chest. I shuddered. How close it had been to his heart.

"Hold still, my lord." I seized the rag from the floor. Too putrid. It could poison the wound. In haste I ripped off a piece of my torn tunic and wrapped it tightly around his shoulder to staunch the flow of blood. "It's a deep wound. It may need stitching. My nurse Aine will have some herbal salve that will soon heal it."

91

"Thank you." Some color flooded into his face as he added lightly, "We're twinned, you and I."

"Twinned?"

He indicated the bandage on my own arm.

"Oh. I see."

As he went to pull down his sleeve his fingers brushed against mine. As if I'd touched the flaming torch, I jerked away.

His lids hooded. I was certain he'd noticed my reaction.

"I'll take you home to Coventry."

"My lady!"

Aine rushed toward me and pulled me close. "Thank the goddess you're safe!"

Her arms felt so warm.

Home. Safe.

"I'm all right. Are you?"

"It would take more than a rope to scare me." She tutted. Her brow creased with concern. "You're bleeding."

I glanced down at Leofric's bloodstained cloak. The fabric had formed a thin barrier between us as we'd ridden back to Coventry on his horse, the dawn streaking the sky, my body fitted into his. His grip still seemed to embrace me. In my shuddering state I hadn't dared tried to ride Thurkill's beast by myself.

"It's the Earl of Mercia who's been wounded. He's Dane-axe cut. Can you help him, Aine? You'll need to . . ."

I spun around. He'd been behind me.

The bower door swung.

The next day I found Lord Leofric alone in the herb garden. Clear and bright, as if the terrifying night at the hut had never been. But hideous visions of Thurkill's leer still played in my mind, keeping me shuddering, and Leofric's sword, flashing silver through the air to find its mark. In spite of the mildness of the day, I shuddered again.

That sword was strapped on his belt now as the sun burnished glints of gold in his hair; turning its color even brighter than my own. His wound had been tended, I was relieved to note. A white linen bandage showed at the collar of his fresh tunic, but he revealed no other battle-scars.

Yet as he swung about I registered that his battle-scars lay beneath the surface of his skin. For a swift moment his river-blue eyes were clouded with sorrow. He'd been remembering his brother Northman. I'd have staked my life on it.

"I wanted to thank you for saving me from Thurkill."

A bleak smile etched his lips. "I need no thanks for fighting a Dane."

He pulled a piece of lavender from a nearby bush. Its clean scent rose up as he rolled it between his fingers. The thin stalk seemed incongruously delicate in his fist. "It's as well Thurkill has gone from these parts without there being too much bloodshed."

I was sick of spilled blood.

Aine had wanted to keep me in bed all day. A mint poultice for the black-and-blue lump on my brow. Witch-hazel salve rubbed on my body. A bowl of bread softened with milk, spooned into my mouth. An herbal cup with mandrake in it. No visitors. I'd heard Edmund outside the bower, remonstrating with her, but she hadn't let him in. He'd sounded frantic about me.

But by noon I'd arisen and hurried into town, my basket full of bandages and remedies. Others had suffered more than I. Setting my trauma aside was the only way to cope. Many had been wounded in battle, from the Middle Lands and Mercia, too. The numbers of injured were fewer than I'd dared hope and most would recover. But some would be maimed for life and too many had lost their lives. The grisly work of burying bodies was almost over and there had been little looting. In the main, the Saxons respected the dead.

But my people were war-weary. Losing fight. Reports had come about the extent of the damage Thurkill had wreaked on our border villages. The attacks had been savage. Much would need to be done to repair and rebuild. And at home even Aine had come to harm.

"You have my gratitude for saving me from Thurkill," I said to Lord Leofric, breathing in the calming aroma of the lavender bushes as I stepped closer. They'd begun to flower earlier than usual. "Not only from me but from all my people."

He bowed in acknowledgment. "I'd warn you not to celebrate too soon this time."

An indignant flush rose to my face, a swift retort to my lips. I'd thought my men had needed to celebrate and believe in their strength. My argument seemed weak as I recalled the feasting and merriment that had left me unguarded in my own hall and allowed Thurkill to take me hostage.

"It was a lapse of judgment on my part." How I hated to admit it. But I was responsible.

"More than a lapse. Coventry isn't safe. Thurkill the Tall wasn't the only Dane who wants your lands."

There was no need for him to tell me I would face many challenges to keep the Middle Lands secure. They'd kept me awake along with Thurkill's leer. "The Danish peril hasn't passed. I know I have more battles ahead."

"They're battles you can't win."

Naked

My pulse began to race. "What do you mean?"

Leofric lifted up the lavender as if to smell it, the contemplative gesture belying the calculation in his eyes as they met mine. "I think you know."

II

Made her cheek flame . . .
——Tennyson [1842]: *Godiva*

"We must discuss the Middle Lands," Leofric said, "now your father is gone."

Flinging the stalk of lavender to the ground he crushed it under his heel. He made a rapid survey of the garden. In the vegetable beds, green shoots were pushing through. A peaceful place. A sanctuary.

"We can't talk here. Come. I will speak with you alone."

"Well?" We were in the hall, a trestle table a barricade between us. A peek at Leofric's grim face had sent the servants scattering.

For a moment he studied me. I tightened my lips.

"The Middle Lands are Engla-lond's heartlands," he said. "They're the center point for Saxon law, or for the Dane law. The way the Middle Lands go, so all Engla-lond will go. The Danes will not relent. They'll come after Coventry again and again. They mustn't take it. Coventry must stay Saxon."

Once again he was telling me what I already knew. It was a habit with him I'd begun to find maddening; treating me as an ignorant child. "Coventry *is* Saxon."

"But for how long? All you've proven so far is that you need Mercia to hold the Middle Lands."

"I've proven no such thing! Coventry would have won the day, with or without Mercian warriors. Long have we in the Middle Lands held off the Danes from the east."

A dismissive sweep of his hand. "Under your father's command."

"And now under mine." As usual my fingers sought the familiar comfort of my braid. The wound on my arm twanged. I wondered if Leofric's wound pained him. If so, he gave no sign.

His short laugh spilled disdain. "You'd be dead if I hadn't saved you. You've just thanked me for it."

"I'd have fought Thurkill off," I lied.

He leaned across the table, his voice low. "You were half naked. Do you think me blind?"

Flames from deep inside my body smoldered through my skin.

"It isn't just Thurkill I speak of. You lack in battle craft. Even more dangerous, you think you know it but you don't. That Danish warrior you fought in the field—I don't wish to diminish your courage, but to leave him injured, ready to attack you again . . . And Thurkill. We both know you don't have the power, the physical strength, to have defeated him. My strength overcame him."

"Only because you didn't give my intelligence a chance," I shot back fast as a catapult. He'd hit me where it hurt most. I was as good as any man. I had to be. Years. Hidden tears. Both daughter and son. For my parents' sake, I'd vowed it. "There are many ways to win a

97

fight, my lord, and the best is by using wits. Brawn doesn't always beat brain."

A bang of his bare fists on the table sent it juddering. In spite of myself I jumped.

He gave a satisfied smile. "Brawn saved your lands, Lady Godiva."

I flung my plait over my shoulder. "Next time I'll use my brains to save my lands."

His tone stayed low but there was flint-fire in it. "There won't be a next time."

My stomach became a milk churn. I stared at him.

"I can't leave Coventry at risk," Leofric said. "It would cost every Saxon in Engla-lond if I did."

"I don't understand -"

"Yes. You do."

Panic engulfed me as realization dawned. Heaving a lungful of air, I searched Leofric's face for a clue, some sign that my suspicions were unfounded. No muscle moved.

"Do you mean to take my lands?" Gripping the edge of the table, I could barely stay upright.

"I don't need to take them. The Danes have been defeated. I've already won them."

Shock stopped my speech. Then fury overcame me, a bonfire explosion. My own fists slammed down on the wood. "You haven't won them! These lands are mine!"

He shook his head as though my outburst hadn't occurred. "Coventry must come under Mercia's rule. It's the only way to keep it safe."

Self-doubt seeped through my veins as if I'd swallowed a hemlock herb draught. Was I equal to the task my parents had left me? "I can keep Coventry safe."

"You're wrong."

"Is this why you came here? What were your true reasons for riding into Coventry as soon as you heard of my father's death? Did you come to aid me, or defeat me?"

His jaw set. "My men and I came to defeat Thurkill the Tall. To save Saxon lands, and Saxons from the Danes who would crush them and make them slaves. That I have done. Keeping Coventry under my command is the only way forward."

"Then you're a thief, Lord Leofric," I hissed. "And a liar."

The coldness I knew to be so dangerous came over him, chilling my skin. I'd witnessed it with Thurkill, in the hut, and Thurkill lay dead.

His voice cooled to a perilous temperature. "Have a care, Lady. I told you no lies. Did I not warn you I came here for Mercia's sake? Did I not warn you the weakness of the Middle Lands threatens what's mine? I came for Saxon good and I won't waver. With only you as their leader, Coventry can't be the Saxon stronghold it must remain."

Sobs threatened but I blinked them back, hard. No weakness would I show to this man. My father left me these lands, this town, this hall.

Through the mist of supressed tears I beheld the hall that my father had built, that my mother had made so fine. The tapestries and bronzes that hung on the walls, the timber beams, painted red, yellow, green, blue, and gold. The dais, the high table. The trestle tables to be laid out to welcome all.

Hall-joy.

I blinked, hard. No weakness would I show the Earl of Mercia.

"You say you come for the good of the Saxons? How can that be if you take a Saxon woman's lands—by force?"

"Would you prefer it had been Thurkill?"

Thurkill's fat talons groping my breast. What would have happened if Leofric of Mercia hadn't arrived . . . I concealed my shudder. "Maybe I would be better off! Am I your prize now, Lord Leofric? I am the spoils of war—for you?"

A long, considering surmise. "Not by force. I leave that to the Danes."

"How noble." Rue in my tone, a bitter-tongued herb. "Yet you, a Saxon lord of the Witan Council, want to take my inheritance."

"No inheritance will remain if I do not. Mercia must be Coventry's overlord, for the Saxon good."

"Never!"

So casual. He shrugged.

Again tears started. I brushed them away from my cheeks before he could see them. "I've let the enemy inside my gates."

"I am inside your gates." A strange twist on Lord Leofric's lips. "And inside them I intend to stay. But enemies . . . that's not my intention."

How could he not expect us to be enemies if he seized my lands?

As if I'd spoken aloud he answered my question.

"Be my wife, Godiva of Coventry."

"You want me to marry you?"

A nod was his only reply.

As if for a weapon I grasped for a response, but none came. A sword, a shield. To attack. To defend. What response could I make? I could only stare.

Leaning across the table, his tone turned almost persuasive. "Let us come together as one. The Danes won't try to take Mercia or the Middle Lands again if our lands are joined."

"You seem to have it all planned out." Sarcasm dripped.

A shrug of his shoulders. "It's a good plan."

"There's a problem."

Boldly I circled the table to position myself squarely in front of him, like a chess piece in the game my father had taught me. Yet my heart beat so loud I felt sure he could hear it.

"I won't marry you, Lord Leofric."

Anger combusted in his eyes, something darker thundering behind it. Internally I quaked.

The blaze passed. His face became granite. "You may find you've no choice."

"I have a choice!" I held my ground. "These are my lands, and it's the right of a Saxon noblewoman to marry with her consent. Do you dare to take that right from me, too?"

"Perhaps you ought to consider what's more important. Your lands . . . or your husband?"

He pulled me into his arms. His lips that appeared so cold in repose were forge-fire as they discovered mine. Melting me, down into my belly, spreading like tongues of flame to liquefy my core.

Struggling to wrench my lips from his I tried to speak, my protest opening my mouth. Instead of releasing me he probed deeper with his tongue. Widened my lips. Bow-bent my body, drew me deeper into his embrace. My legs quivered with threat of surrender.

Heat swirled, rage, fear, and an emotion I dared not acknowledge as I dragged myself away. With shaking fingers I brushed loose strands of hair.

My body continued to smolder. His warm lips. Not cold. The

caress of his tongue. Almost playful. The fire he'd stirred up in the deepest hearth of me.

Ablaze.

Silver and amber. The clasp on my cloak.

Talisman tight, I clutched it.

To withstand fire.

"This is treachery," I gasped.

"This is wisdom," Leofric corrected. "You must make up your mind. Coventry is mine. The battle has been won for it. All that remains is for you to decide whether you'll be my hostage—or my wife."

Hostage! Thurkill the Tall was the enemy who had threatened to take me hostage, not Leofric of Mercia. How could I have let this happen? What had I done?

"So I'm to be your prisoner."

"There'll be no need for that. But if you go out riding, take a guard with you."

"I'm not to be kept under lock and key? Why thank you." Caustic as lye, sarcasm crept into my tone once more. "But if I'm to be at liberty, I could escape."

"You won't escape, Godiva." Leofric said. "You won't leave your lands and your people. Will you?"

12

"You would not let your little finger ache
For such as these?"——"But I would die," said she.
——Tennyson [1842]: *Godiva*

Rushing into my bower I threw myself down by the fire. Heaves wracked my body.

Too many emotions. Anger. Shock. Exhaustion.

Passion.

Still shaking, I grabbed the fire-iron and poked the fire into full life. Red, orange, yellow, blue. The flames leapt and mingled. When I went to the forge to have Ebur shod, the metal would change color until it was white hot. Hammered at melting point to alter consistency. To change shape.

Another heave of my quivering body.

Aine came in and hurried to my side. "Lady Godiva! What is it?"

"Oh, Aine!" I gulped mouthfuls of air.

She smoothed my hair. "Tell me."

Pacing the room, I recounted what had happened. Except for Leofric's kiss, though I sensed she guessed.

"I've failed my parents. I haven't held Coventry safe."

"Come now, that's not true. You're exhausted, that's what it is. What you've been through. It's too much. Here, let me wash your face." She led me to the bench by the window. It was soothing to watch her bustle about, filling a bowl of water from the jug. Gently, she patted my face with a soft cloth, the lavender water cooling my hot cheeks.

"So, Lord Leofric seeks to marry you?"

"He said he was my ally in our fight against Thurkill. He lied to me! He tricked me! He believes the Danish peril is too great for the Middle Lands."

Aine pursed her lips. "There doesn't seem to be a lie in that."

"He didn't tell me he would try to overlord me," I said tartly.

"Mercia is far mightier than Coventry and the Middle Lands," Aine pointed out. "Lord Leofric is an earl, your father was a thane. Lord Leofric is your overlord already."

Aine pressed on. "Isn't Coventry more precious to you than anything else in the world?"

Tearing some herb leaves she mixed them with hot water. "Now, there's nothing better than this herbal mixture of chamomile and sweet mint. Drink it and listen to me."

Obedient as the child she'd brought up, I took a sip of the soothing liquid.

"This fighting has to end. Your mother would have wanted you to put what's happened behind you. To be brave. To move on. That takes real courage."

Slowly, I nodded. I understood what she was trying to say.

"Many Saxon women have done what you are being called to do.

You know the name such women are given, those who marry to end war. *Fripwebba.*"

"*Peace weavers.*" I bit my lip. "I know Saxon women pride themselves on keeping the peace. But that's not the path I was raised for. I'm a warrior."

"But why do you fight, my lady? You fight to bring peace to your lands." Aine said shrewdly. "It's not battle you truly seek. It's peace."

Gripping the herb cup, I was silenced.

Aine picked up her sewing, lying nearby, and began to darn a hole in my tunic. The stitches, even and fine. "The needle can mend. The sword cannot."

"But even if I want to bring peace, it doesn't mean I have to marry against my will," I objected. "I'm a Saxon noblewoman. I can marry with consent. It's my right."

"Yes, it's your right." She was quiet for a moment, deep in thought, though she didn't drop a stitch. "What was your mother's favorite tale?"

"Why . . . the tale of Beowulf." So many nights we'd sat at the high table, in the flickering firelight, listening to the gleeman. "She liked to hear of Queen Wealtheow, the first *fripwebba*, the great peace weaver."

The meaning dawned on me. "Do you mean my mother would want me to choose for my people and not for myself? To be a peace weaver?"

Aine bit off a loose thread. "I cannot say, my lady. But don't think too long on this. It seems to me Lord Leofric won't be kept waiting."

From the top of the hill I could see it all.

The Middle Lands. The land of my people, the land of my cyn. The land I loved.

I'd ridden out as soon as I'd arisen, after another sleepless night. Gone out all day. Spoken to no one, not even Edmund. I needed to consider. To plan.

What was I going to do? Could I marry Lord Leofric? Could I be a peace weaver?

Running my tongue around my mouth, the imprint of his kiss seemed still upon me. His lips had been hot-iron, branding mine with forge-flame. No denying my anger with him for having trapped me. Also, no denying the other fervent flicker awakened below.

Leofric's kiss. The dormant hearth inside me kindled, making me yearn for more. A hungry fire. Seeking fuel.

Yet here on this hill, Edmund had kissed me, too. Surprised me, sent me spinning. Into the whirlwind. Swirling in the vortex. Dizzy. So dizzy.

But Leofric's kiss . . .

Home.

Below in Coventry smoke started to rise from the chimney holes as twilight fell. I knew each chimney, each house, each fireplace, each bench, each family tending the flames, cooking their evening meal. At any door I knocked, I would be welcomed inside.

Leofric of Mercia had my measure. No matter what peril I faced, no matter what harm I risked, I'd never leave my home.

Edmund threw open the stable door. "Why have you been avoiding me?"

I dropped the horse brush. Ebur moved restlessly in the stall.

He yanked me by my shoulder, out of the horsebox.

The wound on my arm stabbed. I rubbed my arm. "That hurt!"

"What's going on?"

"Nothing."

"Don't lie to me. You've always told me everything. What's happened?"

I stared into his mirror-grey eyes, as familiar to me as my own.

"Tell me."

"Lord Leofric has asked me to wed."

"He wants to marry you?"

I gave a rapid nod.

"Is that all?"

"Not all."

"He's annexing the Middle Lands, isn't he?"

Reluctantly, I nodded once more. The ride had cleared my headache, but already pressure again pounded at my temples.

"By God! I knew it!" Edmund roared. "He had this in mind all along! This can't be allowed! Mercia to take the Middle Lands?"

"Mercia did save us against the Danes," I said uneasily. My first thoughts had been the same. *Had Leofric planned it?*

"That doesn't mean you have to marry the Mercian lord!"

"If I marry him, I keep my lands. If not, all is lost."

"So you're going to do it? Are you mad? You mustn't even consider marrying Leofric! You can't trust him! Your parents would never have wanted this!"

"It's a Saxon noblewoman's right to choose whom she would marry. As heiress to the Middle Lands, you must choose wisely."

"My parents wanted me to follow my heart."

"And where is your heart?"

"With Coventry," I said simply.

"Coventry." Edmund almost spat out the word. "Always thus with you. Perhaps your parents did you a wrong to bring you up to talk of nothing else, making you so loyal to these lands."

"Don't speak against my parents, Edmund," I snapped.

"Do you really think they would have wanted you to marry Lord Leofric? Listen to me, Godiva. Let's get on our horses and ride away from here. We'll leave now, today."

He didn't understand what Lord Leofric had grasped immediately. "I can't leave the Middle Lands!"

"But we can't stay here! Not with Mercia as our overlord."

"Nor can I leave Coventry to such a fate without me! My place is here with my people. This is where I belong."

"You belong to me."

My back slammed against the stable wall.

My wrist imprisoned above. My injured arm hanging.

"Godiva. You've always been mine. I've waited for you."

His lips a hot blade against my cheek. His smell, metal clean. I knew Coventry town by sound and smell. He'd led me through the streets, blindfolded. So I knew Edmund.

"So much has been taken from you already. I should have saved you from Thurkill. I'll never forgive myself," he murmured. "Let me save you now. Marry me. Your parents wanted us to wed, you know it."

Teeth sharpened on my neck.

Ravenous. Devouring.

His mouth on mine. Teasing me open . . .

Wrenching my wrist free, I ducked out of his hold and pushed him away.

He staggered.

"What is it?" His teeth were gritted. "What's changed between us?"

My lips felt numb. Everything had changed since Leofric had kissed me. But before that, too.

Edmund cursed. "Were you ever going to marry me? When I asked you before the Witan. Were you going to say yes?"

Numb and dumb. Impossible to reply.

At the feast before my parents left for the Witan, that's when I'd known. In a flash I'd realized I would never marry Edmund. Some kind of foretelling, such as Aine possessed. An intuition, a gift I hadn't recognized.

He must have seen the answer in my eyes.

Fury on his face. Fury, hurt pride. And rejection.

But not complete surprise.

"I'm sorry." A fragment. A whisper.

I should have told him. I knew that. But I hadn't known how.

A crack.

A crash.

Lightning.

In a twist of rage Edmund kicked in the stable wall.

Shards. Splinters.

Knives through the air.

Behind me Ebur neighed and pawed. I shivered away, closer to my horse.

Another furious kick.

A jagged hole. He spun around.

"You've played me for a fool. Led me on all these years."

"No, no! I was confused. I wasn't sure."

"Sure of what? Of me?"

"Please, Edmund! Try to forgive me. We can get beyond this. Be my friend, as you always have been."

"Your friend!" He cursed again. "What are you asking of me? I can't stand by and be your friend if you wed the Earl of Mercia. And you're going to marry him, aren't you?"

I bit my lip.

"Well, I won't watch you do it, whether it's for the good of the Middle Lands or not. I'm leaving. I only stayed here—for you."

"Please, Edmund. You can't leave me. Don't go." He had always been at my side. How would I survive without him?

"There'll be no place for me here. Leofric has his own *cnihts*. I would have been sheriff. I would have been lord."

It was the boy, speaking now, the boy who had lost his lands in the east. The boy who had come to us, frightened, orphaned, alone. The boy I had befriended. The boy I loved.

"There'll always be a place for you in Coventry."

"Serving you and the Earl of Mercia? At the foot of his table? Never. I'll leave on the morrow."

Straw flew as he flung out of the stable.

"Edmund. Wait!"

I raced after him, into the dusk, and skidded to a halt.

Lord Leofric stood in the stable yard.

How long had he been there? How much had he seen and heard?

"*Mercian.*" Edmund sneered.

I froze.

"You've been riding out alone," Leofric said to me, almost idly. "I told you to take a guard."

Somehow I found the spirit to reply. "To protect me or to stop me escaping?"

Edmund broke in. "I'm her guard, Mercian. Her *cniht*. I know your plan to take the Middle Lands. I've been convincing Godiva against it."

Leofric took in what must have been my rumpled hair, my flushed cheeks, and bruised lips. "Is that what you were doing?"

"You've no right to Coventry. A fellow Saxon? To come to these

Naked

lands, under the guise of assistance and take a noblewoman's inheritance?"

"There was no guise," Leofric said sharply. "It's my Saxon duty to defend the Middle Lands. It's my Saxon duty now to hold them."

"You're not needed here," Edmund spat. "Godiva can hold these lands."

"With your protection, I presume." Leofric curled his lip. "I saw that on the battlefield. And where were you when Thurkill took her? She'd be better protected by a Dane."

"Why you . . ."

Cold-glitter. Sparks of fury. Edmund pulled his sword.

"Think carefully." Leofric spoke soft, so soft. Dead calm. Hilt-ready. "Before you make another move."

Edmund. An edge.

Leofric. A wall.

Edmund's lips drew back in a snarl.

In a leap I flew between them.

"Stop it!" I shouted. "Please!"

Edmund's sword flashed in the air and dropped.

Leofric retreated. Just a step.

Edmund spoke through thinned lips. "Are you coming with me, Godiva?"

Quivering like a bowstring, I shook my head.

"Then I can do no more." Bitter-faced, he thrust his sword into his belt. Without another word he strode away.

"Edmund! Wait!"

A hand clamped my arm.

"I'll have your answer, Godiva."

On my boot heel I spun.

I'd find Edmund later, talk to him. We'd argued before. Never like this, but I'd find a way to make him understand.

"You want my answer, Lord Leofric? Then you shall have it. You've told me your terms. Now you'll hear mine."

13

"Alas!" she said,
"But prove me what it is I would not do."
——Tennyson [1842]: *Godiva*

The hall echoed as I entered. Empty and chill. Soon the fire would be lit and the trestles folded out for the evening meal, but for now the vast room was vacant.

Except for Lord Leofric. Waiting on the dais.

I'd insisted he give me an opportunity to change out of my boots and leggings before we had this crucial conversation. Time to prepare myself. In my bower I'd stripped off my leathers, donned a clean shift, a scarlet tunic. Lavender water splashed over my skin.

A quick glance at the missal. A muttered prayer.

An anxious reflection in the polished roundel. A cloth rubbed at the red marks on my neck. A circle of gold looped to hide them, my fingers trembling. Honey balm on my tender lips.

My argument with Edmund had shaken me to the bone. I had to

find him. I had to explain. But first I had to find enough strength to bargain with the Earl of Mercia.

These negotiations were crucial.

Yet Lord Leofric appeared unconcerned as he leaned against the high table, his boots crossed in front of him. "You've come to a decision."

"I have." Breath sucked from deep inside my lungs. "But I have my terms."

On my way back from the hill I'd planned my exact wording of what to say in this meeting.

My prepared phrases scattered like dandelion seeds as Leofric came close to where I stood warming my hands in attempted nonchalance by the central fire.

"Do you think you're in a position to set terms?"

"You think me a mere girl, but you've already been mistaken in me. You thought me not a warrior."

"I'll concede that you can fight."

"Then hear me now." To my shame my voice wavered. With resolution I steadied it. "We must discuss the *morgengifu*."

Astonishment, speedily hooded by his eyelids.

"Must we indeed?"

"Since my father is not here to negotiate for me, I must do so for myself."

Grief swiped its sickle through me once more. Yet again I wished my father by my side. There was a certain humiliation in having to speak to my prospective husband of the morning gift that by our custom was given to a bride the morning after her wedding. More than a mere dowry, it defined the power relations in a marriage, and between the families to be joined in wedlock. Negotiations could be heated and I was sorely unschooled. But I had to bargain for myself. No one else would.

Leofric put his hands together in a steeple. "Go on."

"You can try to take these lands from me by force. But you haven't counted upon the loyalty of my people—to me, not to you. They will not bow to you willingly, not unless I ask them to. Without my command, you'll have internal unrest to add to the external Danish threat. You don't want trouble in the Middle Lands, should I allow you to overlord them."

"Allow me? I don't need their willingness."

"Do you not? Do you want strife or do you want peace?"

Acting as a *fripwebba*, a peace weaver, was demanding as much courage as being a warrior.

His harsh exhalation was almost a curse. "You dare to threaten me?"

"I dare to warn you. If not, you will have more trouble than you bargained for."

"I'm beginning to think that already." His murmur sent a ripple deep in my stomach as if it were a caress.

"Let me tell you my terms." I counted on my fingers. "They are these. First, as my *morgengifu* I keep sovereignty of Coventry as far as the wildwoods of Arden. Coventry will not become part of Mercia to be subsumed under your authority."

"And second?"

"It will be their lady to whom the taxes are paid. It will also be their lady to whom they come for advice and justice."

With great care I'd considered what to ask for. Control of the shire's finances was crucial. It would give me power that I wouldn't possess if I was ruler in name only.

The Earl of Mercia would know that, too.

Lord Leofric stalked away and stared out the window into the courtyard to where two Mercian warriors stood on evening guard. The taller of them was Acwell, his henchman. I wasn't a prisoner, but the sight of the Mercian warriors reminded me how easily I could become one.

Stitching my fingers between each other I waited for his reply.

Had I dared too much? Would he listen to me?

Playing for time, he remained with his back to me. A strategy of his, I'd begun to discern.

When he swung around a muscle twitched in his jaw.

"You want to keep Coventry. The jewel in the crown. And the rest of the Middle Lands?"

"They will be yours." It seemed to slice away a limb to lose any part of my inheritance. But in the dark of night, pacing my bower, I'd come to the conclusion it would be safer for most of my lands to become part of Mercia, especially the border area to the northeast, always vulnerable to Danish raids. For our protection, I had to be a peace weaver.

Who knew what evil still lurked outside our borders?

"This is all you ask?" The word *all* twisted with sarcasm.

"There's something else." The words fell out of my mouth, as fast as pebbles in a hill slide. "If we have a son then he will have Mercia. If we have a daughter, then she will be Lady of Coventry. The title must continue under the female line."

"Lady, you're quick," he drawled. "We haven't bedded yet."

A flush roared into my cheeks that came from my fire-core within. "You mock me."

A negative movement of his head, yet a slant of a smile hovered around his lips. I noted again the line that appeared in his cheek as though it had once been dented in laughter.

"You fight for yourself and on behalf of children you haven't yet borne. Who can't admire that in a woman?"

"Doesn't every she-wolf fight for her cubs? My father was a thane. His rank was not as high as yours, but as his daughter, I inherited lands and title. My daughter must do the same."

Leofric rubbed his jaw.

My heart began to pound. Danger had hemmed me in. Only Mercia could keep it at bay. My bargaining position was weak. Only my resolve was strong.

"Rebels from the Middle Lands at Mercia's borders are the last thing I need," he said at last. "They would be as bad as the Danes."

"Worse."

"Hah." He released another of those exhalations. "For the good of both our lands I agree to your terms."

In relief my shoulders slumped. There was graveness in him I trusted. "I have your word on this? As a Saxon?"

"My Saxon word for Saxon good. But I must give you a warning of my own." He leaned in, his mouth next to mine. "I will be *your* lord."

My stomach somersaulted as if I had taken to the air. So close to him, my lips parted as my body remembered the kiss we'd shared.

Instincts battled within me. An urge to step closer to him. At war with my feet, falling back.

Feet won. I retreated, yet my attention remained on him.

"You will be known as the Lady of Coventry. You shall also be Lady of Mercia."

"It doesn't mean the same to me."

A raised brow. That was all. Then his visage was clear of any emotion I could discern. "There's something you have forgotten."

Moving nearer still, he closed the gap I'd stretched between us.

His breath warmed my cheek. "The *morgengifu* is given to a woman by her husband the morning after their wedding night. Not before. To wed is to gamble. In our language even the words have the same meaning. But the gamble is mine, is it not?"

The blush scalding my face suffused my neck and breasts as I stared at the dirt floor. More than ever I wished my father was alive to broker my wedding. "My *morgengifu* is sovereignty of Coventry. No more and no less."

Lifting my chin, he forced me to meet his stare. A blue flicker. The heart of a flame.

"Such a price suggests great satisfaction with the bride."

"I know what marriage requires." My cool words belied the fire-serpent coiled in my loins. In the cup of his palm I raised my chin higher. "For the sake of Coventry, you won't be dissatisfied."

Edmund's bite marks on my neck. Red, raw. In spite of the gold necklace, he saw them.

Instantly he withdrew his hand.

"Is there nothing you wouldn't do for your people?"

The touch of his skin still kindled though now his fists were clenched by his side.

"I'll do anything."

Speculation in his surmise.

Silence.

"Then we're agreed, Godiva of Coventry."

"Agreed. For the good of my people, for the good of my lands, I'll marry you, Leofric of Mercia."

Yet even as I spoke I trembled at the bargain I'd made.

The marriage gamble was also mine.

14

So left alone, the passions of her mind,
As winds from all the compass shift and blow.
——Tennyson [1842]: *Godiva*

"Faster, Ebur. Faster."

The wind tangled my hair as I galloped across the fields, splashed through the streams.

Yet again I'd disobeyed Leofric's command to take a guard with me.

I had to be alone.

Thoughts clanged and clashed as the Middle Lands flashed past me in a kaleidoscope of sky and land.

Tree, leaf, blade of grass. Farm, barn, hut. Ox, sheep, bird. Man, woman, child.

Each and every one dear to me.

For these I would lay down my life.

We charge the care of Coventry to you, while we are gone. My mother's voice whispered on the wind.

So boldly had I told Lord Leofric my terms for marriage. Against Ebur's flanks my knees still trembled as I thought of it. Had he guessed how terrified I'd been? How alone I'd felt?

Now I was more alone than ever.

With a childish sniffle I wiped my glove across my cheeks. It was more than a week since Edmund had gone, without another word to me, his place at the high table empty, his horse's stall unfilled.

While I'd pledged myself for Coventry, he'd vanished.

Shards. Splinters.

Left me as shattered as the stable wall.

"It's better Edmund's gone, my lady." Aine had said, as I sat slumped by the fire in my bower. "A stable can't have two stallions."

"But to leave without saying good-bye. Don't you know how much Edmund means to me?"

"Playmates as children was one thing, now it's quite another," she'd retorted. "You've grown too close to Edmund. He's like bindweed around a *hollen* bush. It's dangerous. You must stand alone now. You'll see him again, never fear."

Desperately I wanted to believe Aine. Would I ever see Edmund again? What I'd said to him still rang in my ears. There was no way I could revoke my words now. The raw pain on his face, as though my palm had slapped across his cheek, still made me wince. The words had spilled out of my mouth of their own accord, ale from a tankard. I hadn't even known I would say them until they had been said and couldn't be retrieved.

But in the stables he'd frightened me, too.

Ebur began to tire. Leaning down, I slipped off my glove and patted his rough mane. "Time to go home."

His ears pricked backward.

We slowed to a trot.

As I approached the outlying houses of the town, in the distance I made out the shape of Lord Leofric on horseback, his broad leather-clad back unmistakable, his tawny hair bare. He, too, had been riding out alone.

Perhaps he was also wondering at what would come from our marriage. For good or ill, our lives would be joined. To start to accept it, we had to build new lives.

His protection. My peace.

Outside the church I looped Ebur's reins on the lych-gate. Inside, someone, Aine or Walburgha perhaps, had laid fresh flowers on the clay floor at the foot of the cross.

My veil over my hair.

With trembling fingers, I lit two candles.

Fader.

Moder.

Kneeling in front of the painted cross, I missed them so much I could barely breathe.

I had to say good-bye to the old life.

Be brave. Move on. Bring peace.

Wedding vows were holy vows. In a few days' time, I would make them in this hallowed place, built by my father for my mother. When I made my vows to Leofric, I would have to keep them. They would be for life, never to be broken. *A woman must keep her pledge to a man.* Our Saxon saying.

In this place, before God, my vow would be sacred.

Beneath my veil I bowed.

"Surprise!" Beolinda leapt out from behind the bower door.

"Beolinda!"

From my sweaty palm, I released my knife. Instinctively I'd pulled it from my belt.

I'd been deep in reflection as I came home after my time spent in prayer. Seeking guidance. Comfort. Peace.

Just then I didn't need to be reminded of how Thurkill had grabbed me, his dagger at my neck.

"Did I give you a fright?" She giggled. "I'm sorry. I've been waiting for you."

Her sweet rose scent enveloped me as we embraced each other. She'd grown a little plumper, I thought, as she pulled away. But prettier than ever.

"Aine said you were at church. How can you pray so long? Don't your knees hurt?"

My hours of prayer had always been private to me. To discuss my faith always seemed to be a form of pious pride. Dodging her question I asked, "Just what are you doing here hiding behind the door?"

Beolinda giggled again. It cheered me just to see her pretty face, her golden hair shining as bright as coins. "When we heard the news I set out straightaway. Did you think I'd let my closest friend get married without me as a witness?"

My closest friend. No matter how much I cared for Beolinda it was Edmund to whom I had always given that accolade.

"Godiva, you're so sad. Is it your parents? I'm so sorry for your loss."

"I always imagined my parents would be with me at my wedding." Only days away. I cleared my throat.

"And I always thought you would marry Edmund!"

"Things don't always turn out as we expect." Jagged. Chips of wood.

"And Edmund's gone away?" Beolinda's lashes fluttered wide. "Is that right?"

Splinters once more. "Yes. He's gone."

"Where?"

"I'm not sure. Perhaps to the Angle Lands."

"Did he leave any word?"

"No." I changed the subject. "It's good to see you."

"I'm amazed to find you marrying Lord Leofric of Mercia. I just met him in the courtyard when I arrived. He isn't what I expected. He's so stern."

Stunned to find I hated Beolinda speaking badly of Leofric, I bit my tongue. I supposed she would find him stern; he'd probably barely spoken two words to her when she arrived at the hall. He'd barely spoken more than a few words to me since I'd agreed to wed him. Retreated again. He always seemed to be in consultation with his warriors. It bothered me more than I cared to admit, but I disdained to begin my married life discussing my future husband behind his back. I'd made my bargain and I would keep it.

"Perhaps you'll be my wedding attendant in the church." I had no one else to stand up for me, not anymore.

"I'd love to! Is there a special gown for me to wear?"

"Nothing special," I laughed. Beolinda hadn't changed, at least. It came as a relief. "You can carry flowers, perhaps. It's only going to be a simple ceremony."

She tucked her arm in mine. "No, Godiva. It's going to be a special ceremony. Very special, indeed."

With Beolinda for company I wasn't so lonely, though Edmund's absence continued to ache, a wound slow to heal, like the battle cut on my arm.

I missed him more than I could say. And when Beolinda went home I'd be alone. With my new husband.

A man I barely knew.

An idea had come to me.

I would get to know Leofric.

We were going to be wed. Perhaps if we spent some time together, I might be able to break through the barrier between us. We couldn't spend our years of marriage as strangers.

I'd ask him to ride to the Forest of Arden with me, I decided, as I filled Ebur's water trough, avoiding the empty stall next door where Edmund's horse should be. I'd taken yet another long ride across the fields. My restless body craved exercise as my wedding day drew closer. Beolinda hadn't wanted to ride, even though she used to when we were younger. It had been Edmund's company, not riding, she'd enjoyed. Edmund who'd spurred me on to more daring feats on Ebur's back as we raced across field and plain.

Ebur butted me with his nose.

"Ebur."

He butted again.

"*Ebur.*"

Twisting around, I went to push him away.

In a hay bale in the corner of the stall, silver glistened beneath the straw.

Avoiding Ebur's back legs, I crouched.

Yanked it out.

The weight of it sent me stumbling back on my haunches as I crouched down to haul it out.

A sword. Massive, two-edged, silver, the hilt inlaid with gold.

Crossing to the stable door, it took both hands to hold it up to a slant of afternoon light. The carved patterns on the blade glimmered in the sun.

It wasn't a sword that belonged to anyone from the Middle Lands. Perhaps the carvings were of Mercian design. I frowned. I had seen Leofric's sword, the one he used in battle, and it was plain; plain and strong. Perhaps this was a ceremonial sword, to use on our wedding day. I knew a bridegroom carried one to signify that he would defend his bride. Did he know it was here, hidden behind the hay in Ebur's stall? Or was it lost?

Testing its weight, I swung it. I'd never held such a balanced blade before. It sang.

Dragging the sword behind me I went to find Leofric.

He was in the hall, deep in conversation with his bodyguard Acwell. As I entered they stopped.

"Leofric." I called him by his name alone and not his title now. It still tasted strange. But it was a step forward, at least. "I must speak with you."

Acwell bowed and left the room. The immense bulk of the man always unnerved me, and we had rarely exchanged more than a few words. Still, he was always courteous.

Leofric seemed abstracted. "What is it?"

My arm wound twanged as I lifted the double-edged sword above me. It had almost healed, but not quite. "I found this."

The effect on him was extraordinary.

"Where did you get it?" Across the room he came and grabbed me by the forearms, his fingers digging into my flesh. "Who gave it to you?"

The metal sword tip clattered against the floor as I pulled away from his painful grip.

"No one gave it to me. I found it in Ebur's stall. I thought it must be yours, misplaced."

"In Ebur's stall? That's where you found it? In the stables?"

"Yes."

"In your horse's stall. Not in anyone else's."

"I just told you. It was in Ebur's stall hidden beneath some hay."

A blue blaze. Fire danger. "Put it back. Exactly as you found it."

"But isn't it your sword? It doesn't belong to anyone in the Middle Lands, because I've never seen one like this before and . . ."

"Put. It. Back." Each word a slap against my skin.

"But . . ."

"You heard what I said." With a swirl of his cloak he stalked over to the window.

The sword almost slipped from my fingers as I stared at him, open-mouthed. Why was he behaving toward me in such a way?

Unexpected tears pricked as I returned to the stables and hid the sword beneath the hay bale. Even burying my face in Ebur's soft mane didn't comfort me.

By dawn the next day, the sword had gone.

15

Robed and crown'd,
To meet her lord . . .
——Tennyson [1842]: *Godiva*

I reclined in the wooden tub. In the warm water my hair swirled like riverweed. Tendrils entwined around my hips, my thighs, my wrists, my arms.

Aine poured in another kettle of hot water from the fire, sending steam rising to the starry bower ceiling. "A bath fit for a bride."

A bride.

Tomorrow I would be a bride.

Now Aine added yet another bunch of spruce leaves to the wooden tub. Deeply I inhaled the pine scent. It was both invigorating and relaxing.

Next she started to scrub at my skin with a cloth that seemed to have some kind of crushed pebbles wrapped in it, fine as sand.

"Ouch!" I protested. "Aine! That hurts!"

She took no notice, just rubbed harder. "Your skin will be lovely and soft."

"What's left of it," I grumbled. But I knew there was no point arguing with her. She'd scrubbed my fingernails and behind my ears as a child in much the same manner.

Finally Aine stopped scrubbing. My whole body tingled. My skin glowed rosy pink in the firelight.

Oil came next from a green glass bottle, added water-shimmer. Glistening rainbow pools on the surface. Into its silky smoothness I lowered my body deeper, immersing my shoulders.

"That's lovely."

"You needed the scrubbing first. Now soak. Then we'll wash your hair."

Obediently I fluttered my lashes closed. Aine was always extra tart, a sour green apple, when she was worried about me and trying not to show it.

I knew what made her tart-tongued.

We were both nervous.

Tomorrow, I would be a bride.

The Earl of Mercia's bride.

"Put. It. Back."

My lids snapped open.

It was as though he was in the bower with me his words rang so loud in my memory. For a moment I wondered if Aine had spoken, but she was sideways to me, folding out linens on the bed. Bright new linens. Fine white linens. For my bride night to come.

My bride night with Lord Leofric of Mercia, whose furious face was imprinted in my brain.

The double-edged sword. Where did it come from? Why had it made Leofric so angry? I'd barely been able to sleep or eat since I'd found it. Beolinda had asked me what was wrong, but I hadn't been able to tell her. She probably assumed it was pre-wedding nerves, darting about like damselflies in my stomach.

Once again I forced myself to relax and breathe in the soothing pine scent of my bathwater.

Yes, I had pre-wedding nerves. Would not any bride?

But to marry a man so hard, so cold, so angry with me made it so much harder.

"To wed means both to promise and to gamble. The wager is mine, is it not?"

Leofric's dry tone.

A wager on whether the bride would breed.

I delved for the soap. Spruce and lavender, a concoction of Aine's own. It smelled delicious.

I'd wished my father with me while I'd negotiated my wedding terms. Now I wished for my mother.

It was the bride bath custom for the secrets of a good marriage to be passed down from mother to daughter while the bride washed away her maiden status in her ritual bath. Purified by the cleansing process, she would be made ready for what was to come. The duties of a wife, rites to be followed when a married woman, advice on how to please a husband . . . I needed these, but I would have to do without. There was magical knowledge, too, women's wisdom I'd heard muttered and whispered, though I knew not of its truth. How to guide a man without him knowing he is guided. How to advise him while letting him still be master of the hall. How to live with his moods and pleasures, to alter and shift them. How to keep him in thrall in the bower. Whether my mother practiced such arts, I knew not. My father had loved her for his whole married life, that much I knew. It had been in his surmise, both tender and passionate after years together, in his many caresses, in the throatiness of his speech. But my mother was gone, her marriage secrets with her.

The soap slipped from my grasp.

Sliding down I plunged beneath the water, turning my hair to slippery tendrils.

With one hand Aine wrenched me up out of the water as if she were saving me from drowning in the sea.

"A cold rinse. To stimulate your system. That's what you need now."

"Aine! Not a cold rinse! No!" I spluttered, trying to duck.

The jug of chill water splashed, spilled down my neck and onto my breasts, turning their tips to darts. The rosemary sprigs and apple blossom petals mixed into the rinse stuck to my wet skin.

Sending my hair swirling like a dog shaking its fur, I laughed aloud.

Droplets danced into diamonds in the firelight.

It felt good.

Aine lifted up the wedding garland and set it on my hair. Raising my hand I scented my fingertips on the petals.

Day's eyes. The flower that opened to welcome the morn.

For new beginnings.

Wheat.

For fertility.

Clover.

For wealth.

Aine set great store by such things. The water in my pre-wedding bath had been fragrant with the nine sacred herbs: mugwort, betony, lamb's cress, chamomile, nettle, crab-apple, chervil, thyme, and fennel, for our pre-wedding baths were traditionally both holy and cleansing.

I didn't argue.

My marriage would need all the luck and blessing it could get. Since Leofric's anger at me over the sword, I'd avoided him. I'd not try to make friends. Once, while I was in the courtyard, I thought I saw him observing me from the hall, but there was no one at the window when I examined it more closely.

Could I marry him? My fingers clenched on the garland.

Taking my hand away from it before I spoilt her work, Aine clasped it in her calloused fingers, her grip reassuring.

"Here, my lady. Let me add one more herb. Close your eyes for a moment."

"But . . ."

"Just close your eyes, child." Her tone was the same that had made me always wash behind my ears. Obedient, I pressed my lids tight as she reached up and added something to the garland.

"There. You can open them now."

For a brief second, I swore I caught sight of a woman standing by the window. I blinked. It must have been a trick of the light, yet longing overwhelmed me.

Unshed, I gulped the tears that threatened. "Oh, Aine. I wish my parents were here."

Would I have been marrying Leofric if they were? Or would I have been marrying Edmund?

"Your mother would have been proud." Aine said, as if sensing my unspoken question. "You must be a peace weaver now. But remember, my lady, the threads of the marriage cloth are strong. Your vows will bind you to the earl and he will be bound to you. You'll have to take the joys and sorrows that come once you are wed."

Joy and sorrow. I had witnessed both in my parents' marriage.

"Lord Radulf and Lady Morwen—their love was tested, through trial and time," Aine went on, as if guessing my thoughts. "That's the way marriage grows. It must grow through grief, it must grow through pain, and it must grow through anger."

"Through anger?" This was unexpected advice. I grimaced. The way we had already begun, it seemed anger would certainly be part of a marriage to Leofric of Mercia.

Aine smiled. "You don't think anger fiber of the marriage cloth? It's one of the strongest strands. Don't be afraid of its power."

Standing up, I reached for my belt, a thin leather plait to waist my long linen tunic, woven fine and embroidered around the yoke in patterns of green leaves and gold thread. A broad band of blue around the hem in honor of Our Lady. Made creamy with age, it had been my mother's. Remade to fit me. Aine had tutted over it, wishing she had more time.

But it was beautiful.

"No, my lady. Not that belt."

Aine reached for a linen packet and passed it to me.

Weighing it, the parcel was heavy, the linen rough-woven. Inside, I found a chain belt, long loops of carved yellow metal, clasped with two golden eagles.

"Lord Leofric sent it." Aine answered the enquiry that must have been writ all over.

"Do I think right? Is it made of gold?" My question trailed away as I ran my fingers over the loops.

"It must be, in full or part. No other metal has that weight, my lady. Here. Let me help you put it on."

The belt clung to my hips, the clasp falling just below my navel. In an instant, it made my tunic rich and grand.

Aine grunted in approval. "Quite the Mercian Lady now."

"I'm Lady of Coventry first." Quickly I slid my mother's silver keys onto the belt. No Mercian belt, no matter how fine, would make me forget my allegiance to the Middle Lands.

The ceremony. A blur.

Surely someone else, not I, Godiva, walked through the streets of Coventry from the manor, down the main street, past houses hung with cloth ties and wreaths, to the cries and good wishes of the townsfolk who gathered outside every door and window. Surely someone else heard Walburgha's bawdy shout for my happiness, saw Wilbert's grin as he hushed her, and noted Tomas the tanner's scowl. Surely someone else entered the church ablaze with beeswax candles, and walked slowly to the altar, where Lord Leofric stood in front of Brother Aefic.

Under the cross, the old monk remained solemn-faced even while the crowd made a joyous hum as I passed through.

Beolinda stood at the left side of the altar, early rosebuds in her hands.

And Leofric. My groom. A sheep's snowy fleece across his broad shoulders. At his side the hilt of his sword gleamed, as was the custom. If any sought to take his Saxon bride, they would pay the price.

I lifted my veil.

He took me all in, submerged me in his river glance: my garland of blooms, my braided hair with day's eyes tucked in here and there, my summer cloak clasped high and proud around my neck by the watchful sparrow-hawk, the double eagle–headed belt clasped around my waist. A smile, perhaps some softening of his features, some flicker of appreciation . . . I cannot deny I sought it, hoped for it. Would not any woman at the end of her bride walk hope for the same? But he turned away toward the wooden cross that hung on the wall in front of us.

And so, beneath the cross where my mother had prayed so many times, I moved to stand beside him, my body taut as a bow-string.

Perspiration pooled at the base of my spine. The church was warm, too warm, almost suffocating.

Brother Aefic began to speak in Latin, yet I could barely comprehend the words. It seemed a foreign language, not one I had spent years learning as a child. *Deus . . . nuptialis . . .* phrases floated above. We, too, spoke as part of the ceremony: Leofric, controlled, unmoving. I, determined not to tremble, in a tone that rang around the rounded walls, clear as a bell. I didn't look at him; I didn't need to, so strong was his presence beside me. Only after the end of the ceremony did he give a swift breath out.

Brother Aefic led us to the church door. We stood on the threshold, half in, half out, the towns folk gathered by. In the old Saxon way, he took our hands and placed them in a hand-fast, the simple touch, the sacred human knot that had for centuries been enough to hold a man and woman together for life. It wasn't the Latin Christian words the monk had spoken, but Leofric's clasp that made me come to myself at last.

His grip said more than any words.

To this man, I am wed.

"Do you follow the wedding cake custom in Mercia, Husband?"

Leofric sat beside me at the high table on the dais. Fire glow lit up the tapestries and bronzes hanging on the walls, gilding the timber beams richly carved and painted in scarlet and ochre. More symbols had been added now. On the beam above and on the wood panels of our chairs double-headed Mercian eagles had been carved next to the wings of the Coventry sparrow-hawk.

Husband.

How new the word tasted. Determined not to let it ferment, I had seized it immediately, yet to my surprise in my mouth it tasted sweet as honey mead.

Leofric's hand rested on the high table, covered with the finest linen, but now scattered with crumbs and empty platters. "It's the same in my home, *Wife*. We, too, have cakes and ale."

What was in his tone? Irony? Mockery? Or something else?

"They make honeycakes, too?" I forced myself to focus on the ritual being carried out in front of us. One by one, each of the wedding guests came to the front of the hall carrying a small, flat cake. Placing the cakes on top of each other, it formed a tier that grew higher and higher by the minute. Down the hall servants were filling cups and horns with *bride-ale*, brewed for this day alone.

"The recipes are the same in Coventry and Mercia, no doubt," Aine commented. She was sitting beside me at the high table in spite of her protests. With three places left absent by my parents and Edmund on the bench, I needed Aine there, no matter what her rank. She was more committed to the proprieties of our status than I. It was with some reluctance she had taken her place on the dais, her best red tunic bringing out the russet of her cheeks. Farther down the table, Beolinda sat flirting with impassive-faced Acwell, the strongest of Leofric's bodyguard.

Walburgha bustled up and placed her golden cake on the growing tier. Her cake was bigger than the others. The tier wobbled alarmingly. She admired it with satisfaction.

"Made that for you this morning, my lady. Added extra honey for sweetness to mine." Leaning over the table she winked. "Delicious, it is, and may it bring you luck in your marriage, and many fine children, we hope."

"Thank you, Walburgha." My reply sounded faint.

Beaming, she addressed Lord Leofric. "Mind you take care of our lady. No one is near good enough for her, that's what we've always said, but I suppose, you being an earl, you'll do, even if you are from Mercia and not from these parts."

Leofric inclined his head. A glimmer of amusement, soon gone.

"Good luck to you, Lady Godiva!"

"Best wishes to you both, my lord and lady." Wilbert came up behind his wife and taking her by the arm steered her to their place at one of the trestle tables.

"God's blessing." A farmwife from a nearby village added her cake to the tier. I often stopped to visit her as I rode to Arden.

"Thank you." I smiled.

My people were so happy, so pleased to see me wed. After the battle-scars and losses of good men in the fight with Thurkill, they needed the festivity, the cheer. I suspected they were also comforted by our new alliance with Mercia and Leofric's reputation and strength. They didn't guess at the battle being fought inside me.

Drumming started on the tabletops.

"A toast!" The cry came from a Mercian warrior at one of the tables below.

"Was Leofric hail!"

"Was Godiva hail!"

I was Lady of Coventry. The sacred act that had been my mother's of offering our feast cup full to the brim was now my task.

I hadn't expected it to be my wedding cup.

I raised the silver goblet shimmering with amber.

Filled it to overflowing with feast mead. Spiced. Offered it to Leofric.

He grasped it. My fingers, too.

Rough.

Warm.

For a moment he seemed to caress the cup.

Over the edge of the goblet our stares met.

"Good health! *Was hail!*"

He bowed.

Lifted it to his lips. And drank.

"To my bride," he said, when he was done.

A hint of a smile. A creased cheek.

More mockery?

"To Coventry," I said.

The smile vanished.

He released the cup.

"Good health! *Was hail!*" The cry came again.

I lifted the goblet.

And drank.

16

Unclasp'd the wedded eagles of her belt,
The grim Earl's gift;
———Tennyson [1842]: Godiva

Aine pulled the woolen blankets lined with cowhide over the windows. Around the bower candles set shadows dancing around the walls. She had covered the floor with clean rushes, pressed lavender between the linen sheets, piled apple boughs high beside the fire.

Fruit smoke wafted through the air. It didn't soothe me as I remembered my bold promise that Lord Leofric would be satisfied after the wedding night. How far from that certainty I was now. It echoed with the emptiness of a *beor* boast.

"You're nervous, my lady."

I twisted a tendril of hair in my fingers. "I don't want to be, but I am."

"There's no need." Aine lifted the garland from my hair. "You and Lord Leofric are well matched."

"How can you say that?"

"I've seen you together and I know you well enough. There'll be passion between you, that is, if you don't hold yourself back." One by one, she plucked the day's eyes from my long braids.

"He forced me into this marriage!"

"But you set your own terms. You've made your choice. Listen to me on this, and listen to what your body whispers to you. It will not lie."

Flushing, I remembered my response to Lord Leofric's kiss. There'd been no lie there to the heat he raised in me. "I'm only doing this to have children for Coventry. It is my only reason."

"Then you must be passionate. Passion begets children. Whether you can carry a babe to full term is a different matter, as your poor mother knew, but passion leads to conception of a child. If a woman is cold it's harder for her to conceive." She took up a brush. "Now let me attend to your hair."

While she loosened my braids and began long strokes I feverishly contemplated what she'd said. *Passion.* I had to allow its fire to light in me. For Coventry.

Footfalls came outside the bower door.

"Open the door, Aine," I squeaked.

Lord Leofric entered. He'd removed the wedding shearling from his shoulders but I saw beneath his cloak that he still carried his sword.

Aine bowed. "Shall I leave you now, my lady?"

I gulped. "Thank you."

With a final nod of encouragement, she left the bower, closing the wooden door behind her. Slowly, still not speaking, Leofric went to the door and drew the heavy beam across.

There's no escape. I'm his prisoner now, just as I was with Thurkill.

As if reading my mind he came and stood in front of me where

I sat by the fire. "I am no Dane. Do you come to me willingly this night?"

"I will do what I must for my people."

His mouth. A twist again. "Our agreement does not ask for more."

Only the crackle of the fire could be heard as he cast off his cloak before turning to me.

"Your hair is the color of mead."

Honey-colored he meant. It skimmed my thighs.

Honey-limbed I became as he reached out and ran his fingers through the loose tresses, then down my neck, and upward, to cup my chin in his palms. As if to memorize it, he stared into my face. Coiling strands of my hair in his fingers, he pulled me to him, entwining us, his mouth seeking mine.

Passion. I had to allow it in me.

With my lips and body I rose to meet him. Now my fingers found his hair, sliding through its surprising softness, my lips parting against the hardness of his mouth as he searched me with his tongue. I could still taste spice on his lips.

Down. Through the thin linen shift he found my breast with his teeth. I gasped.

He pulled back. Under my shift he caressed my thighs and my hips as he lifted my shift above my waist. Taking it over my head he dropped it to the floor leaving my body bare.

My breathing quickened.

He twisted away.

My heart sank.

Didn't he like what he saw? My skin goose fleshed as though I'd been ducked in an icy river. I thought he would find it pleasing, with my smooth white skin, unmarked except for the battle-scar on my arm, my legs muscular from many hard days' riding, my pre-childbirth slender waist, and my breasts, not as large as some of the village girls, but full as ripe russets. Didn't my youthful body meet his expectations?

"My lord . . ." My whisper a sliver of shame.

He turned.

A glint in his raised hand.

Petrified to stone.

No! Every woman knew of what some men were capable when alone with a woman. Every woman knew the risks; had seen the scars, both physical and mental. Some men even thought it their God-given right to chastise, to correct, and to enforce that a male would be head of the house, of the marriage bed.

How wrong I had been to trust Leofric of Mercia!

Edmund had tried to warn me.

"He's a Saxon lord," I'd said.

"That doesn't mean you can trust him."

Leofric himself.

"I must give you some warnings of my own, Lady. I will be your lord."

He'd told me, but I hadn't understood. I would have believed Thurkill the Tall a wife-beater but Leofric of Mercia? The way he had kissed me, the way I'd responded . . .

My instincts hadn't warned me. I hadn't intuited it, body or soul.

My gaze fled to the barred door.

His step forward.

Breath strangled.

My step away.

Reaching for anything to aid me, a fire poker, an axe . . .

Closer, he moved. Revealing the golden Mercian belt I'd worn for the wedding, he clasped it around my naked waist.

The metal of the belt was warm against my skin, but not as warm as his fingertips, sliding upon my skin as he set the belt in place; that molten heat I hadn't expected. The eagles just below my navel, their beaks pointing to the tender part of me that lay below.

In a single swift movement he lifted me off my feet. Swung me into his arms. Laid me on the bed.

Under his long-cast gaze. My naked body.

He unclasped the belt.

He didn't speak.

As he unclothed.

My husband.

His silver sword.

Double-eagle domed. Cast aside.

His belt.

Brown. Studded. Slid through his hand.

His tunic.

Wool, dark, rough-woven. Ruffling his tawny hair as he lifted it over his head.

His shift.

Unmarked. Linen, fine-woven. Removed.

Chest hair. Golden.

Muscle. Sinew-stretched. The Dane-axe cut still livid.

Skin. War-toughened. Battle-scarred leather.

His malehood.

I swallowed my gasp.

Of such a size. I had never seen.

He came to the bed.

He didn't speak.

On top of me.

Heavy. Warm.

He didn't speak.

His breath. My own. Great shallow gasps.

His lips opening mine. Seeking, sucking, tasting.

His mouth on my breast. Teasing, suckling, biting.

His hands between my legs. The place no man had ever touched. Rubbing, stroking, gently bruising.

He didn't speak.

His fingers hard inside. One, two, three. Searching, prodding, pushing.

He didn't speak.

And when the huge shaft of him went deep, so deep . . .

And as the weave inside me ripped and tore . . .

And as the pain came, rose up and fell away . . .

He didn't speak.

And so I bit my lip.

And didn't speak.

Pale pink fingers of light edged the blankets covering the windows. Leofric lay next to me, the linens tangled around us.

In the soft morning light I peeked at him. He appeared younger than when he was awake. In repose, his face lost its harsh edges, revealing traces of the boy he'd once been. An urge struck me to trace that jaw with my fingertips, across his cheekbones to where the lines gently fanned out from his closed lids.

But he'd awakened.

Crystal blue. Sunlight on water. "You rise early."

"The dawn is my favorite time of day."

"I, too, like the dawn." He raised himself, the sheet falling away. In the morning light, the swirls of hair on his chest were darker than they'd appeared the night before. They'd glinted golden in the candlelight.

I ought to be grateful. He'd been gentler than many men would have been, I suspected. The rust-colored stain on the sheets meant my virginity wasn't in doubt.

Yet his sheer size . . .

I bit my lip.

He stared at my mouth as my teeth caught at the tender flesh.

In the rose-gold light of dawn he reached for me.

And turned me.

His lips on my core.

As if he knew.

As if he understood how much he'd hurt me. As if he licked my wound.

I tensed.

He lapped.

His mouth became a healing balm on the tender place his shaft had made.

I gasped.

Then a sigh.

Juddering through my body.

Harder. Deeper.

Lips.

Tongue.

Teeth.

He sucked the marrow of me.

Another gasp. Another judder. Another sigh.

I'd never known such pleasure.

My back arched, my mouth opened.

And in return I took him.

By instinct, between my lips.

Full. Deep. Strong.

I took him in.

He moved as if to jerk away.

Stopped. Stayed. Grew larger.

Hard. Unyielding.

Yet smooth-skin sheathed. So unexpected.

The smell of him.

Musk thistle.

My lips rubbed. My tongue licked.

The taste of him.

Sea-fed. Whelk-wash.

Down my throat.

While from below waves made by his lapping tongue came over me until we split apart.

Our breathing the only sound. Except for a skylark, summoning the morn anew.

Judders still ran through me as we lay together.

Silently he rolled away and reached over to where his belt lay cast aside on the floor. My eagle gold beside it.

A small leather pouch. He held it out it to me.

"The *morgengifu*. Your morning gift."

My brow furrowed. "But we've set our terms."

Coventry. Was he revoking our agreement?

He shrugged and pressed the package into my palm.

Slowly I untied the long cord.

A ring. A dull gleam of gold. Carved swirls. A large, smooth gem in the center, egg-shaped. I held it up to the light.

The gem glowed red as a wild cherry. "It's beautiful."

"A ruby."

I'd not expected such a courtesy of him, just as I hadn't expected the pleasure he'd given me.

I slipped the ring onto my finger. "Thank you," I said, made shy. "Where did it come from?"

"It was my mother's. It's Mercian made."

So he'd brought it with him to Coventry. The eagle belt, too, he must have had with him. He must carry them with him always, a family keepsake.

"And now you give it to me."

"Does it fit?"

"Almost. It's big." To hide my sudden bashfulness I twirled the ring, traced the carving with my finger. "I'll take it to the blacksmith."

He made no reply as he swung himself out of the bed. Some morning modesty made me avert my attention from the part of him my lips had wrapped only minutes before.

Instead my gaze fell on my bride garland that Aine had laid on the table by the window. The day's eyes were curled and dry. It was then I noticed the last herb Aine had added, it's pointed leaves like a star and a purple button in the center.

One-berry.

For passion.

For true love.

17

Ever at a breath
She linger'd, looking like a summer moon . . .
——Tennyson [1842]: *Godiva*

The last of the sun slanted on my face as I sat in the herb garden. Laziness had become my companion, a languor, a strange kind of sleepiness that made me sit in the sun contented as a kitchen cat. Herbs were growing: sage, rosemary, lavender, and rue. My lashes had been closed as I breathed in their fragrance and listened to the fieldfares call overhead. Spring was departing and soon summer would come. All around me newness and greenness had flourished from the coldness of the winter earth.

And from me.

The Danish threat still hovered, yet I felt so safe in the garden. Cabbage moths fluttered past. The wind gently murmured.

His protection. My peace.

With Leofric as an ally, serenity and calm had come to Coventry and the Middle Lands at last. And to me.

Daily I still fretted about Edmund. I'd expected to hear from him. A letter, a sign. Nothing. The days drifted by like the clouds floating overhead.

My waking hours were full, acting as both lord and lady, picking up the reins of my parents' governance. Managing the hall and stores, settling disputes, collecting taxes, holding the *althing*, making visits. I thought I might clash with Leofric, but he kept his promise. He didn't interfere. At times, I wished I hadn't been so determined to be in charge, alone. My parents had formed a partnership, relied on each other. Often I wanted to ask my husband questions, seek advice. But pride forbade it.

Leofric was busy, too. Letters and messages came from Mercia and elsewhere. He didn't share their contents with me. He spent many hours answering them and in consultation with his *cnihts*, especially Acwell, who continued to unnerve me. Their conversations always ceased when I was present. After one message Leofric took a short trip away, I knew not where. When he returned he came straight into my bower, still in his travel garb, horse scent on his skin.

No longer did he prefer to sleep in the open air.

For with each day that passed by came its dark twin night. My skin heated thinking of those nights. Each shadow hour had been a discovery. A revelation of the intensity of pleasure one person could bring another.

On the mattress. On the floor. Against the bower wall.

Clothed, unclothed.

In my mouth. In his mouth.

In front. Behind.

Dawn. Dusk.

Midnight.

Again.

Again.

Again.

"Marriage agrees with you, my lady," Aine said.

My honeymoon was over. A month had passed since my marriage to Leofric, and I knew now why it had that name. Not for the sweet mead we drank at the wedding feast to celebrate our troth, but for something else: another kind of sweetness that made me liquid at the core.

Yet he did not speak.

Was I the kind of woman who needed sweet nothings murmured in her ear? Did I need protestations of love? Leofric had married me. We were husband and wife. Bodies, joined.

Yet he did not speak.

"It's not as I expected it to be," I said to Aine.

With a smug expression she paused in her herb cutting. "It's as *I* expected. I knew it would go well for you in the bower as soon as I saw you and Lord Leofric together."

My cheeks warmed. "Oh Aine—"

"There's no use saying 'Oh Aine.' I know a satisfied woman when I see one. There's something about the eyes."

I evaded her shrewd glance. But it was so. My whole body tingled from Leofric's searching hands and lips. His caresses made me helpless in his arms, only able to pleasure and be pleasured, using my hands and lips in return. Thought dissolved in those nights we spent together, only wild sensation remained.

Yet he did not speak.

Leaning against the wooden bench, I released a sigh. No, I could not deny our match at night. When he reached for me our bodies came together in a rhythm that seemed to be known by both of us by instinct.

And yet the more I knew of his body, the less I knew of his mind and heart.

In a new habit I'd formed, I twisted the ruby ring Leofric had given me on my finger. The closeness we shared in the hours of darkness didn't entirely disappear during the day. Sometimes I sensed him studying me and the heat of our nights would rise up yet again to tint my skin: my breasts, my neck, my cheeks. But there was still a distance between us, as far as when I had first seen him from the watchtower, a lone rider breaking out in the distance. Even in the brightness of first daylight when we awoke and he so often took me again, I would search his expression. Yet I couldn't read what feelings lay there. Those windows to his soul were shuttered as tight as windows on Coventry's main street on a cold night.

So easily now I could envisage in my mind the set of his mouth, the firm lips, the hard jaw, the expression that gave nothing away, even as his stare searched mine. I'd started to know his face as well as I knew my own. Not only the appearance of it, but also the touch of it: the temperature of his skin, the roughness of his jaw, the line of his brow ...

Restless, I began to pace the plant yard. The scent of herbs was growing stronger each day, as the earth began to warm and new shoots of green life pushed through the soil. Leaning down I touched a green bud growing at the edge of the grass, a primrose, its leaves tightly clasped its colored center.

"Is it different, Aine? For men and women, do you think?"

She snapped off a sprig of rosemary. "It depends on the man, my lady. Some men can close off part of themselves. They just fill their need, like thirst, or hunger."

Was Leofric one of those men who were able to separate their minds and hearts? I rejected believing it so. Was it merely my woman's vanity that made me feel there was something more being created between us, something more than a simple slaking of Leofric's hunger, or thirst? Sometimes, there would be a kiss, or a touch, that surely it was impossible for a man to give to a woman without feeling. I shouldn't ask for more. Considering our alliance had been forced upon me, I should simply be grateful that the physical side of our relationship was one of passion, not of pain. It could have been a hardship, just as I had feared on my wedding night, when I'd seen the chain belt in his fist. Instead there were some nights when I could barely wait to hear the lifting of the latch as he entered my darkened bower.

Aine got to her feet with a grimace. She'd been complaining of bone aches during the winter months. I hurried over to help her with the willow basket. After patting my cheek, she picked up the herb basket and disappeared into the kitchens.

I stared after her. Aine believed some men were able to separate their bodies and their hearts. Would it last—what Leofric and I had begun to create between us? I didn't mean a child for I sensed I hadn't conceived. Something else had been conceived in me. In my heart, something had seeded.

Why did I care to know this man's soul, this man who had caught me in a trap? But a truth was growing in me with the spring.

Just as my body yearned for Leofric each night, my heart was beginning to yearn for his.

After dinner, the gleeman took up his usual place in front of the fire. For the first time since the festival of Easter we had supped on hare stew. Many of my people, Aine included, still celebrated the Christian feast as well as honoring Eostre, our goddess of spring. Since hares were sacred to Eostre they would not eat them until after her feast day.

Moonstones laced my neck. More milky-clasped my sleeves. A gold-trimmed tunic. I dressed for him.

The gleeman bowed. "What will you have tonight, my lord and lady? A song on the harp? A poem or a riddle? The tale of the battle of Maldon?"

On the high bench, Leofric sat beside me, his thigh close to mine. The leather smell of his clothing was familiar now, as was the more intimate scent that was just his. It drew me to him, an invisible potion.

With a clink of metal on wood he placed his goblet on the table. "What would you hear, Lady?"

My mouth had gone dry. I took a sip of the ale that had replaced our nightly mead now our honeymoon was over.

"Please make your choice, my lord."

"I haven't heard Beowulf of late. Of the battle against the monster Grendel. Even if it is an old Danish tale, it's still the finest."

An unexpected knot of grief choked me.

"What ails you, Godiva?" Sometimes his voice was as gentle as his night touch.

"A recollection of my mother."

A glimmer of understanding flashed between us. "What is it you recall?"

"Her words of comfort when I cried out in the night."

The intensity of his surmise held me tight as an embrace. Leaning over to me he spoke soft. "Have no fear. If you cry out in the night I will hear you."

His breath fanned the sensitive skin below my ear, sending shivers through me. "Then I won't be afraid, my lord."

He picked up his goblet again.

"Leofric?" I twisted the ring on my finger. I still had not taken it to the forge to be made my size. "It's beautiful out of doors, now that spring has arrived. Will you come with me tomorrow, as I ride abroad in the Middle Lands?"

"Where do you think to visit?"

"The Forest of Arden."

He surveyed me over the rim of the cup. "Arden."

"It's my favorite place. We could ride there together. It's not too far from here."

At his brief nod of consent I couldn't hide my smile.

Loudly I clapped. "Let us hear of Beowulf."

The gleeman began. It didn't pain me to hear it, as I had feared. Instead, when he came to the lines:

Awesome Earl; since erst a whelp
fund-shorn found, was offered help.
Waxed under welkin, won worth-prestige
until all areas we edged with were beseiged
over the whale-road, wide wealth did they bring:
gave up their gold. That was a good king!

Sideways at Leofric. Awesome earl. I smiled.

18

Cry down the past,
——Tennyson [1842]: *Godiva*

"Congratulations on your marriage, my lady!" The farmwife bobbed and ushered her children forward. "May the god and goddess bless you!"

From Ebur's saddle I leant down and took the primroses offered by one of the children. The girl smiled shyly before going back to clutch her mother's apron, with its pockets full of seeds and tools.

"How beautiful! Thank you. How goes it with you?"

"We've planted the spring crops. We hope there'll be a better harvest than last year. It wasn't a good year for us, nor was the year before."

In sympathy I nodded. "Let us pray for a good harvest this year."

"We will, my lady. And for blessings for you and your husband." She bobbed at Leofric, but her smile she reserved for me before we rode away to the cries of the children, their shyness gone, shouting good-bye.

Our horses drew parallel. "Your people love you," he said, over the sound of their hooves as we slowed to a walk.

"Don't the people of Mercia love their lord?"

"They respect me." Leofric glanced at the sun-dappled fields, full of green life. Everywhere was brimming with new life now: lambs and calves in the fields, baby birds chirped in their nests, and small animals rustled in the bushes. The Middle Lands were at their best in the spring. Hawks circled above. Under a cloudless sky we'd ridden through the villages, clustered around the common lands and out into the farming lands, where more homes were scattered. All the way folk had waved and called good wishes to us.

"The people of the Middle Lands are loyal. I prize loyalty above all things," I said, my head held high with pride.

"But what if you are loyal to the wrong things, to the wrong people?"

"Mine are good people."

"Mine are good, too. But Mercia is a harsher place than this."

"There's no land as beautiful to me as the Middle Lands, but we can't predict what each year will bring. It can be feast or famine."

"*The ploughman feeds us all.*" He quoted the old Saxon saying; one my father oft repeated, too, I recalled with a pang.

"We've had some hard times. Our last few harvests were scarce." It had worried my father.

"We've had many bad harvests in Mercia." Leofric's face turned grim. "Famine has been hard on my lands. When I was a young boy there was a time when year after year, the crops failed. Then there was pestilence affecting the cattle. I'm determined, in the future, to have the wealth and stores to ride out difficult times." He gave his horse a slight kick to urge him on. "But let's not talk of difficult times this day. How far to your woods of Arden?"

"Not far."

He gave me an odd glance. "Before the battle for Coventry. You stood on your horse's back. Can you do that while riding?"

For a moment I hesitated. What I could do with Ebur had a strange, secret power. I didn't speak of it, nor show it for fun. Edmund had witnessed it, for the gift had come to me as I grew. Whether I would have the same connection with any other horse, or only Ebur, I knew not. All I knew was I guarded it as most precious.

Yet I wanted to tell Leofric.

"Yes. While cantering, but not in a gallop, of course."

"Will you show me?"

He must have seen my uncertainty.

"It's of no matter."

"No! I'd be pleased to show you." I'd worn a light, short tunic and leggings today. Not my leather. But I could still do it, no matter what I wore.

Into a trot I pulled Ebur ahead. Leaning down I whispered the words to her. Ancient words. Ancient whisper.

Releasing my feet from the stirrups, I clambered up on the flat of the saddle. For a moment I knelt, finding my balance, my head and shoulders poised like an arrow into the breeze. Then I was on my feet.

Knees bent, I locked my pose. Keeping my head high, I allowed my legs to absorb the impact of Ebur's every step.

Trot hastened to canter.

My arms outstretched, we flew.

Birdsong trilled from me as we soared across the plain. The wind laughed into my hair, chuckled against my cheeks. My lashes fluttered closed as I became the whisper, became the wind.

Naked

Too soon it was over. Beneath the saddle Ebur shifted. Sensing my balance about to change, I jumped low, my legs astride, and propelled myself back into the saddle.

Leofric galloped up behind me. With a pat of thanks and praise I reined Ebur in.

Ebur gave Leofric's horse a nudge as they drew beside us and stopped.

"I've never seen such a thing before." Leofric's words were understated, but in his visage admiration blended with understanding.

This rider knew the whisper, too.

"It's Ebur," I panted, still short of breath. "Not me."

"Perhaps."

His huge black horse. Like Ebur, an exceptional animal.

The stallion had an unusual name: *Wyrd*.

"Your horse's name. Where did it come from?"

"I named him myself. Fate is its meaning, as you well know." Leofric flashed me one of his rare smiles. "I take fate into my own hands."

The stallion leapt forward.

Magic sparkled in the sunlight, falling on the leaves as we reached the edge of the Forest of Arden.

Leofric stroked Wyrd's neck as we tethered our horses. "This is a sacred place."

"How did you know?" Arden was the home of our ancient spirits but it wasn't common knowledge beyond our borders. Many still came to worship in Arden on holy days, but only those who lived in the Middle Lands.

A shrug was his only reply as we went deeper into the forest by foot, the oaks, elms, and poplars whispering their mysterious welcome. Yet I swore he bowed as we entered the deep green grove.

"It's believed these woods are haunted," I told him.

He lifted a brow. "With whose ghosts?"

"With the ghosts of Saxons past. Once, when I came here with Edmund, we heard terrible squealing sounds and I thought it was a ghost! But it was only a sow from one of the villages. Some of the farmers let their pigs run free, instead of keeping them on the common ground with the sheep and cattle. There are mushrooms in these woods that the sows love to find."

Still no word from Edmund.

Deeper into the wood we came to a ley, a small clearing dappled with light. By a huge fallen log I laid out the loaf of bread, cheese, and ale Aine had packed. I felt strangely shy as we sat together, our backs resting against the wood. We hadn't spent many hours alone together by day, or shared a meal alone. There were always others with us at the hall. I offered him the loaf. Its smell told of its freshness; it must have been baked that morning.

With a nod of thanks Leofric tore off a piece, his fingers gliding briefly over mine. I knew those hands now. Gentle yet strong, I knew how they could play upon my skin. Yes, I had come to know those hands each night he spent in my bower, but I knew not enough of his life.

"Have you a forest such as Arden in Mercia?" I asked, with the shyness still upon me.

"We have Sherwood Forest. It's deep and green, and full of hiding places, to those who know them. It was in Sherwood my brothers and I were outlaws."

"Outlaws? In your own land." I'd heard of such things. It angered me.

His face darkened, as if he was no longer sitting in a patch of sunlight, but had moved into the shade. "My brothers and I went there to hide. We were there for many months. We survived on wild nuts, fruits, and berries. Sometimes we found wild mushrooms or ate what we could hunt."

It suddenly became hard to swallow my bread. He spoke as if it were matter of fact, but fruits of the forest could barely have sustained the young, growing man he must have been. "When Thurkill took Mercia? Is that when you hid in the forest?"

He inclined his head. "When Thurkill took our halls and when he outlawed us in our own lands, we had to flee quickly, and we only had a few horses and arms with us. But we built up our strength to take our lands once more. Thurkill thought he had defeated us, but he was wrong. I will rebuild Mercia, and our great cities." He gazed beyond me into the woods, but I sensed he didn't see its deep greenness. It was his cities he saw.

"I will not stop until Mercia is as mighty as it should be." Spoken in the woods, his vow had a sacredness that made me shiver. "After Northman was killed, I swore to rebuild our homeland."

My heart contracted. He'd lost his brother, his way of life, and his home. I'd lost my parents to Thurkill but at least I hadn't seen our hall burn.

Leofric had saved me from that.

"My father dreamed of building in stone," I said. "He dreamed of a castle. And my mother used to say, *Better to have castles made of wood than made of air, Radulf.*"

Leofric smiled; the unexpected boyish smile that seemed to go straight to my core. "And what did your father say to that?"

"He said dreams must come first."

"*Dreams must come first.* And what would you build?"

"My mother believed we should build a church before we rebuilt the hall. She always wanted to have a stone church for Coventry. A church should be the first stone building, she said, for a church is for everyone. She and Brother Aefic long planned it. One day I hope to build it in her memory. I would make it so fine that all the townsfolk would want to come. I would build it with glass windows as they do in the great cities."

"So buildings made of dreams do last," he murmured. "The dreams of your parents have become yours."

"Perhaps dreams are passed down along with lands."

The brooding set of his jaw came as he stared again unseeing into the trees. His recollections had returned to his brother, I guessed. "Was Northman with you in the Forest of Sherwood?"

The darkling shadow passed across his face. "He led us there; my family and those who remained loyal to us. He was, after all, the eldest the future ealdorman. It was why he was called Northman. It's a Mercian name. We are proud, in my family, to be men of the North."

"He was not earl, as you are?"

"I am the first earl. King Canute himself granted me the title."

"That night in the hut. You asked if Thurkill and the other man I heard talking about *huscarls* mentioned Canute. Why?"

"Canute is gathering a force of Saxon nobles around him. He calls them his *huscarls*."

"A bodyguard?"

"Of a kind. More like *cnihts*, perhaps. They make to Canute their allegiance."

"Surely these *huscarls* are traitors to the Saxon cause," I said passionately.

What good Saxon would betray his heritage and make allegiance to the Danish king on our English throne? I couldn't fathom it.

Leofric shrugged. "Perhaps some would call them traitors. Perhaps they're simply being expedient in troubled times."

"But to ally with the Danes." They'd been our enemies for years. My mother in particular had loathed their very name.

"War makes strange bedfellows," Leofric said. "So does peace."

I gulped some ale. "What do you think of Canute?"

"He's a clever man. He listens well; unusual for a king. There is a story being told of him. Many of the courtiers fawn over him, telling him he is all mighty, all powerful. But Canute told them if that was so, surely he could control the tides. Then he took them to the edge of the water, and showed them that the waves of the sea did not obey him. Those fawning courtiers were made fools." He smiled briefly. "My brothers like that story."

"Yes, you have younger brothers too, you told me."

"Edwin and Godwin. They're both much younger than I, close to your age."

Reaching out he cuffed my wrist. With his other hand he put a finger to my lips.

"Do you hear that?"

Silent, I shook my head. I couldn't hear anything except the rustling of the trees, and in my ears the sound of my quickened heartbeat at his touch.

"Come." Raising me to my feet, his fingers slid to take me by the hand. With soundless steps on the fallen leaves he led me to the edge of the ley.

Crouching behind a low branch, he pulled me down with him. "Over there."

My gasp was louder than it ought to have been but it didn't disturb the deer, a female. With gentle but watchful gaze she surveyed the forest for beside her was a fawn. Still young, the fawn stood on wobbly legs, gazing with its huge brown eyes, seeing the world new.

How long we stayed there, watching the doe with her newborn, I do not know. Beside me, Leofric barely moved. I saw the outlaw in him then, the readiness to spring in the coiled energy of his body, so close to mine. He seemed intent upon the deer, his expression less guarded and his face relaxed. There was softness in him I hadn't suspected in a man usually so armored.

I reached for him.

I caught him off guard but not for long. Released from his clothing his speed matched mine as he twisted, slid against the silvery base of a poplar tree and pulled me down onto him, finding my center with the speed of a spear. My tunic rucked over my thighs as my legs clasped him. Face-to-face, eye to eye, lips to lips now, our arms around each other. With a gasp I brought myself down harder onto him so his swelling force filled me. There was no pain anymore, that had long passed between us, just a rubbing rhythm as we rocked together. We didn't speak, there was just the rocking movement we made and then the explosion, deep within me and I cried out, my head thrown back. Again and again, his hardness driving me into frenzy until at last he joined me, in a great last shuddering cry.

We became still. His rough breathing and my own still coming in great, shallow gasps faded into the sacred silence of the trees.

My hair had come loose. Pushing a strand from my forehead I made to roll away.

He caught me by the forearm.

"What are *your* dreams, Godiva?" He sounded hoarse.

"My dreams?" Aftershocks of passion still heaved through me.

"You spoke of your mother's dreams becoming your own, of building a church for Coventry. Is that all you dream of?"

Was that all I dreamed of? Could he not sense in the yielding of my body the feeling growing within me? Did he not feel, too, what was between us, become as holy as a vow? "The good of my people is my dream."

Thrusting me aside he was on his feet with a suddenness that startled me. "Your lands are all that matter to you. How well I know."

His spurt of anger stung like nettles on my bared thighs.

Scrambling to my feet, I covered myself with my tunic. "Isn't it the same for you? Everything you've ever done is for Mercia. Why, you've just told me so."

"Then we're alike." His lips set hard. "We both care only for our lands."

Wheeling around, he stalked away through the woods.

19

We rode back to Coventry in silence, my knuckles white against Ebur's reins. Why hadn't I taken my opportunity in the wildwoods and told Leofric of my feelings? Pride had stopped me, and pride was a sin, Brother Aefic always said. Now Leofric had become a stranger to me once again.

The gates of the courtyard were wide open. As we rode inside, a young man barely out of his teens came running out of the hall door. "Leo!"

Leofric leapt off Wyrd's back. "Godwin!"

The two men embraced, tight as bear cubs.

"My brother." Leofric's face was alight in a way I hadn't yet witnessed. "You're here sooner than I expected."

He hadn't told me he expected visitors from the north. He never shared the contents of his letters. I bit my lip.

The younger man laughed. Not as tall as Leofric and slighter in build. His hair was fair and his eyes were the same blue, yet they were friendlier as they lit on me as I slid off Ebur's saddle. They lacked Leofric's hot, bold glare. "Did you not think news of your marriage would bring your brothers to your side?"

Some unspoken communication passed between them.

"Not both of you," Leofric said.

"Edwin didn't come. We guessed you would want one of us to stay in Chester."

"You guessed right."

"It's been a long journey. Edwin and I squabbled like children over who would make it. But there's someone else who refused to be left behind."

As Godwin spoke, a young woman in a tunic as red as the ruby on my finger came out of the hall. I almost gasped as I saw her, so beautiful was she. Pale-skinned, dark-haired, her dark eyes glowed at Leofric.

"Elfreda!" Leofric went straight to her side.

She clung to him. "I had to come."

I'd been standing aside watching the reunion, clutching Ebur's comforting mane. She slid me a sidelong glance from those dark eyes.

"This is the Lady Godiva who is now my wife." Leofric's tone revealed nothing. "Godiva, this is my brother Godwin, and our neighbor, the Lady Elfreda."

Elfreda's smile. Radiant. "More than a neighbor, I hope, Leofric."

Leofric's smile. Gentle. "Of course."

I stepped forward and clasped each of their hands in turn. Godwin's was warm. Elfreda's soft as butter. Suddenly my fingertips felt rough and coarse.

Godwin beamed at me. "When the news came that Leofric had married we were overjoyed."

"And full of curiosity," Elfreda added.

"We have only brothers in our family," Godwin explained. "So you're especially welcome as a new sister-in-law."

"Thank you. I have no brothers or sisters of my own." Though Edmund had been fostered with us so young. He'd filled that gap.

"Now you have me and you'll have Edwin too, who sends God's greeting." Godwin roared with laughter again. "I'm much the better brother, I think you will find."

I laughed too. It was impossible not to like Godwin, though I was not so sure about Elfreda, who continued to gaze at Leofric with unmistakable adoration.

Godwin addressed Leofric. "You'd agree, Leo?"

"All are equal among brothers."

The same expression of grief passed over their faces. *Northman.* They both still grieved for him. The laughter in the younger man's eyes vanished. Leofric's jaw set to granite.

"We must have a feast worthy of brothers to welcome you." Into my voice I brought a note of jollity I was far from feeling. "But you'll want to rest first. You must be tired, Godwin. And Elfreda." I nodded at her politely. She gave a small smile.

Godwin grinned, his humor restored. "Nothing a few hours on the mead-bench won't fix."

Leofric clapped the younger man's shoulder. "Give me the news from Mercia, Godwin my brother. Then you shall have your mead."

"I'm sorry. We're leaving you out of the conversation," Elfreda said to me, as we dined at the high table.

With a start I glanced up from my platter. I'd been crumbling bread on my trencher as Leofric, Godwin, and Elfreda had caught up on old times.

In honor of our guests our evening meal had been a roasted lamb dressed in a minted sauce. Then the gleeman had taken his place in front of the fire and begun to sing. The mead cups had been filled.

As Godwin drank his promised mead a change came over Leofric. In his brother's presence I saw a new side of him, a younger, happier side.

My heart smote me. I hadn't thought of Leofric being a stranger here, nor made allowance for it, I realized with remorse. So self-assured, he'd given no indication that he may desire to be in his own lands. Yet as with the beautiful Elfreda, he and Godwin talked of names and places I knew not, I understood he missed his home as much as I would miss the Middle Lands.

"I'm sure you have a lot to discuss," I said.

"We do. But we'd enjoy hearing about your lands too, Godiva."

She smiled shyly at me, her eyes soft-glowing as topaz.

A wave of near hostility overcame me. How horrified my mother who raised me to practice good Saxon hospitality would have been. Elfreda was my guest, and there was no reason to dislike her.

Yet Leofric regarded her with such gentleness.

"Perhaps you will show us your town while we are here?" Godwin broke in with a merry smile. "I hear it grows fine."

"Of course." I nodded. Forced a smile in reply. Churlish to refuse a guest.

But with the excuse of headache, I soon left the hall for my bower.

Leofric didn't come to me that night.

For the first time since our wedding he didn't visit my bower or my bed. The honeymoon is a sweet month, I reasoned with myself, as I tossed and sighed, but it cannot last.

Why had I believed it would?

In the darkness I stared up at the roof of the bower. Herbs hung above my bed, something Aine had put there for fertility I presumed.

It would be of no use if my husband did not come to my bed.

Round and round, I twisted my ruby ring. We hadn't married to become soul mates, the way my parents had been. Yet the longing in me had put down roots, to truly know the man I had married, the man Godwin and Elfreda knew so well.

But Leofric did not come.

Nor did sleep.

20

And nodding, as in scorn,
He parted . . .
——Tennyson [1842]: *Godiva*

Godwin hurried toward me across the courtyard, his face alight. "Where are you going, Godiva?"

"Into Coventry." My sleepless night had left me craving fresh air and exercise. Every sound, whether footfall or owl call, had sent me sitting bolt upright, hoping for Leofric's lift of the bower latch.

"May I come with you? You promised to show me your town. I hear Coventry is growing apace."

Perhaps company would keep me from brooding.

"It would be my pleasure," I said politely. Churlish to refuse a guest.

Together we left the hall and walked along the main street. He had an easy step and an air of eagerness.

Home pride filled me as I pointed out the sights.

"That's our water mill." The huge wheel sloshed. "We're planning to build another. And that's—"

I halted. Godwin wasn't listening to my commentary. His focus was on some of the young girls, soft-skinned as buttermilk, who as they passed were giving him shy and inviting smiles.

"I don't think you're listening to me," I laughed.

"The girls of Coventry are so pretty. But not as pretty as their lady. Now, you were showing me the sights. What's that over there?"

Again I laughed at the low, thatched round house he indicated. "You know exactly what that is, Godwin. It's the town tavern."

"Is it? Now that's a sight I must see."

"It's only midafternoon."

"Never too early or too late." He seized my arm. "To the tavern, sister-in-wed."

Inside the dim room, with a huge hearth fire and leather shields along the wall, the mead-benches were full for the time of day. Some of them, farmers in for the market, gave me furtive glances. No doubt they ought to be in the fields.

The innkeeper hurried over. "Lady Godiva!"

"God's greeting to you. This is Godwin of Mercia, Lord Leofric's brother."

"I hope to sample your wares," Godwin put in.

The innkeeper bowed and rubbed his hands together. "God's greeting, my lord. We have some mead made from the finest honey, some ale, and some bog-myrtle *beor* brewed by my wife. The best in the Middle Lands."

I hid my chuckle. I knew Walburgha didn't think so. She claimed her *beor* to be the best.

Godwin slipped the innkeeper a silver coin that made him beam. "Two tankards of your finest ale, if you will, with my thanks."

Naked

We sat at a low table beneath a pair of drooping deer antlers.

The innkeeper brought us brimming goblets.

Godwin smacked his lips. "This seems very good."

"You sound quite expert." I grinned.

"And hope to become even more so." Godwin lifted his brimming tankard in a toast. "*Was* Godiva *hail*. Long life and a long and happy marriage to my brother."

"*Was* Godwin *hail*." I raised my own.

"You're close for brothers," I said, after a sip.

"It's not always that way, but it is with us. I think it's because we were forced to flee together. You know of that?"

"Leofric has told me a little."

"Probably not all." Wiping the froth from his lip Godwin turned grave. "Leofric took the brunt of the hardship we faced. He cared for us, his younger brothers, often at his own expense. I saw him go without food more than once. It hardened him, our days as outlaws, but there are few men as loyal, brave, and true as my brother. Leo, we call him between ourselves, for his lion heart."

"*Leo*." The nickname suited him.

"The years we spent together as outlaws brought us closer together than many brothers are. If it hadn't happened, we would all have been separated, and sent as squires to different Saxon nobles. We may never have seen each other again."

"So in Mercia you brothers stayed together."

"And the bond between us grew. That's why it was so hard when Northman was killed, especially for Leofric. When Northman died, he did not just lose his brother, he lost his best friend. They are quite a few years older than Edwin and I. So the loss of Northman was greatest for Leofric." Godwin paused to wave for new tankards. "I'm chattering like a midwife."

"Please." I sipped more ale. "I want to know."

He slanted me a squint that told me his good-natured pose hid something more. He seemed to sense my need to know more of his older brother. "When Northman died, I wasn't sure Leo would recover from the blow. We had vowed, as brothers, to return Northman to his rightful place in Mercia. But he died before his lands were his own again."

"And Leofric became earl."

"His vow is to build Mercia up again, to a land worthy of his memory."

"He is intent on that, I know." *Oh, how well I knew.*

"And he will do it. Leofric is the most stubborn of us. Even when he was a child, he would not give way, once he had set his mind to something. Once Leofric has decided upon his course, he refuses to give in."

"I can believe that." *Only too well.*

"And you, Godiva?" Godwin slipped the innkeeper another coin as new tankards of ale arrived even though I hadn't finished my first. "Are you as stubborn as a mule—or should I say, as a lion?"

"I can be. I'm sure it's a fault."

He gave me an admiring glance. "I see few faults in you."

He was flirting with me, but there was only fun in Godwin.

"You're not what I expected," I said impulsively.

"What did you expect?" He made a mock grimace. "Did you think all the men of Mercia as stern as Leofric? We're not, you know. It's a shame really, for Leofric. He was made old before his time, with all the pressure of Mercia on his shoulders, when he stepped into our older brother Northman's shoes. We even thought he was going to marry . . ."

Godwin gulped his ale. About all else, he'd chatted freely, but this had truly slipped out and now he tried to drown it in ale.

"Marry . . . whom?"

He took another loud gulp. "Oh, Northman was always meant to marry Lady Elfreda. She has extensive lands next to ours. Our fathers were good friends and Northman and Elfreda were intended from the cradle. When Northman died Elfreda was heartbroken. And of course Leo was devastated, too. They spent a lot of time with each other. They comforted each other. Elfreda is one of the few who can get a smile from Leo."

"Oh." Suddenly my ale tasted flat. "She's very beautiful."

"North and Leo always called her *Doe*. For her eyes, you see."

Elfreda's eyes were soft brown. She was as gentle as a doe, too, I sensed. I pushed my tankard away. Is that why Leofric had watched the doe with her fawn in the woods? Had he been thinking of Elfreda?

Godwin was still speaking. "We all thought that Elfreda's marriage would be made with Leo instead of with Northman. But it didn't turn out that way. We heard that Leo had married you."

"I'm surprised Elfreda made the long journey from Mercia," I said carefully.

"Oh, she'd do anything for Leo. She's been living in Chester with Edwin and me. She says she can't leave motherless boys to care for ourselves."

"I see."

Godwin gave me a keen glance. "You grieve your parents, too, Godiva."

Beneath the jollity was a young man who had also known loss, hardship, and battle.

"I miss them," I admitted. "It's hard to be alone."

My parents. Edmund. All gone.

"I miss how life used to be," I said.

"What were your pleasures in the Middle Lands?"

"Riding. Dancing." I laughed. "Sometimes both together."

"I understand you're an excellent horsewoman."

"I have an excellent horse."

"A horse that dances?"

"Ebur can do many tricks. She can prance and dance, but that wasn't what I was thinking of. I can do a dance with a rope, or a horsewhip."

He goggled. "You dance with a whip? I've seen dances with sticks and shields and even hobby-horses but never with a whip."

"Not anymore. I haven't done it for a long time. It was just for fun with my family."

And with Edmund. We'd loved to dance.

Godwin slipped his arm through mine. "You have a new family now."

"Thank you, Godwin."

There was no way to explain I felt more alone than ever since Leofric had walked away from me in Arden woods.

In the plant yard Elfreda found me knelt beside an herb bed, digging. Weeding had seemed the perfect work to relieve my frustration at the situation with Leofric. Two more days had passed and two more nights, but he had not revisited my bed. Instead, he spent the nights in the hall, with Godwin and the other Mercian men.

"Your gardens are beautiful."

Her soft leather shoes were tiny, I noticed as she stood beside me, her ankles fine and delicate. The hem of her shift was embroidered with gold thread.

"Thank you." Unclenching my fingers from the trowel I ensured my accents remained gracious as I angled my neck toward her. "I'm sure the grounds of your own hall are very fine."

"They are much more extensive than these but yours are much nicer," she added hastily, as if fearing to offend. Yet perhaps she meant to be condescending. "But I couldn't dig them myself, as you do."

"You probably wouldn't enjoy it."

With a yank I pulled out a root of mugwort.

"Oh but I would! I'd love to do all the things you do. You're so self-sufficient. Leo tells me you also ride as a warrior!"

In my dirt-covered apron I clambered up. I was taller than she. "I'd do anything to defend the Middle Lands."

She shuddered. "I hate to fight. Perhaps I'm a coward."

"I'm sure you're not."

"I'm sure I am." Hesitant she stepped closer, her glittering hem catching the light. "Can I help you with your gardening, Godiva? I'd love to learn."

Part of me wanted to say I would appreciate company. But the need was greater in me to be alone.

"Your clothes aren't suitable for outdoor work."

"Oh." She appeared downcast. "I understand."

To my surprise I felt a pang of remorse as she walked away.

The next day, I was once again in the herb garden when a gentle call came from behind me.

"Godiva?"

With gritted teeth I drove my trowel hard into the earth. Craning my neck I arranged my face so that my irritation would not be revealed. Again, I had sought solace in the herb garden. Again, I was to be disturbed.

"Elfre..." My words fell away as my mouth dropped open. Standing in front of me Elfreda was wrapped from neck to knee in a voluminous homespun seed apron, similar to mine, but hers was huge, dwarfing her tiny size. In the pockets she had a fork and trowel.

"One of the servants loaned this apron to me." She beamed. "I so wanted to help you and when you said yesterday my clothes would be ruined, I asked in the kitchen if they would help me. Look!"

From beneath the apron she poked out her foot, no longer shod in fine leather, but in wooden clogs, again many sizes too large. "They gave me these as well. I paid silver for them," she added quickly. "I wouldn't deprive anyone of their shoes simply because I want to garden with you. Please let me help, Godiva. Would you teach me? I don't know what to do but I'll do exactly as you say."

How could I be unkind to her? It was akin to kicking a newborn pup.

"I'd love you to help me, Elfreda."

Her beaming smile grew even wider as she knelt beside me.

"I'm weeding grasses away from these herbs," I explained. "You can recognize sage, can't you? By its paler, softer leaves? See, they've got almost a fine down on them."

"Oh yes. I know sage."

"That's all you need to do."

"That's all! Why, I can do that."

Copying my posture, she began to weed without another word.

In the brown earth, the ruby on my finger glowed red as a drop of heart's blood. I ought not to wear it while gardening, my bare hands yanking the root tendrils, soil gritted under my nails. Dirt traced the engravings around the gem, tracing their golden patterns to dark shadow. Since Leofric had given it to me as part of my *morgengifu*, a symbol I hadn't expected, I'd not been able to remove it.

Naked

The ring still needed to go to the blacksmith in town to be made smaller. Leofric's Mercian kinswoman had been of a larger size than I. But I hated to take it off to have it altered, even with the troubles between us.

Everywhere I went, I looked for him. Searched the hall for his height the moment I entered. Sought a glimpse of him on Wyrd's back, hard riding across the plains. Hungered for his touch at table. Listened for his tread across the courtyard. Yearned for that unexpected grin.

Nothing.

I comforted myself that his business with Godwin kept him from me. But in the Forest of Arden a connection had broken between us, a twig snapped. Now, distance widened between us by the day.

Once more I focused my attention on the task in front of me. My serenity was being slowly restored with Elfreda at my side. It wasn't the same as when I was alone out of doors, when every rustle in the trees or bird call shifted the silence that I reveled in, a deep silence that filled a need in me. Elfreda's presence beside me with her gentle breathing and careful handiwork altered my sense of awareness. It was companionable to have someone near.

A spasm of grief threatened. I blinked, fast. I missed my mother. She had gardened with me in this way, in tranquil peace, but there was no other friend or family member who cared for it except Aine. Beolinda hadn't been very interested in anything that would dirty her skin and Edmund hadn't done women's work.

Where was Edmund? Had he traveled to the eastern Angle Lands, found kin of his own? Was there anyone left who knew him? Was he traveling alone somewhere, out on the roads, in a strange place? Had he found work and shelter? Was he safe and well?

"Do you have brothers and sisters, Elfreda?"

"No." She wiped the back of her hand across her cheek, leaving an endearing smear of dirt. "I had a brother once who died as an infant, but that is all. Like you."

"Though I have no brothers or sisters I have good friends. As good as family."

"Childhood bonds are not easily broken," Elfreda said.

Edmund's angry face flashed into my mind. The bonds between us had stretched like fraying rope but were they broken?

"Leofric, Edwin, and Godwin have been brothers to me," Elfreda confided next. "And Northman, of course."

Northman. They all spoke his name the same way, the Mercians, a mixture of pride and sorrow that separated like oil and water. Only time would blend it.

"The brothers of Mercia are close. I've rarely heard of such fraternity."

"That's why it's so dreadful there are such terrible rumors in Mercia and spreading across all of Engla-lond, too, I believe."

"What rumors?" I had heard nothing of this. "What is said?"

"Dreadful things. The idea that Leofric would betray . . ." Elfreda shuddered. "It's too terrible even to speak of."

"Betray whom?"

"No." Fiercely she moved her head from side to side. "I cannot say. Even to speak of it is wrong."

Curiosity burned inside me but I didn't press her. Tears were hovering at the edge of those long, dark lashes.

"You're doing well with your weeding." I changed the subject. "You've almost cleared that row of sage."

"Have I done it correctly? I've been careful. I so want to be as capable as you are, Godiva."

A rueful laugh escaped me. "I don't always feel capable."

"But you've fought battles." Her lashes lifted in admiration. "You held back the Danes from Coventry."

The battle for Coventry may have been won but I wasn't winning the battle currently raging inside me. I wished I'd found the courage to speak more of my feelings to Leofric. Yet some reticence curtailed me.

Or lack of courage.

"I didn't fight the battle of Coventry alone. I had strong men beside me."

Edmund.

Leofric.

Oil and water, too.

"Godiva." Elfreda's expression became anxious. "There's something I want to ask you."

"What is it?"

She took a deep breath. "I'd so like us to be friends."

The wind rustled in the boughs of the oak tree.

"Friends? I'm not sure we can be friends."

Elfreda's cheeks colored as pink as marshmallow flowers. "Oh."

Her head drooped as she went back to her weeding.

With a laugh I stopped her trowel.

"You're as kin to Leofric, are you not? Since Godwin has sworn to be a brother to me, if they are also brothers to you . . ."

Her face lit up as though she were a day's eye found the morning sun, as my meaning dawned on her. "Do you mean we could be like sisters?"

"Yes, Elfreda." I squeezed her fingers. "We're sisters, now."

———————

The evening meal had ended. Once more Godwin had made the hall rafters ring with laughter. I was grateful for it with Leofric glowering silently next to me at the high table.

Over the previous days I'd begun to know Elfreda better, and Godwin, too. We'd ridden out beyond the town, though not as far as Arden. Elfreda was the gentlest girl I'd ever met. Her adoration for Leofric and his brothers shone out whenever she spoke. Barely a sentence came from her lips that didn't begin Leofric, or Northman, or Godwin. I had to admit I encouraged both Elfreda and Godwin in telling stories about Leofric, about his youth and boyhood. I lapped them up like a kitten at milk.

I wanted to know Leofric of Mercia, but not the earl. I wanted to know of his tumbles from his horse while learning to jump, of his climbing back on with a broken arm determined to jump again. I wanted to know of the way he would leap into rivers from high rocks and emerge laughing, sleek as an otter in a gurgle of water. All this, Elfreda and Godwin told me. I wanted to know that in spite of his time as an outlaw, Leofric wrote and spoke Latin as good as any monk. He'd learnt Danish, too, Godwin said, to outsmart his enemy.

But all this, before Northman had died. Before Leofric had become the stern man I knew. The grim-faced earl at table now.

The gleeman took up his place in front of the fire.

"Could we have dancing tonight, instead of singing?" Godwin enquired.

Leofric glanced up from his goblet but said nothing.

"Dancing?" I asked. We hadn't danced in the hall since my parents had died.

"If you'll allow it," Godwin said.

"We know you're still in mourning," Elfreda added. "But dancing might make you happy again. If only for a while."

They cared for my happiness. My lids prickled. "I've no objection to dancing."

Inhospitable to stop the pleasure of others. But no dancing for me. Beneath the table my feet seemed stuck in mud.

Elfreda clapped. "Wonderful!"

Godwin jumped up. "Come and dance, Godiva!"

"Not tonight, Godwin." I'd rarely felt less like dancing.

"But you must," he insisted.

"Will you dance, my lord?" I asked.

Godwin chortled. "He won't, will you, Leo? He hasn't danced in years."

Leofric picked up his goblet again. "Don't let me stop you."

I stared down at my empty trencher on the table, flecked with crumbs.

"Please, Godiva." Elfreda pulled my sleeve. I wore a favorite blue tunic tonight. Not as rich as Elfreda's embroidery, but fine nonetheless. "Come and dance with us."

An invitation.

Churlish to refuse a guest.

I raised my head. In their eager faces I saw real affection I'd never expected to witness again.

Family.

Hall-joy.

Beneath the table my toes twitched.

I wanted to dance.

My arms outstretched I leapt to my feet. "Bring the pipes and drums!"

Commotion filled the hall as the lower trestle tables were pushed aside to clear the floor. The hall wasn't as full as it was on a feast day, but there were plenty of folk. Warriors, townsfolk, servants, all

formed a ring. Wilbert and Walburgha, at dinner in the hall that
night, and even Acwell, Leofric's grim bodyguard, joined the dance.

The gleemen began to play.

A rhythm first from the beating drum. Then it came, the call of
the pipes.

The call no feet could resist.

I peeped at the dais. At the table Leofric sat alone.

Across the hall his gaze gripped mine.

As if he held me in the dance.

Stock still, I stood, unable to move.

Then Elfreda grabbed my hand, Godwin the other. In the ring
we began.

Glee of dance and song,
And battle-throng—Battle, dance and song!

The gleemen chanted to the beat of the drums.

Fire! Fire! Steel and fire!
Oak! Oak! Earth and waves!
Waves, oak, earth and oak!

Verse after verse, until we were all puffing and panting. The ring
surged in and out like waves. Elfreda glowed, Godwin laughed. Walburgha wiped her perspiring cheeks with a kerchief. Wilbert beside
her, surprisingly nimble.

We danced and danced and danced.

The music changed. A new song started. Again the pipes called.
Another dance, till my feet began to ache with joy.

Naked

In partners, in pairs. Godwin, Wilbert. Back in the ring. The circle formed, broke, reformed and broke again.

"Godiva! Here!"

Godwin threw me a horsewhip. Who knew where he'd found it. Perhaps he'd brought it with him to dinner.

Instinctively I caught it, single-handed. Black leather, fine-tipped. A handle, a tail. As long as I was tall.

"Clear away! Give her space!" Godwin shouted.

"Godwin, no," I protested.

"Please, Godiva! Show us the dance of the Middle Lands!"

The other dancers backed away. I was alone in the circle.

The drums started pounding.

My feet found the beat.

Above my head I cracked the whip.

A cheer rang out, laughing and whooping.

In the circle they began to clap in time.

In a spiral I began to dance.

Twirling, swirling, around me the long tail coiled. Loose, tight, in, out, over, under. Leather on air, leather on earth, cutting high, swinging low.

It never caught me. Faster than the whip I twisted and turned my body and hands chasing each other.

"Godiva!"

"Godiva!"

Skipping, jumping, a rope, a loop. Inside the spiral.

"Godiva!"

"Godiva!"

In time they clapped, on and on. The drums beat faster and faster.

All that I kept inside me, fire, stars, sparks.

The whip became a comet, streaked across the sky.

The drums began to slow. I came to a halt.

The crowd cheered.

Dizzy and breathless, I glanced up at the high table.

His place was empty.

Leofric was gone.

"Leofric."

Holding a candle aloft, his face was half light, half shadow as he stared down at me lying in my bed. "I didn't mean to frighten you."

"I wasn't asleep." After my dance, when he'd disappeared, I'd come away to my bower, my heart and feet heavy. Tossed my head on the pillow.

He found me undesirable.

Yet even now, I longed for him to blow out the candle, to come to bed and lay beside me, as he had done so many times during our sweet month. But he made no move to take me into his arms. He simply studied at me as I lay, my hair fanned out on the linen.

At last I broke the silence. "I like your brother."

"Godwin has the gift of making friends easily."

"Has he gone to bed at last? I thought he would drink mead all night."

Is that what you have been doing these past nights, Leofric? Do you drink mead with Godwin until the early hours? Why do you not come to me? And where did you go while I was dancing for your eyes alone?

"Godwin sleeps now." Leofric's tone gentled. "So does Elfreda."

"I like Elfreda as much as your brother."

A smile. A private, soft, indulgent smile, that tore at me in spite of my growing fondness for its cause. "They're two of a kind."

When he focused on me his expression seemed to harden. "Since you're awake there's news I wish to tell you."

"Please." Shifting aside, I made room for him in the bed, my movement an invitation. He moved closer. The leather male scent of him. Desire flooded me.

Touch me, I wanted to beg. *Touch me, the way you touched me during our honeymoon. Take me, as you did in the Forest of Arden.* But he did not. The coldness and distance that had come between us hung like an invisible tapestry, separating us from each other. I didn't know how to tear it down.

Placing the candle on the table beside us he remained standing. "All is not as it should be in Mercia. My brothers have done their best but I've left my land in their care for too much time. They need me in the north. I've lingered too long in Coventry."

He'd lingered too long with me. That was what he meant.

"When will you go?"

"On the morrow. There's no reason to delay."

Turning away into the cover of darkness, I bit my tongue. I kept my tone as water cool as his. There would be no weakness from me even as my deepest woman-self reeled at his news.

"Will you be away for long?"

"I can't say."

Why did I feel as if he was lying to me? Why didn't he confide in me the urgent business in the north? Could I not to be trusted?

"Acwell will stay here in Coventry as your bodyguard," Leofric said.

"Edmund is my bodyguard." Whether he was in Coventry or not, that title still belonged to my friend.

Leofric moved the candle. In the sudden darkness his expression was indiscernible.

"Now you will have Acwell. You're not to ride out alone."

Acwell. That silent brute of a man. Yet I sensed his loyalty to Leofric, his Mercian lord. If Leofric had asked Acwell to watch me I'd never have a moment to myself.

Hard, I set my lip. Why, I'd ridden unattended in the Middle Lands for years. It was a pastime I treasured.

"Do you understand me?" Leofric grabbed my wrist. "Thurkill is gone but there are other enemies ready to take his place. Peace is not yet won."

There was wisdom in such wariness, I knew it. A lull, perhaps, but no real rest for any Saxons while the Danish king was on the throne and the Dane law strangled half of Engla-lond. The Middle Lands with its vital position would always be desired. Who knew what evil plots were being made. Only through my alliance with Leofric had I any hope of keeping the shire safe.

"Promise me," he demanded, when I made no response. "Promise me, for the love of your land."

I wrenched my wrist away. "All right!"

Thurkill had terrified me more than I cared to admit. Nightmares of him still plagued me, though they never came when Leofric slumbered beside me.

It wasn't Acwell I wanted. An internal whisper.

"So you're leaving with Godwin and—Elfreda?"

"Yes, they'll come north with me. When I return, we need to discuss some of the ways Coventry has been governed. Your father's methods differ from mine."

When he returned. At least he did not plan to stay away.

"And . . . will you . . . sleep . . . now, my lord?"

Was that a flicker of warmth in his expression? In the candlelight I couldn't be sure.

For a moment he hesitated, as if weighing something in his mind. "There's much I need to do if I am to leave for Mercia in the morning. I'll sleep in the hall with the men. With Godwin."

Anger ignited in my brain as the rejection set in.

"Of course." I lifted my chin. No disclosing how much he'd hurt me, the space I had made for him beside me turning cold. Or how many shadow hours I'd spent waiting, hoping, praying he would come to me. "I understand."

"The Danes know that the Middle Lands are now under Mercia's protection." His lids were hooded. "You can hold Coventry in my absence?"

"I've told you before. I can hold my own lands." My assertion came out more waspish than I intended.

Wax spattered as he seized the candle. "It seems you don't need me after all."

The bower door slammed behind him.

"Leofric. Wait!"

21

And all the mothers brought
Their children, clamouring, "If we pay, we starve!"
——Tennyson [1842]: *Godiva*

The candle dripped away its dim light. Needle in hand I sat alone in my bower, my ruby ring glinting in the firelight as I stitched. In the weeks that Leofric had been away I had taken up the task of completing my mother's tapestry, a hanging she had planned for our hall, depicting a woodland hunt such as those my father had often enjoyed. Her embroidery was fine and delicate; I wielded my needle more like a blade. I would never be as skillful as she had been. But I hated to leave her work unfinished.

With a sigh I rethreaded the needle with a length of green silk to finish a cluster of leaves. Leofric had been gone for weeks but for each week it seemed as if a month had passed. The days were long but the nights . . . The nights were longer still.

When he'd come to me in the night before riding north with Godwin and Elfreda I'd called after him. I didn't know if he hadn't heard or just ignored my plea. If my husband had come back into the bower then, I'd have told him of my feelings, taken the chance. But once again the chance had slipped away.

More than once, at sleepy dawn, I found myself reaching out for him in my soft bed. My body craved his. Part of me now could only be filled by him, nothing else. A hunger, a thirst unquenched. I longed for him. In the darkling hours I lay awake. And if I did sleep, my dreams were full of him, so vivid, so colorful and full of passion, that when I awoke I would find myself in a tangle of blankets, my body aroused. I could still scent the leather of him on the linen. For weeks I hadn't let Aine wash them.

The sensations, the feelings he'd aroused while he'd been in Coventry had grown stronger while he was away.

His body. My body.

In the bed, on a sheepsskin on the floor, against the wall.

The Earl of Mercia had vanquished my bower.

His skin. Leather-battled. Tanned hard. A survivor. Yet pale and smooth in those private places I'd explored by lip and fingertip.

His breathing. Even-chested. Reassuring in the night.

A yawning stretch upon awakening in the morning light.

Intimacy. Shared. Sacred.

What I missed most.

Dropping the needle I rubbed my temples. My head ached. Was he missing me at all? Or had he forgotten about me the moment he had left the Middle Lands and crossed the Mercian border?

It gnawed away at my very bones. I'd shown him my homeland, taken him to my beloved Arden. I wanted to see his great cities: Chester, Derby, Nottingham. I wanted to ride out with him to Sherwood Forest, discover the secret places where he'd hidden as an outlaw. To travel to the north would have been an adventure. I was the Lady of Mercia now, of shires I'd never seen. Yet he hadn't wanted me with him.

And Elfreda. His *Doe*. The woman he'd planned to marry, if he hadn't needed to marry me to keep his northern lands Saxon safe. Perhaps he was in her arms now, relieved to be away from the wife he had been forced to take for duty. In the short time she and Godwin had been in Coventry, I'd grown fond of her. It had been a wrench to say good-bye.

Yet night-dreams visited of Leofric making love to Elfreda, caressing her with his hands and lips in the same way he caressed me.

How could Leofric not love that soft, gentle girl-woman? Although she was older than me in years she had a soft girlishness that would never fade. That softness, an eagerness and enthusiasm for the world. Being with her each day would be seeing each day anew.

Elfreda. A prize. A wife fit for an earl, with all the womanly virtues. She wouldn't argue with Leofric, make demands, parry and fight.

He called me a battle-maid.

Headstrong. Willful. Defiant. I knew my own shortcomings.

So much attention I'd given to having been forced to marry Leofric, I hadn't given any to the fact that he'd been forced to marry me. Would I have been his first choice? Would he have chosen me over Elfreda, if not for the greater Saxon good?

Aine came in carrying a pile of firewood. "The hour is late. You'll strain yourself, my lady. You should go to your bed. Rest."

"What's the point, Aine?" Rolling it up, I thrust my embroidery into its basket. "I don't sleep well anymore." Each night I stared at the stars painted on the ceiling. I had counted them all many times over.

"You're indoors too much of late." Aine glanced at the *briw* of mint and carrot cooling in its wooden bowl. I hadn't been able to face the broth that was usually my favorite, or the grain bread and fresh butter on the slab beside it. My *oxymel* health cup, made of honey and vinegar syrup, stood untouched. "You don't eat, you don't sleep. When was the last time you went out riding?"

"I don't care to ride." Still, I felt a pang. I had been neglecting Ebur.

"You haven't ridden abroad in the Middle Lands for weeks now, and you know it was your parents' practice to do so. It's your duty."

We charge the care of Coventry to you, while we are gone.

For their honor. For the good of our lands.

Be brave. Move on.

"I'll go tomorrow."

My spirits lifted as I rode out of Coventry and into the rolling green farmlands beyond the town, with Acwell riding behind. As I'd anticipated, he never seemed to let me out of his sight. It made me miss the ease of Edmund's company as my bodyguard all the more.

The summer air was warm against my face, the sun dazzling the ripening *korn* fields. The roadsides bursting with *hagathorn*, wild garlic, and primroses, the shady oak and hazel copses were cool and inviting. Aine had been right, as usual. I felt better as soon as I was out of doors.

Determinedly, I tried to avoid thinking about Leofric as I rode. But I hadn't taken this path since we had ridden it together on our way to the Forest of Arden.

Arden. The hours we had spent there were imprinted on my mind, my soul, my body. We had become as close as a man and woman could be that day, or so I'd believed. There'd been a powerful holiness when we made love in that sacred grove. The crackling of the leaves as he—

I wouldn't ride to Arden.

Leaning down I urged Ebur on, outriding my thoughts. At the farm where I'd stopped with Leofric I sought out the farmwife. She was standing near the barn.

Ebur snorted as I came to a halt. I smiled. "How goes it with you?"

"We're pleased to see you, my lady." She appeared more tired than she had in the spring, her face thin, almost gaunt. "But all is not well here."

"What's happened?" Swiftly I reached for my sword. I'd begun to ride armed and armored since Thurkill's abduction. Never again would I be caught without defense. "Not warriors from the east? Not Danes?"

Leofric had urged me to stay my guard. Suddenly, Acwell's presence on his horse behind me became reassuring.

"No Danes. It's the harvest. The crops last year were as poor as we have ever known."

The harvest had been bad, I knew, but not to this extent. I frowned. "How much grain do you have left?"

"Not much, my lady. It's nigh on June, and I'm worried we won't have enough for June, let alone for July. Not for our cattle or for us." She leaned forward. "We won't last the hungry month."

The hungry month. That was the name July went by if the hay and grain ran out. Not just farmers were affected. When grain was scarce, the price of it went sky high and many in the town became unable to afford it. And I had sat in my bower, refusing my food!

Shame tensed my muscles. Ebur shifted beneath my seat. "Are there others who are in the same position?"

"There are farms that have less grain than we do. There's a shortage throughout the Middle Lands." The farmwife glanced over at her children playing with knuckle bones outside the barn door. She whispered. "I fear our children will starve."

Naked

"No child will starve in the Middle Lands," I replied fiercely.

Her apron twisted beneath her anxious fingers. "My husband worries night and day about the weather. He needs to get the grass cut and dried before the rain can spoil it, to feed the animals. There is not much hay remaining in the barn and the grain bin is almost empty. Soon we will have nothing to eat or to sell." Her expression became imploring. "My lady. We won't be able to pay our taxes."

Reaching out I clasped her thin hand. "My father never took taxes from a starving man. Nor will I."

Tears brimmed in her eyes. "We aren't starving yet. But we might be if we must sell all our grain to pay our taxes."

"Taxes. Do you think I seek your money at such a time? As you eke out your food it's famine we must fight, together, just as we fought the Danes. We've beaten poor harvests before."

"Oh my lady!" With her apron she wiped her cheek.

"The next *althing* is soon. Please come, and bring your husband, and tell others in these parts to come, too. I'll listen to you all about the harvest, and about the taxes."

"Oh thank you, my lady. We'll come. Thank you!"

With a heavy heart I rode away. The Mercian bodyguard Acwell had been listening intently. He followed hard on Ebur's hooves.

The Middle Lands were in need and I hadn't known. How disappointed my parents would have been in me. I would waste no more time sitting in my bower hoping Leofric would return.

As Ebur galloped I sent a promise flying into the air. Famine would not beat my people. I could only hope my help would be in time.

I stood on the dais in the hall and raised my palm flat. The center fire was unlit, for the summer air was warm and no hide hung over the windows. But still the air felt stuffy.

Crowded in front of me were many anxious faces, both town and country folk, almost to the rear of the hall, threatening to spill out the doorway. The farmwife was at the front of the crowd, her weather-beaten husband beside her. Tomas the tanner sidling at the back as usual. His feaberry eyes darted too often toward me.

Acwell hovered near me, watchful.

"Welcome, good people of the Middle Lands. The *althing* for the shire of the Middle Lands has begun. Who will speak first today?"

"I'll speak, my lady." Wilbert pushed forward with a bow. "But I don't speak only for myself. I speak for all the townsfolk, in the villages, and out on the farms. It's the poor harvest, my lady. We all face famine."

"We'll go hungry!" Walburgha cried.

Noise and consternation broke out among the crowd.

"I won't be running my water mill," said the miller, "if there's no grain to be ground into flour. Then how will I feed my family?"

"It isn't just that we're short of grain this year." The farmwife appeared even thinner than days before when I had seen her at the farm. "We've had a few bad years in a row."

"Probably going to have a few more, too, if I read the land right," added her husband.

"Goes in sevens, doesn't it?" Walburgha put in. "Seven years of bad crops, there usually is, and we've a few more to go if the saying be right."

"We'll starve!" Someone called again from the rear of the hall.

"Have you ever gone hungry in Coventry?" I asked.

Mutters of no were heard, though many didn't sound convinced.

"Not in Coventry, never!" said Wilbert stoutly.

"Then you must have faith in me!" I cried. "Have we not already defeated Thurkill the Tall, a fearsome foe?"

"It's true. We have!" called the miller.

Tomas the tanner moved to the front. "Yes, we defeated the Danes."

Wilbert snorted with disgust. "I didn't see you fighting."

"I had the toothache," Tomas said indignantly.

"The toothache!" Walburgha shook her fist at him. "I'll give you the toothache."

"Pray, don't argue between yourselves. If everyone in Coventry is to survive the hungry month, and beyond, we must stand together."

Walburgha gave one last shake before attending to me.

"The famine that we face is severe," I said. "Last year's crops were bad, and for a few years now we have struggled. We have also had to use our resources to fight Thurkill the Tall and the Danes. I know times are difficult for you all, especially families who lost men in battle."

Compassion softened Walburgha's expression. She had a stout heart. "There are quite a few families in need."

"On the farm next to ours, the children are doing the farmwork for their mother, who is expecting another baby. Her husband died in the battle against Thurkill, God rest his soul." The farmwife crossed herself.

There were certain to be many more stories such as these. "How many will not have enough food for the hungry month?"

Almost three-quarters of the group raised their hands.

Many more than I had suspected. I bit my lip. Stepping away from the crowd, I reached over to the table and took from it a good Saxon loaf, round and flat, made from coarse flour ground at our own mill.

Holding it in my two hands, I raised it high. My ruby ring glinted.

"Here is the loaf! Here is good bread: grown, milled, and made in the Middle Lands. In our Saxon way your lord is your loaf giver. I am your lady just as my father was lord. My father was your loaf giver and so shall I be."

As red as blood my ring flashed as I tore the loaf in two.

Silent now, the crowd waited. I heaved a breath.

Lowering the pieces of bread, I met as many frightened expressions as I could. Resolute. Only Tomas looked away.

"No one will starve in the hungry month. In Coventry, the loaf is shared, rich and poor alike. I will not collect the taxes until this year's autumn harvest."

Relieved babble broke out.

Claps and cheers.

"Was Godiva hail!"

"You're a saint like your mother, Lady Godiva!" Walburgha dabbed her cheeks.

"And as wise as your father!" called Wilbert.

Carefully placing the bread on the table I noticed my tense fingers had made dents in the crust.

I addressed the crowd again.

"Please, I have more to say. I ask that if you have any stores you share them with others in need."

Tomas gave a belligerent swagger.

"What, if we've been sensible enough to put stores away we have to share it with those who haven't?"

"Who'd want your stores, Tomas?" Walburgha cried.

"I guess we know who's got something tucked away to keep for themselves!" The weather-beaten farmer at the front took a step toward Tomas. "And I guess we know where to find it, if we're hungry!"

Tomas slunk away.

"It's up to each person to share what they will." I wasn't surprised at Tomas's selfishness. "But our way in the Middle Lands has always been to care for one another. I trust that will not change."

The crowd muttered their approval.

Wilbert nodded. "That's the way it should be."

"Aye, that's how it's always been done in Coventry," the miller agreed.

"We will face these times of hardship together," I promised. "You're not alone, good people. I am your lady, and I will never let anyone in my lands suffer. Coventry did not burn, and Coventry will not starve!"

"To Coventry!"

"*Was Godiva hail!*" Wilbert shouted.

The folk cheered.

As the crowd gathered, loneliness unexpectedly consumed me. I clutched at the edge of the table, the weight of their faith in me heavy on my shoulders.

I longed for my parents.

I longed for Edmund.

For Leofric.

"My ring is missing!"

Aine paused in stoking the fire. "What's missing, my lady?"

"My ring! The ruby ring Lord Leofric gave me!" I searched frantically around the bower. Cloak, tunics, shifts, shawls. Hurled out of the clothing chest.

"Where did you last see it?"

"I had it at the *althing.*"

"Perhaps it got caught in your cloak. It could be hanging by a thread." Aine shook the mantle I'd been wearing.

On my hands and knees I sifted through the rushes on the floor.

"Stop it, my lady. Get up. Let me search for you."

"No, Aine. I must find it. I must. The ring was loose. I didn't take it to be mended in time. Oh, why didn't I take it?"

She hauled me up. "I'll have the servants search. Someone may have picked it up. They'll guess it's yours and they'll return it."

"I don't believe I'll see it again."

"Of course you will. We'll find it."

"It's a bad omen."

Aine's dark eyes were fixed on me, her expression inscrutable.

Slumping down by the fire, my fingers traced the empty place the ring had been. A white circle branded my skin.

"It's gone forever."

"My lady. You're making too much of this. You'll grow ill if you carry on so. You need to get away from Coventry for a while."

"I can't leave Coventry!"

"Your mother used to visit the monks at Evesham when she was troubled and needed help."

Evesham monastery. There my parents often sought advice and aid for the poor.

"The monks may know ways to help, during the hungry month." I sat up. "I could visit Beolinda on the way." Her father had been a good friend to mine. He might have some useful advice, too.

"You need a change from these bower walls, my lady."

And I needed the monks' wisdom. Leofric was gone. I was alone. I had no one else to guide me. "We'll go on the morrow."

22

Not only we, that prate
Of rights and wrongs, have loved the people well,
And loathed to see them overtax'd . . .
———Tennyson [1842]: *Godiva*

Beolinda hurried out the door to where I stood, Ebur's bridle in my hand. We'd been traveling for hours. Saddle-sore and weary, I was relieved to spy the thatched eaves of her family hall, set in a valley shaded with elm trees, now in full leaf. It was smaller than our hall in Coventry, with just a few houses and barns, but its aspect was particularly fine.

"Godiva! I wasn't expecting you!"

A butterfly the color of black and flame darted around me as I laughed. "It's my turn to give you a surprise, Beolinda. I hope you don't mind putting us up for a night. I didn't have time to send a message. We're on our way to the monastery at Evesham."

"Of course you're welcome to stay the night!"

Pink-cheeked, she laughed, too, but her attention strayed across the courtyard as though she searched for someone.

"Is your father at hall?" My father's friend. It would bring my own father closer to me. My heart lurched. He might be able to give me advice on how to cope with the hungry gap as my father would have. My father had always managed to keep peace during famine, even though some barns in the Middle Lands still held grain, while others would be forced to scratch for enough for a meal. Some had enough money to pay prices forced sky high for the last of the crops, some had no money at all. Inequality always revealed its ugly face at such a time. Hunger could drive a man to many things, even thieving from his neighbor. I'd heard of such crimes and of the harsh punishments meted put at *althing* meetings—the loss of thieving hands. Somehow, my father had generally managed to avoid this in Coventry, at least that I could remember. I desperately wanted to achieve the same—or avoid having to mete out such justice. Would I ever be able to lift my sword and cut off one of my own people's limbs? *No.* I would have to ensure my people didn't go hungry, to be driven to such acts.

"My father isn't here, nor my mother or sisters. They're away all making visits."

"Oh? Where have they gone?"

"To the east."

My parents had often traveled to call on friends and relatives in the warm summer months. I'd gone with them, many times.

"July is a good time of year to travel," I said easily, when Beolinda offered no more information. She still appeared anxious, her fingers in her mouth. "Are you sure it isn't a problem having us here, Beolinda? With your father away?"

Aine was behind me on her brown mare and Acwell, still sticking to me like sap. They would need to be fed, too. Had I been hasty, calling unawares? How inconsiderate I'd become. Was even Beolinda's family short of grain?

Beolinda seemed to come to herself.

"Of course not." As she looped her arm through mine I smelt her sweet rose scent, heightened by the summer heat. "Leave your horse to one of the grooms, Godiva, and come indoors. How tired and pale you are. You must sleep in my bower tonight."

We left Beolinda's hall early in the morning. A red sky bloomed.

"Red sky at night, shepherds' delight, red sky at morning, shepherds' warning," Aine muttered as we rode away.

I was glad to continue our journey to Evesham. Even though she'd been hospitable, I'd still sensed Beolinda's lack of ease with me. I assumed there was a matter troubling her she didn't want to share. Not famine, I prayed. If barns were already emptying, the Middle Lands were in greater trouble than I'd feared.

Acwell's horse drew up to mine. The journey with him had been pleasant. Against all expectations, Aine seemed to enjoy his company. You never knew with Aine who would gain her approval. For my part I'd grown used to him, to value the reassurance of his solid bulk.

And he was a link to Leofric.

"Have you always been in Lord Leofric's service?" I asked carefully. Acwell's reserve didn't encourage questions. But the urge to speak of Leofric overwhelmed me.

He nodded curtly.

"Then you were in Sherwood Forest?" I prompted.

Another nod. Then he surprised me by saying, "I served Lord Northman."

So he'd known them both.

"What manner of man was Northman?" I pressed. The grief that cloaked Northman from view forbade me asking such questions of Leofric, or even of Godwin or Elfreda. Yet my curiosity was growing over the brother who still made such an impact. His presence seemed as potent dead as alive.

Acwell shifted his reins from one hand to the other.

"Lord Northman was a leader such as all men would follow," he said after a moment.

"Like Lord Leofric," I said.

Acwell hesitated. "Lord Leofric is not a man to seek power though he carries the burden of it."

"You don't think the earl a natural leader?" I felt amazed by Acwell's response. I'd known Leofric had assumed the mantle of power from his elder brother but he'd never seemed uncomfortable with it. Quite the contrary.

"You misunderstand, my lady. A leader such as Lord Leofric is one to be trusted. He has the loyalty of every good man in Mercia."

A man to be trusted. I wondered then what had been Elfreda's meaning when she spoke of rumors against Leofric in the north.

"They were hard days in Sherwood, were they not?" Once again my question was leading.

"They were hard. But they are gone." Acwell yanked on his horse's reins. "I'll check the road ahead. If I have your leave."

With good grace I bowed. Our conversation was clearly over.

Yet again Acwell surprised me. Leaning close he murmured, "Don't ask too many questions of the past, my lady. It does more harm than good."

His horse thundered away.

Brother Aefic beamed as his tunic swished across the earthen floor of the chapter house. "God's greeting, Lady Godiva. We're pleased to welcome you to Evesham, my child."

From Beolinda's hall we'd sent word of our coming.

My hands outstretched, I went to him. At the sight of my bare finger, I winced. My ring hadn't been found in spite of Aine's hopes. I could not get used to its being gone. None of the servants had seen it. Being without it made the honeymoon I had shared with Leofric seem even more distant. A wife without ring, child, or husband.

"I came to seek your help, Brother."

A brief clasp, swift and reassuring as a benediction.

He indicated a wooden bench where I could sit. On another he seated himself and pulled it close. "What can I do to help you? You know I am always at your service, just as I was for your parents. May their souls rest in peace." He crossed himself.

Grief stabbed me, as it always did when my parents were mentioned. What they'd been through . . . "Their loss stays with me."

"Their love stays with you." He gently reframed my words. "It won't leave you, just because they're gone, my child. Love is eternal."

I hadn't thought of it that way. Continuing to remember them was a way of continuing to love them. It comforted me.

Brother Aefic cradled his stomach and smiled at me, in the same way he had when I had gotten a Latin lesson right. "There's trouble in Coventry that brings you here."

The monk shared Aine's uncanny knack of knowing what was going on without being told.

"No Danes at least. For now, the Middle Lands are safe under Mercia's protection." The defeat of Thurkill the Tall would have spread far and wide. Though Leofric had guarded me against complacency, even if others sought to seize my lands, Leofric's strength and strategy . . . my faith was in their power. My lands were safe with him. The Earl of Mercia was a powerful ally. At least my marriage had served that purpose. Yet the victory felt hollow inside me. I brought myself back to the purpose of my visit.

"The hungry month approaches, Brother Aefic, worse than ever, we fear. I've made law that our people don't have to pay taxes until the next harvest."

"The reduction of taxes was often Lord Radulf's practice in time of famine."

"And now mine."

The monk frowned. "But you're not collecting the taxes at all? My child, that's very charitable of you. It's more relief than your father gave, I believe."

For a moment I wondered if I had been overgenerous. *No.* What I had done was right and I would stand by my word. "There's been so much hardship in the Middle Lands in recent months. We lost houses, barns, goods, stock as well as lives in the fight against Thurkill."

"You'll be rewarded for your charity, I'm sure. Your mother would be proud. Her devotion was an inspiration to many."

"You know she hoped to build a stone church in Coventry one day. It was her dream and my father's."

"Your parents were most generous. A stone church would be a great gift. There are brothers who have traveled to Rome and brought to Engla-lond holy relics of the saints. How fine it would be to house such a relic in Coventry! But I'm sounding worldly. We don't need stone buildings to do God's work in the world."

He chuckled as he rubbed his shaved head, a gesture I'd often seen him make. As a child I'd asked him if he had lost his hair. Shaking with laughter, he had told me it had been lost many moons before.

"The bees will help us." He chuckled again. "You must see our beehives while you're here."

The monks paid their taxes with honey wealth. I'd always loved their hives.

"My old nurse Aine will want to see them. And a Mercian body-guard is with me, too."

"They will need to sleep in the servants' quarters."

Acwell wouldn't approve. He guarded my bower door like a hound. Nor would Aine. Of late she'd taken to sleeping beside me on a pallet on the floor.

"You haven't been accompanied by your husband Lord Leofric?"

"He's in his own lands, in Mercia."

"When is he coming south?"

"I'm not sure. There's been plenty for me to do in the Middle Lands," I added quickly.

"I understand." Brother Aefic said kindly. "I'm glad you have come to Evesham, my child. We will help all we can with the famine. But grief is wearying. Rest here with us and regain your strength. Care of your health is a duty. When you're stronger, you can go home."

"Thank you, Brother Aefic." Perhaps some time away from Coventry would give me the respite I so desperately needed.

I could no longer face my empty bower.

"Their honey tastes good," Aine said reluctantly as we strolled through the garden, not far from where the beehives stood, shaped like vast golden baskets. The bees hummed through the warm summer air. Behind us the monastery buildings with their thatched roofs glinted in the sun. "Though I could get more from those bees than the monks do, I'm sure. I'd say a charm, that's the way."

"I don't think the monks would approve," I laughed, pushing the veil away from my face. I'd covered myself as we'd gone close to the hives though Aine hadn't bothered. She swore she'd never been stung and never would.

"What's wrong with telling the bees? *Settle down, victory-woman, never be wild and fly to the woods. Be mindful of our welfare and the goddess will be good.* That's all you need to tell the bees, and they'll never swarm you. My charms and herbal remedies work just as well as these monks' medicines, if not better."

"Their beeswax candles give strong light." Each night I'd lit sweet-smelling tapers, marked with lines for each hour, and scented with candle-wyrt, in my quiet room. When I'd blown out the flame and lain in my narrow bed I'd been able to sleep. My mother had slept in such a cell, too. I seemed to sense her presence in the peaceful monastery.

Be brave. Move on. That's what she would have wanted. Let the pain and suffering diminish.

"I asked the beekeeper how they roll their candles. I offered him the recipe for my *oxymel* in exchange, but he said he didn't want my witchery. Witchery!"

Not all the monks were as tolerant of the old ways as Brother Aefic.

"That sign language they use," Aine went on. She'd taken to chattering of everyday things of late, to soothe my troubled mind, I suspected. "What's wrong with words, I ask you?"

Again I laughed. It had taken me a few days to recall the monks' sign language, too, especially at mealtime in the refectory. While one of the monks read the Bible aloud in Latin, we ate in silence. To ask for wine, two taps on the fingers. To pass the butter, three strokes on the inside of your hand. For pepper: knock one index finger on the other. For salt: shake your fingers together. Edmund and I had learnt the hand signs along with our Latin. We'd used it as a secret code. Just between us.

"The food is good, too, Aine."

We'd supped on fresh vegetables from the garden made into thick soups and stews and my appetite had grown. Their *briw* of new picked green peas, mixed with eggs and bread crumbled in, was one of the finest I'd ever tasted.

"It's wholesome enough," she replied. "This rest has done you good and I'm glad for it. I've been worried about you, you've been so listless."

"I hope you've rested too." To my relief Aine appeared to have gained health at the monastery. She'd been through so much with me.

"Rest in this place? With all the bells ringing and smoke burning and singing throughout the day and the night?"

"Prime, terce, sext, none, vespers, and compline," I recited.

"Candle, taper, wick, candle, lantern, and lamp," Aine retorted. "That's what we call our prayers in the Middle Lands. It was good enough for your mother."

My mother had often visited Evesham and traveled home restored. I understood why now. The quiet and contemplation suited me, too. Unlike Aine, I'd found the rhythm of prayers and the chanting of the liturgy soothing, though I hadn't attended all the services.

Brother Aefic's advice had been sound. What he'd told me, in essence, was to remember the good times, the joy, the love. Healing would come by dwelling on my recollections of happy childhood days with my parents and their cherishment of me. I'd grown up surrounded by love. The warm weave was a mantle of protection I could wear any time I needed.

I'd taken walks and observed the monks at work in the surrounding field or sat indoors watching the scholars as they copied manuscripts in the scriptorium.

Eliza Redgold

"Why don't you try again with the beekeeper?" I suggested to Aine. "Perhaps you can tell him I would appreciate their candle secrets to light our hall in Coventry." All the monks had been so kind to me, out of respect for my mother and father.

"That might work. I could try again. He's down by the beehives now, encased in a hundred veils, so scared of being swarmed. I'll go now, my lady, if you don't mind."

"Of course not. Don't get stung, Aine."

Aine snorted again. "No bee will ever sting me."

She bustled down the garden path toward the hives.

Plucking a dandelion from the grass, I sat down on a garden bench, my face to the sun.

A cuckoo called overhead. Cuckoo's day had come and gone, when the bird's first song was heard, heralding summer to come. Soon they would fly away to warmer climes.

Would I see Leofric again before the cuckoo flew?

"Godiva!"

"Edmund?"

"Over here!" A voice hissed from behind the shield of an elm tree.

"Edmund!" At once I ran across the lawn behind the tree and flung my arms around him. All the love I had for him, the love that had grown up with us, brimmed like ale froth the moment I saw him.

Hauling me behind cover of the trunk of the tree he held me close. The sapling slightness was completely gone now. In our time apart he'd filled out. Yet he was still not as broad as Leofric, whose chest was solid as an oak.

Edmund held me out by my elbows and examined me hungrily. "You're as beautiful as ever, Godiva. More so, if that's possible."

I'd almost forgotten how handsome he was. Such a Saxon, Beolinda always sighed. His face was more tanned, contrasting his blond

208

hair against his skin. There were new lines around his mouth. They only emphasized the blade of his lips.

Lightning.

"I've missed you so much. Nothing was the same in Coventry without you."

Edmund's empty seat at the table. His vacant horse stall. His bay stallion, gone. It had smote me every time I passed. Our horses had been stabled side by side since we were children.

His grip crushed the dandelion bloom I held. "I had to see you. I hated the way we left things between us. I've missed you, Godiva."

"You left so quickly. We didn't say good-bye. I thought I might never see you again."

"I had to go."

The jagged hole in the stable wall. "You frightened me, Edmund."

Slivers of mirror glass. "I lost my temper. Not with you. I loathed your plan to marry that man."

Distance stretched between us as I stepped back. "That man is now my husband."

"Because you had to wed him."

"Yes, but . . ."

"It's all right," he interrupted. "I understand why you married him. Your people come first."

I stared down at the broken dandelion stem in my hand. There was no way I could begin to tell Edmund about the feelings I had for Leofric. The feelings that grew stronger and stronger as every day passed. I barely knew what to make of them myself, the mix of longing and desire, anger and regret that churned through me. Hot, cold, warm, chill.

"Where have you been? Did you go to the Angle Lands?"

"Not yet. I plan to. I've been all over Engla-lond. But I need to go home." He flashed a bleak smile that tugged at my heartstrings. "Once I thought Coventry was home."

"Coventry *is* your home."

"Not anymore."

I bit my lip. "You're still angry with me."

"No. I'm not angry."

"So where did you go?"

To my surprise he shook his head. "I can't tell you. It isn't safe for you to know."

"Not safe?" What could he mean?

"You're being so mysterious! What's the matter?"

"I have to speak to you alone." Hilt-poised he peered past the poplar tree. There was no one in the garden, as far as I could see.

"You've got a bodyguard with you, haven't you?"

"Yes, Acwell is with me," I replied, puzzled. "One of Leofric's men, you met him."

"Don't let Acwell know you've seen me. Or Aine. She's here with you, too, isn't she? Will you promise?"

Reluctantly I nodded. I never kept secrets from Aine.

"Meet me here tonight, when everyone has gone to bed."

My heart began to drum. "But why?"

Edmund's grey eyes stared into mine. "You're in danger, Godiva."

The full moon globed the night sky as I slipped into the monastery garden. Lavender from the herb plot filled the air with their delicate scent and the nightjars had begun to call. It had been easy enough to slip out. Acwell and Aine were in the servants' quarters. The monks had retired to their cells.

"Edmund," I whispered. Suddenly I felt frightened. "Edmund! Where are you?"

"I'm here." His blond hair turned to silvered fox in the moon-light as he stepped out from behind the shadowy poplars. His dark cloak billowed.

The night air was chill. With a shiver I pulled my own cloak closer.

"I wasn't sure you'd come."

"Of course I came! What did you mean today when you said I was in danger? Tell me!"

Edmund trod closer.

"I'll do better than that. I'll show you."

With a swish, from beneath his cloak he pulled out a sword and held it up to the moonlight.

"Have you ever seen one of these?" he asked.

Two, edged-golden-hilted. I gasped.

"You have seen one, haven't you, Godiva?" The sword glinted like fire as Edmund brandished it. "I thought so. It's a *huscarl*'s sword."

My thoughts flashed back to the night Leofric had rescued me from Thurkill. The two men outside the hut had been saying *huscarl*. I'd asked him about it in Arden.

Edmund brought down the sword, resting its tip on the grass be-tween us.

"The *huscarls* are members of King Canute's secret army, the most powerful men in Engla-lond," he said. "They're an elite mercenary force."

"They're nothing but traitors!" I exclaimed. I'd said the same to Leofric.

Edmund's lips thinned. "The Saxons who have joined the *huscarls* have been given great privileges, lands, titles, money. They're forging a new Engla-lond in alliance with the Danes. You'd be surprised who has joined them. Has Leofric ever talked to you about the *huscarls*?"

Uneasily I nodded. In Arden, Leofric had averted my question about whether the *huscarls* were traitors. He'd talked about expediency.

"King Canute has proclaimed that warriors who bear a two-edged sword with gold inlaid hilt will be admitted into his chosen guard," Edmund said. "It's their secret symbol."

"A secret symbol," I echoed. "How did you get one?"

"I can't tell you." He stared into the night, his mouth a grim line. "Let's just say I've crossed paths with a *huscarl* myself. And you've seen one of these swords before, haven't you?"

Reluctantly I nodded.

"Where did you see it?"

"I found one in the stables."

"At your hall? In Coventry?"

The *briw* I'd had for supper rose up in my gullet. "Yes."

"It's as I thought." Edmund sheathed the sword. "There's something you have to know, Godiva. Leofric is a *huscarl*."

"No!" I stumbled as though Edmund had struck me with the flat of the two-edged blade. "Leofric's a Saxon through and through. He'd never join King Canute's secret force."

"How else would he have become an earl? Quite a feat to go from being a Saxon outlaw to one of the highest titles in the land. I didn't want to tell you but there are tales of Leofric abroad in Engla-lond."

"What kind of tales?"

"Leofric is responsible for the death of his brother."

"No!" My hands flew to my ears as if I could block out Edmund's words. "That's not possible! He loved his brother! Northman was killed by Thurkill the Tall."

"Thanks to Leofric. He betrayed Northman so he could rule Mercia himself."

Naked

Elfreda's revelations in the herb garden floated back to me. *Such terrible rumors in Mercia . . . dreadful things . . . too terrible even to speak of.*

Doubt crept into my limbs like a cold breath of fog. I pulled my cloak closer.

"How do you think Leofric got his lands restored to him, a Saxon? And there's something else."

Another chill of trepidation. Fingering my skin.

"When Leofric arrived in Coventry after your parents had been killed." Edmund leant in. "Convenient. Just in time, wasn't he?"

Again my hands clamped my ears. To shut him out. I refused to listen to another word.

"Leofric's mad for power, don't you understand?" Edmund grabbed me by the arms and shook me, as if trying to wake me from a dream. "You've got to listen. I'm your oldest friend, you have to believe me. He promised King Canute his brother's life and he delivered it. He's involved in all kinds of terrible plots. Against you, against the Saxons. He's a *huscarl*."

"No." The word was weaker this time.

"What do you really know of Leofric?" he demanded.

What did I know of him?

The image came. Leaning over me in the rose-gold dawn.

I knew his body.

But did I know his mind?

The husband who never spoke to me even in our most intimate moments. Only in Arden had we exchanged confidences and then he'd drawn away.

"Godiva." Edmund shook me again, as if I were a doll made of hemp rags. "I came to warn you. Your husband can't be trusted. He's plotting against you."

Wrenching free I flung myself away.

Edmund seized my shoulder, spun me around. "You have to listen! For your sake, Godiva, for the welfare of your people, for Coventry. Be wary of Leofric!"

The monastery bell tolled for compline.

In the scriptorium, all was quiet and peaceful. The room was small, with only a few wooden desks and chairs. On a carved stand stood an open Bible, the letters black, its illuminated colors bright. Red, yellow, blue, green, gold.

My mother's missal had been made here. I sat and watched the tonsured monk working at his desk by the window, to catch the light on the manuscript he copied. Slow and steady. A quill dipped in ink, a scratch across the page. Another dip, another scratch.

Dip.

Scratch.

Dip.

Scratch.

The night before in my cell I hadn't slept. Edmund had stolen away as the bell had tolled for prayers. Numbed by what he'd told me I'd stumbled back to bed in my monk's cell, his words a hell-torment in my mind.

What do you really know of Leofric?

Leofric is a huscarl.

He's plotting against you.

"No!"

I'd spoken the word aloud. The monk looked up, bemused, and then down at his work, serene.

Dip.

Scratch.

Dip.

Scratch.

Could what Edmund had said be true? I'd seen the *huscarl*'s sword in the stable at Coventry. I'd found it myself. And when I'd taken it to Leofric . . .

Their remembered voices swirled and quarreled.

Where did you get it? Leofric.

I came to warn you. Edmund.

Put. It. Back. Leofric.

Your husband can't be trusted. Edmund.

Dizzy, I clutched my hands to my temples. Surely Leofric was unable to feign his sorrow over his brother's death, the sorrow I'd witnessed in the Forest of Arden. The sorrow that had drawn me to his arms, my lips to his, our bodies pressed against the tree . . .

And my parents . . . Ambushed. The Danes. Lying in wait.

Be wary of Leofric!

Had I made love with a Saxon traitor? An assassin? A murderer? A *huscarl*?

Could my body have betrayed me?

I shivered as if in a crypt.

"Lady Godiva."

The scriptorium door had opened. So deep in my tortured thoughts I hadn't noticed.

Brother Aefic hurried inside.

"We've been hunting for you everywhere, my child. I have news for you." Puffing, he wiped his brow. "Lord Leofric has returned to the Middle Lands."

23

She sought her lord, and found him, where he strode
About the hall, among his dogs, alone . . .
——Tennyson [1842]: *Godiva*

"Home at last."

We'd left the monastery the day Brother Aefic had given word of Leofric's return. I'd not seen Edmund again. But before he vanished into the shadows he'd promised to keep me in his sights. Somehow. It made me relieved to know he still watched out for me.

I'd missed the reassurance of him beside me.

Acwell cantered up. "I'll ride on to the hall, my lady, if you will allow."

"Of course."

Making the gesture of his clenched fist across his chest, he bowed and galloped away.

He was going to Leofric.

Leofric.

My heart wanted to gallop, to race, to reach the hall as fast as I could to see him, to run into his arms.

Be wary of Leofric!

As we entered the main street I slowed Ebur to a walk.

"There's something on your mind, my lady." Aine said, pulling on her pony's reins.

"I'm fine, Aine."

"You can't hide anything from me. Your health began to improve at the monastery. Got some color back. Now you're as white as Ebur."

As usual I wanted to confide in Aine. But I'd promised Edmund to keep it between us.

All the way on the long ride from Evesham I'd considered possible courses of action. I still hadn't decided how to approach Leofric, whether to tell him what I knew.

Would it put me in less danger?

Or more?

Nervously I twitched my braid over my shoulder. When I saw him I'd know what to do. I had to trust my instincts. "Come, Ebur."

We entered the main street.

"God's greeting!" I called to the miller and his wife who were both standing outside the grain stores.

They looked away.

Puzzled, I shrugged. Perhaps they hadn't heard me.

Farther along the street, inside the forge, the blacksmith was hard at work.

"Good day!" I shouted, as I always did, over the wheezing bellows.

Again, there was no response. I frowned. Instead of replying to my greeting or even coming outside to check Ebur was well shod, as he often did, sparks flew as the smith continued to bang at the horseshoe he had on the anvil.

Aine's lips tightened as she pulled her pony nearer to me.

Outside the tavern where I had taken Godwin, two farmers stood.

I waved.

They turned their backs.

Aloud I gasped. Never had I been shunned in Coventry. Never, since I was a child, clinging to my mother's skirts, had I not been greeted with kindness and affection.

Ebur halted as if sensing my distress.

"Walk on."

On the other side of the street, Tomas the tanner came toward us. The wave of hatred that emanated from him almost knocked me from Ebur's saddle.

"So much for your promises!" he snarled as we passed.

"What can he mean?" I asked Aine, aghast.

With intense scrutiny she surveyed the street. "I don't know."

Aine appeared bewildered. Even she didn't understand what was happening.

Suddenly I wished Acwell hadn't ridden on. But the very idea I needed a Mercian guard in Coventry was appalling.

Inside my gloves my hands began to sweat. I yanked them off.

"All is not well here in Coventry," Aine murmured. "Stay close."

Stay close? In my beloved home? I gripped Ebur's reins. He picked up pace.

With relief I spotted Wilbert and Walburgha outside the hall gate. They nodded and then made to hurry past.

"Wilbert? Walburgha?"

Reluctance in every step, they stopped and slowly trudged back to me. Wilbert had his focus on the ground, as if the earth were about to sprout. Walburgha's cheeks were mottled.

"What has happened?" With a thump I slid off Ebur's back, stood holding the reins. "What's the matter?"

Wilbert's mumble was incoherent.

"Oh, Lady Godiva!" Walburgha burst out. "We cannot pay!"

"Pay what?"

"The taxes, my lady! We can't pay!"

"Didn't you understand me at our town meeting?" Why, there must have been a misunderstanding. That explained it. "There's no tax due. I understand your troubles."

"But, my lady, the new tax law!" Walburgha cried.

Mystified I stared from one to the other.

Wilbert glanced up. "Lord Leofric sent word from his sheriff, my lady. We're to pay the same taxes as they pay in Mercia."

"What?" Aghast I staggered against Ebur's side, clutched his mane.

Leofric had done this? The information wouldn't sink into my unwilling brain.

Coventry was my *morgengifu*. My sacred gift.

He'd promised me, consecrated the vow in the intimacy of our marriage bed.

Pledged with my body.

Against Ebur's flank I swayed.

The street seemed to blur around me. My pulse thudded in my ears.

In Ebur's dark iris I saw my distress reflected.

Against his rough coat I rested my cheek, matching my breathing to his until I could speak again.

"You say the tax has been raised."

"That's right, my lady." Walburgha put her hands on her ample hips.

"The taxes in Mercia are much higher than Coventry's have ever been." Wilbert scratched his chin. "But Lord Leofric says we must pay the same as them in the north, bad harvest or no."

"We'll starve!" Walburgha tugged at my sleeve. "We'll all starve if we have to pay it! We'll never survive the hungry month!"

"We don't know how we'll find the money." Wilbert pulled Walburgha away from me. Pride stiffened his spine. "We'll try, for we have always paid our taxes in Coventry."

"The people of Coventry have always been true in their tithes. My father never asked more than you could pay."

"For so long we've had such a fine lord and lady, Lord Radulf and Lady Morwen, may their good souls rest in peace," Walburgha wailed, crossing herself. "In some places, I've heard tell that families put their children into slavery to pay taxes. Children as young as seven, sent to work for taxes! To think that it would come to this in the Middle Lands!"

Children of the Middle Lands, slaves. My people, slaves.

And what harsh justice would have to be meted out by me if any thieving or wrongdoing occurred.

My sword. A limb. I shuddered.

Wilbert's shoulders drooped. "I suppose things change."

"Not in Coventry."

Hope shone from their faces as they gazed at me.

"When my father died, I promised that justice would always be done here in Coventry. Am I not your lady? That hasn't changed."

"But the new law, Lord Leofric . . ." Walburgha objected.

As if I crushed wheat, I ground my teeth. "This new law will not stand."

Wilbert appeared doubtful, his head on one side. "I hope you can talk to him, my lady."

"No one will go hungry in Coventry," I vowed, as fervent as if I stood in the church, the painted cross high above. *Suffer little children to come unto me.* My mother's favorite Bible verse. In the name of my mother, in the name of Our Lady, in the name of the great mother of all, no child would suffer under my rule.

"Tell all in Coventry and the shire." I mounted Ebur's back. "Don't be afraid. Trust me."

"We've been so worried!" Walburgha broke in.

"There's a lot of anger, my lady," Wilbert said reluctantly.

"I'm sure of it."

No one could be angrier than I.

In the hall Leofric sat behind the long table on the dais. He was alone except for two grey wolfhounds at his feet. As I approached, one gave a low growl.

No growling dog would stop me.

"How dare you!" I'd wondered what I would say when I saw Leofric. Now I knew.

The dog barked.

"Aeobald. Stay." Leofric's gaze roamed over me. Aine had commented on my pale face and the dark circles of fatigue smudged above my cheekbones. Once I'd wanted to appear beautiful for my husband, on the night we were wed, on the sweet *mead*-nights that followed. Now I cared not what he thought of my appearance.

"God's greeting." His tone was measured.

"God's greeting! How dare you greet me in the name of God! Did you think I wouldn't find out what you've done?"

Leofric stood up behind the table, his knuckles on the wood. I had forgotten how tall he was, how broad in his cloak. An oak tree, I'd thought him.

"You speak of the taxes."

"Coventry's tax, you have raised without my assent. How dare you demand money my people cannot pay!"

"I intended to speak to you on this when you returned. But who knew when that would be?"

His hypocrisy made me gasp. "You question my return when you've been gone to Mercia with no word? What reason can you have for raising the taxes?"

"There's good reason, if you'll listen to it." A wolfhound at his side, he came around the table. He'd grown a beard, thick and tawny brown. It hid the strong line of his jaw, the line I'd begun to know so well. I fought down my instant yearning to run my fingers through it, to find that line again. There was weariness in his visage, too, deep tiredness brooding like heavy clouds above his cheekbones.

"The taxes for Coventry and Mercia must be the same." His tone remained even, though his eyes held that dangerous spark, the heart of a flame. "Since our marriage, our lands are now joined. We can't ask one part of our lands to pay more than the other. This is the only just way."

"The taxes of Mercia are much more than my people have ever paid!" Tears smarted beneath my lids. I blinked them furiously away. "Your taxes are high because you're trying to rebuild. But why should my people suffer! The hungry month is coming. They'll be lucky to have enough to eat with the poor harvest we've had. And we have had to fight Thurkill."

The dog barked again. Leofric seized its rope collar.

His hands clenched the dog's rope before he released it. Tongue hung out, the dog stood by him, panting.

"You had to fight Thurkill?" Leofric blazed. "If Mercia hadn't come to your aid you'd be at Thurkill's mercy right now."

"You're no better. You're plundering my land!"

The flame in his eyes turned to ice. "Have a care. You go too far."

In the woods of Arden he'd told me what it had done to him, seeing his lands ravaged. He'd confided in me just once.

"Leofric, please." Swiftly I changed strategy. "Our lands are joined. Don't you remember the promise you made me? Coventry is my marriage gift." I'd paid for it with my body. "You swore you would let me rule Coventry as I saw fit."

"I swore that I would let you rule Coventry as long as it was for the greater good of the Saxons," he shot back.

"Are my people not Saxons? Would you see them starve?"

"There are Saxons starving in Mercia. Or do you think only of yourself? Your land? What you want? Many more Saxons suffer in Mercia than here in the Middle Lands. My lands are much greater than yours, Lady. I must make laws that benefit all."

"I am thinking of my people!"

"Not well enough." Beside him the dog bared his teeth. "The only way forward is for Saxon lands to be strongholds, to regain their might. Do you not see the danger all around you? Would you prefer your people paid taxes to invaders instead of their Saxon chief? That's what will happen if the Saxons don't become mighty again."

"Might! Power!" My body trembled with rage. "Is it all you think of? What about *good*? What about *justice*?"

He cursed. "I've experienced enough injustice to last a lifetime. I don't make these laws lightly. They're made to benefit all Saxons."

"Your laws don't benefit the Saxons of *Coventry*! Mercia and the Middle Lands are still separate lands, are they not? Or are we all called Mercia now?"

Flinging free my cloak I grabbed the hilt of my weapon. I'd traveled wearing my blade and breastplate to Evesham and back. I'd even had my blade with me in the monastery garden when I met Edmund at nightfall.

"You're in my lands, my lord."

Immediately Leofric's gaze flew to my sword.

Straight and high, I drew it, singing. The gem on the hilt flashed its amber warning.

"Do you forget, Earl of Mercia? The hawk-eye is mine. Coventry doesn't belong to you. Coventry belongs to me."

"Coventry is yours." He cursed again. "You want it one way, my lady, but not the other. You didn't complain when Mercia came to the aid of the Middle Lands in your battle. But now the Middle Lands will not aid Mercia."

"I didn't ask you to come to our aid!"

"You accepted my offer of help and my offer of marriage. You didn't turn me away." Undeterred by my drawn sword he came so close I could see the sweat on his brow, though no fire was lit in the hall.

He moved so near I smelt the leather of him that had scented my sheets. "Nor did you turn me away from your bed."

In my mind I slammed out the instant image of him, reaching for me in the gold morning light.

The sword shuddered in my fist.

Leofric seized it.

"You play at ruling your lands, Godiva." He hurled the sword away, sending it clattering into the embers of the empty fireplace at the center of the hall. Clouds of ash swirled upward. "Don't you realize you shouldn't have stopped the taxes? You're weakening the wealth of your lands. We have our own taxes to pay in turn, including the heregild to King Canute."

"So Canute's your master?" My question weighed with meaning.

"He's our king." Leofric didn't respond to my bait. "The taxes must be found, or in the end your people won't thank you for it."

I bit my lip. On my journey home I'd been wondering if my father would have done the same as I had done. Even Brother Aefic, the good monk, had implied my father wouldn't have been as lenient.

"They won't be alive to thank me," I replied uneasily.

"They can always find their taxes, if they try hard enough. That's how it's done in Mercia. It's the only way to make a land strong."

"Leofric." Another deep breath. I had to stay calm. "I've been riding across the Middle Lands. If you could see what I've seen, the suffering that could come, you'd never be able to do this."

"You've been riding across the Middle Lands?" His mouth twisted. "That's what you've been doing while I was away?"

"Weren't you informed? Hasn't Acwell just made his report?" I asked sarcastically. "Forgive me if I visited as many of the villages and farms as I could. And now I have been to see the monks at Evesham."

"You've been to see the monks," he repeated in a mocking tone.

"Yes. Brother Aefic helped my parents many times, and gave them wise counsel. I went to ask him what to do."

"That's who you sought out, is it?"

"Yes." Why did he sound as if he didn't believe me?

Sweat chilled my skin. Had Acwell, my hound-guard, seen me with Edmund in the monastery garden? Did they guess at my suspicions?

"Godiva." Leofric's voice turned soft as summer leaves in Arden. "Is there anything you want to ask me?"

I hesitated.

This was my chance.

This was the moment.

To tell him.

To trust him.

I opened my mouth.

Edmund's warning tolled.

Be wary of Leofric!

The moment sped past, fast as an eagle wing.

"No." I said. "There's nothing I want to ask you, except to change your mind about the taxes."

Leofric's lids hooded. "I won't change my mind. They must remain at the sum I have set."

"Leofric! You must repeal this law!"

"I will not." He wheeled around to face me. Even beneath his beard I could discern the set of his jaw.

We charge the care of Coventry to you, while we are gone.

My hands folded a prayer, my fingers beseeching.

"Please, Leofric, I beg you. Children will starve. Please."

"Our lands must be kept safe for our own children."

"You talk of our children now?" A bitter laugh escaped me. All the children in the Middle Lands were as my own. I was their lady, their loaf giver, their mother. Didn't he, a Saxon lord, understand my sacred task?

He dragged me into his arms. "Do you seek to deny me my rights as your husband?"

Hard, his lips came down on mine, his beard scratching against my skin. Wrenching his arms around me he pulled me to him, his body as hard as his mouth.

My warrior mind fought him.

My traitor body loved him.

That's what my lips told him, as my mouth opened against his,

Naked

while with his tongue he searched inside as if for the words I would not say. That's what my breasts told him, their arrow tips pointed through the linen of my tunic, aiming for the touch of his hands. That's what my hips told him, ground against him, seeking the spear of him inside me. That's what my legs told him, hardly able to stand.

With a cry, with all the will left in me, I pushed him away.

His breath was as ragged as my own.

"Leofric," I whispered. "Will you lift this tax?"

He didn't speak. I held my life-breath.

Slow. So slow.

"No."

Tears threatened to engulf me. I swallowed them back. "I understand now. I let the enemy inside my gates."

And my heart added a broken whisper.

"I've told you before." Leofric's hands were clenched at his sides. An emptiness in his expression, a gauntness in his cheeks, as if he were tormented. But I knew now the silent tomb of his heart. So cruel. So cold. "I don't seek to have us enemies, Godiva."

With a smash I threw wide the oak door. "Then you're too late."

24

I reached my bower before the tears came.

They coursed down my cheeks over my chin, down my neck. A torrent, a river, a stream, so fast I couldn't halt the flow. I tasted them: tears of rage, tears of lust, and tears of pain that came deep from my heart, as if an arrow had split it in two.

How could it have come to this? Sobs consumed me as I collapsed onto the bed, where we'd shared so much. The secret scent of him, long gone on the linen. Washed away.

I loved him. I loved Leofric of Mercia with every thread of my being. The feelings that had kindled with his touch, igniting my body, had flamed into my soul. They'd flickered into life when he'd ridden into Coventry, even before, when I'd first heard his name. But it was of no consequence when my feelings had begun.

My heart was his.

To think I'd started to dream that perhaps he might love me, too!

I cast a sour laugh to the stars painted on the roof of my bower, the stars I'd stared at on our wedding night when he'd taken my maidenhood. I'd been wrong, so wrong, to think he had any feelings for me.

It wasn't possible to be so cold, so cruel and have any love in his heart. The passion I'd imagined we'd shared. It had never touched his heart as he'd so powerfully taken mine.

Tears continued to flood down my cheeks. How deeply I'd been mistaken in the man I'd married! The warmth I thought I'd glimpsed in his eyes, the heat from his hands that burnt their trace on my naked skin . . . they were nothing. I'd been making shapes from shadows. His heart had remained ice cold. The tender man I'd glimpsed if only for a few moments wasn't the real Leofric of Mercia. The real Leofric was the heartless tyrant who refused to listen to my pleas.

The nights of passion we'd shared had all been part of the bargain.

I'd lost the wedding gamble.

He'd won.

He'd come for my lands. He'd plundered my body and seized my heart.

To accuse me of caring only for Coventry, when all he cared about was Mercia, his own lands, his own wealth in the north. My people, my lands could perish before he would let his people suffer.

If Edmund was right, power was all Leofric wanted. No matter how he got it.

Hands clenched, I staggered to my feet.

In the sewing basket beside me, skeins of thread had become tangled. Surely my snarled emotions weren't true love's design. Love, hate, fury, despair. Back and forth like the shuttle of a loom. Was this love's warp and weave or a tangled web that I would never escape with honor?

A woman must keep her pledge to a man.

I'd married Leofric; I'd made my vows to him. Solemn Saxon vows in the church of Coventry, before God and all my people.

My people. They would believe I'd betrayed them.

"My lady . . ."

Aine had come into the bower, her footsteps soundless on the rushes.

"My lady, you mustn't weep so. Too many tears. You'll make yourself ill."

"Aine! Oh, Aine! Lord Leofric has—"

She gathered me in her arms. "Hush. Calm yourself."

"I can't . . ."

"Come now. Perhaps it's not as bad as it seems."

"Not as bad as it seems! How could it be worse than this? My people will suffer at my hands!"

"Your people believe in you." She pushed the damp hair sticking to my cheeks. "They trust you. You'll find a way."

"There's no way out of this! I should never have married Lord Leofric! I—I hate him!"

Aine crooked a half smile. "Do you?"

"Yes! I hate him for what he's doing! And—and—Oh, Aine!"

As if I were a child again, Aine stroked my hair. "Come now. I know your heart."

"The way he looked at me . . . the way he touched me . . ."

"The body doesn't lie."

"The body *does* lie! Leofric lied to me; he hasn't kept his word! You don't know what's being said of him!"

"What's being said of Lord Leofric?" Aine almost shook me. "Tell me."

"No, Aine. I mustn't. I can't." Too dreadful to speak of. As Elfreda had said.

Traitor. Assassin. Murderer. *Huscarl.*

"My lady! Trust yourself alone to do what needs to be done. No one else."

"But what can I do?"

"That's the question. Think of your people now as you've always done and not of yourself."

"I can't do anything! I'm trapped!"

"A peace weaver is never trapped." Seizing my tapestry needle from the basket, she thrust it at me. "Trace the pattern. Follow the thread."

The needle pierced my palm.

"Don't give up, my lady," Aine urged. "Find a way."

The smoky hall was crowded but there was muted chatter at the trestle tables. The gleeman was silent. All eyes of the household upon me, I sat up on the dais.

My own eyes were sore as I blinked. Aine had bathed them with chamomile water, removing their redness at the rims. I wanted no telltale signs in front of Leofric. In a deep blue tunic, trimmed with gold, I had dressed myself with care, my hair brushed and braided. But no jewels.

Not feast. Famine.

Since the mealtime horn had blown, Leofric spoke not a word to me. I darted a swift sideways glance at him. There were no signs of hurt by my anger, in the devastating way I'd been hurt by his. He drank more ale than usual as he exchanged words with the Mercian warriors. Acwell sat to one side of him, avoiding my vision.

A board of bread lay in front of me. The piece I chewed I could barely swallow. It left the taint of ashes on my tongue. I dropped it onto my plate.

Lady.

Loaf giver.

At last Leofric addressed me. "You do not eat."

"How can I eat?" Tears threatened again; I forced them back with a tilt of my chin. The Earl of Mercia would never witness me crying. "When soon many will have no food?"

Beneath the beard a muscle worked in his jaw. "The folk of the Middle Lands will get through the hungry month."

"Many will not. Many will die."

With both hands I shoved my trencher of food away.

As he followed my movement, his gaze landed on my bare finger.

Tight as a carpenter's vice, he seized my culprit hand. "Where is your ring?"

"Lost," I faltered. It still upset me that it had vanished. "It was my own fault. The ring needed to be made smaller by the blacksmith."

I hadn't been able to bear to remove it.

"Where did you lose it?" His question as taut as his hold.

"I'm not sure." In the town, in the fields, in the garden. It could have been anywhere. I'd searched and searched.

He dropped my fingers as if they burnt him. Gripping his silver tankard, he drained it dry.

"Leofric."

The tankard still in his grasp, he jerked his head toward me. His hearth-empty eyes gutted my soul.

"Will you repeal the law?"

The tankard slammed down onto the table. Froth spilled onto the linen tablecloth. "You try my patience. Have done. Do you dare to challenge my leadership further?"

"A strong leader lets his people starve?"

His teeth clenched. "Give. This. Up."

His clipped accents reminded me of when I'd found the *huscarl* sword. I had blindly obeyed him then. This time I would not.

"Never. I'll do anything to protect my people."

In the curl of his beard he lifted his lip in a sneer. "Just what would you do?"

"What must I do?" My tone pitched high as a gleeman's song. "Must I lie down my head in your lap, as the peasants do, when they become a slave? I will do it. Must I starve? I will do it. Must I ride through the streets in only my shift like a penitent? I will do it. All these things, I will do, to save one child from starving in Coventry."

Our glances clanged. Sword. Shield.

"You would do such things?"

Under the table my fists tightened. I nodded.

His scorn knifed through me. "A penitent's ride? You wouldn't shame yourself in that way."

"You don't believe me? I'd make such a ride, if it means you repeal this law."

Speculation flared as he stared at me. I knew that look.

Then he clicked his fingers. The serving boy ran to his side. "More ale."

The serving boy poured, his hand shaking.

In a single gulp, Leofric drained it and slammed the tankard down on the table. "Again."

Once more the boy poured.

He drained that, too.

All chatter in the hall had turned as quiet as church prayers. From the tables below folk began to listen and watch openly.

Leofric threw down the tankard. It rolled off the table, onto the floor. "You say you would ride, but you would not."

"Are you saying I don't keep my word?" Each word I made a dart. "I can assure you, my lord, unlike some, I always keep my word."

His glare scorched, but mine was equal to it.

"You wouldn't shame yourself in that way. You would ride through the streets, of Coventry, in only your shift? Like an adulteress? Like a *whore*?"

As if he had struck me, I reeled.

This from the man to whom I had pledged my body.

For the sake of Coventry.

With my breath came courage deep from my lungs. "It would be no shame to me to save my people."

He leaned so close I could almost lick the ale from his tongue.

"And would you ride—naked?"

The hall hushed.

Naked.

The word slithered through my brain.

So silent now, my uneven breathing sounded as loud as a gleeman's song. To have every man and woman in the town stare upon me . . . instinctively I raised my hand across my breast.

As if a draught of ice air had found me, a shudder ran through.

I bowed. A prayer. "I would."

My head stayed low as I waited.

Waited.

Waited.

Then his reply came, soft as an assassin's footfall.

"Ride, Godiva."

Gasps flew to the roof of the hall.

As if on an axe-block I could barely lift my neck.

"You dare me to do this?" My words were broken shards when finally I could speak. "You dare this, of your wife?"

Leofric seized my ringless finger. "I see no wife."

He flung down my hand.

"You speak cruelly, my lord." My response a thread. Ragged, ripped, as if with his knife he'd stripped me. "But hunger is crueler than words and that I won't let my people face."

In my mind a voice came pure as a needle of light.

Fripwebba.

Peace weaver.

Clutching the edge of the table, I staggered to stand and face the stunned expressions at the trestles below. Their mouths were agape, lids wide.

"Hear me, good people of Coventry and the Middle Lands. This cruel law must be repealed. You have heard Lord Leofric's vow. Now hear mine." I choked. Too difficult to go on.

Fripwebba.

Peace weaver.

I raised my head.

"Tomorrow, on the midday bell, I, Godiva, will ride."

Ride, Godiva.

Never had a night seemed so long.

Had Leofric really spoken those cruel words? His anger still made me quake. I'd witnessed coldness in him before, but this was different. His blue eyes had been frozen lakes as he looked at me, as if he loathed me, as if he hated the sight of me.

He didn't love me. If I'd been uncertain after our argument about taxes, I was certain now. He wanted to see me humiliated. No, he didn't love me.

It was worse than that. I bit my lip. He must despise me to make such a dare. My sob groaned into agony.

That it had come to this! Now that I knew I loved him the ride would be harder still. For it was the end—the end of all my cherished dreams and hopes, the end of my secret desires, for the passionate love we might share. My ride would take me away from him, and there would be no turning back.

Ride, Godiva. I shuddered. Strange gawks upon me. Taking stock as if I were cattle in the market square. How could Leofric have held me in such low esteem as a wife to think that other views upon me didn't matter?

My youthful body, my smooth white skin, unmarked except for the battle-scar on my arm, he'd caressed. My legs muscular from many hard days' riding, he'd split apart. My pre-childbirth slender waist, he'd gripped as he thrust. My breasts, full as ripe russets, he'd suckled. Didn't he care that other men would see my body? What did that make of him as a husband?

I jerked upright. The stamp of heavy boots across the courtyard.

Not Aine. I'd told her I needed to be alone. Though she wanted to argue, she'd respected my wishes.

The footsteps stopped. I sensed rather than heard someone standing by the door.

"Leofric. Leofric." My soul-call sounded.

No knock at the door, no hand pushing it open.

"Leofric. Leofric."

Not words.

It seemed hours as I held my body still, like a deer in the sights of a hunter.

Naked

Then came the sound of footsteps again as he walked away.

I fell against my rag-filled pillows. My mouth dry, my heart a husk.

No reprieve.

Tomorrow, I would ride.

Naked.

25

Then she rode forth, clothed on with chastity:
——Tennyson [1842]: *Godiva*

"Your hair!" Aine shouted behind me. "Wait, my lady! Your hair!"

With a start, I came out of my reverie. It had all flashed before me: what had led me to this fateful hour, to this fateful ride.

"My lady! Your hair!"

For a moment, I didn't understand. Then I realized what Aine meant me to do.

I released my braid.

My hair fell in waves of golden brown over my body, covering me in a living cloak. Tendrils caressed my shoulders, curled over my breasts, vined my waist, curtaining my hips. Only my legs were left white against Ebur's coat.

"Forward, Ebur."

Toward the gates. I clutched his mane.

The wind lashed my skin. Over my shoulder I threw a desperate peek toward Aine. She stood alone in the courtyard, a statue, my garments clutched in her hands, the golden belt glinting.

The church bell continued to toll the hour, each peal a shock of doom. No other sound, just the wailing wind and the four-steady clatter of hooves.

Ebur's hair rubbed the tender skin inside my thighs. As I waited for the last peal of the bell, I forced myself to sit proud, shoulders firm, neck straight. I was a warrior. A battle-maid.

Courage is known after the battle is won, Leofric had told me, before we faced Thurkill the Tall.

My courage wouldn't fail me now.

Yet all at once I was seized by an overwhelming urge to give in. To go backward, not forward. To avoid the prying squints, the leers burning on my naked flesh. The townsfolk, many of them I'd known since I was a child. Walburgha, Wilbert, Tomas the tanner. At the last name I shuddered. How could I show myself naked in front of them? What of my rank? I was the daughter of a Saxon thane.

My parents. They would have wanted me to do my duty. But would they have wanted me to make this ride? Of that, I was uncertain.

Perhaps I wasn't bringing honor to Coventry, but shame.

Shame. I licked it on my lips, tasted its vinegar on my tongue. Only moments before I'd told Aine I would feel no shame bringing justice. Now my head drooped like a harebell on a stem.

I'd been wrong. So wrong.

Another chime.

Shame billowed over me now, as the wind tugged at my hair, the gossamer shield that hung so precariously over my body. Only golden-brown strands covered the private parts of me, floating over my breasts, taut as sails against the wind, reaching its tendrils between my legs, the most secret place of all, that had only ever known Lord Leofric's touch.

My husband.

The wind watered my eyes, as my throat constricted with the sharpness of a dagger scrape. My husband had brought me to this. He hadn't come to my bower in the shadow of night, or in the morning clear, to stop me from making this terrible ride. He didn't regret his dare. And yet I felt no anger toward him. Not now, in daylight. The blaze of fury that had been flint-fire in my loins, the cruel words we'd exchanged—all that anger, all that rage, had vanished. All that remained was the love I had for him, the love, the powerful love that I knew now would never depart.

Love for Leofric. Love for my parents. Love for my people.

The last chime of the bell.

She rides!

A cry. I heard it from beyond the wall. A summons to line the streets, to call, to laugh, to jeer.

Ebur. So slow as I approached the gates.

From inside the courtyard I peered ahead. The gates, the arches, the street. How long it stretched, how straight. How narrow the way.

I knew Coventry blindfolded. I'd walked it so with Edmund. He'd promised to stay near, to watch out for me. But he must be far away. My eyes must stay open wide.

More tightly now I gripped Ebur's reins. Sensing my tension, he picked up the pace.

Another glance over my shoulder. No one in the courtyard now, nor in the stable yard. Aine had disappeared. I was alone.

But not for long.

Fear tossed my stomach.

As soon as I passed through the gates, it would begin.

The people would come to watch me. Would they throw stones, as if I were indeed a fallen woman, making a penitent's ride for her sins? Penitents, at least, had a linen shift to cover them, while I had only my hair.

In the pale yellow sunlight I shivered. The chill in my body became nothing compared to the fear ice-spearing in my heart.

Courage, Godiva. Some stronger part of me murmured to the self whimpering within. *Courage. You have faced battle against Thurkill the Tall. You can face this.*

No hiding.

No shame.

A gust of wind sent my hair haloing as I sent a prayer soaring into the sky.

Not of beseeching. Not of sorrow.

But of thanksgiving.

For Coventry. For the Middle Lands. For the land of my people, the land of my *cyn*. For the land I loved.

"Forward, Ebur."

Under the arches as the bell stopped. My breath ballooned within my lungs. Ebur clopped on, slowing to a walk. Bracing myself, I squared my shoulders.

My eyes slammed closed.

I forced them open.

Through the arches.

An empty street.

Eerie silence.

No jeers. No laughs. No onlookers.

It was market day. Why was the street empty?

And then I understood.

My people hadn't betrayed me.

The cry I'd heard.

She rides!

Not a call to look, but a call to hide. To run into shops and houses. To slam their doors. To pull their curtains and shutters eyelid-tight.

One by one, house by house, the people of Coventry had turned their gaze away.

Tears rained down my face, onto my neck, down my breasts. A mixture of relief, love, and gratitude.

I'd not failed my people.

They'd not failed me.

Not just one or two had bowed their heads in mercy, averted their gaze, glanced away out of respect. Each and every one had refused to observe my bared body.

Hawk high, I lifted my head. No shame now. Only pride in being the lady of such a people. My Saxon people, who loved justice, had observed a greater law. Not a law handed down from above but a law risen up from their hearts.

Another gust of wind lifted the veil of my hair. This time no fear pricked my skin, no trepidation trickled down my spine. I needed no shield from prying eyes in the streets of Coventry, for there were no prying eyes to see.

In a surge of elation I lifted my arms into wings, my hair a banner unfurled. Sensing my joy, Ebur raised his great body up on two hind legs, his white mane flying like feathers in the sky.

We dropped back down to earth. Beneath me Ebur continued his steady journey. Still there were no jeers, no laughter, no mocking calls. Not a child played, not a dog barked. Only the sound of the wind, and Ebur's hooves as one by one I passed.

Past the stopped water mill.

Past the silent tavern.

Next to the tavern was the house where Tomas the tanner lived. Just the thought of his feaberry eyes, the licking of lips—as I passed by I shuddered, as if cold water had been thrown on my naked limbs. His gawk upon my flesh would have been terrible to bear. But no, he too was inside his home. I would be spared his leer.

A movement caught my attention. A chink of light from behind the shutter.

A phantom crawl over my skin.

An imagining? I rode on.

Past more houses.

Into the square. No cattle. No sheep. No wrangling between shopkeepers and farmers to get the best price.

Past the carpenter's shop. Closed.

On to the forge. No fire. No bellows wheezing.

Past Wilbert and Walburgha's thatched house. Smoke from the central chimney but the door shut tight.

The end of the road in sight. With relief my shoulders dropped. The journey home to the hall would be so different from when I'd set out, when I'd not known what the good people of Coventry would do for me. I wanted to call out and thank them. They'd understood. They did not blame me anymore for the taxes being raised upon them. The way they'd shunned me when I had traveled from the monastery . . . how hostile and angry the townsfolk had been then.

But to do this—they loved me, just as I loved them. How grateful my parents would have been to the people of Coventry. And I would never be able to repay them for their kindness.

The wind blew harder, whirling my tresses above my head. How shamed I would have been if all eyes were upon me! Now I let the wind blow.

Honor had clothed me.

The love of my people was my garment.

Light as gossamer, invisible as air. Unseen.

Fripwebba, the wind whispered.

Peace weaver.

At the end of the street I stopped in front of the church and revolved.

The sign of the cross.

My ride hadn't cost my modesty, or my pride. Yet these were nothing compared to what I'd lost forever.

Dejection took hold. Slumped my shoulders, bowed my head.

Leofric. My husband.

I'd saved my people and lost the man I loved.

26

The little wide-mouth'd heads upon the spout
Had cunning eyes to see . . .
———Tennyson [1842]: *Godiva*

Shaking, I huddled by the fire in my bower.

My bare feet had found their way home.

Wrapped in a horse blanket, I'd seen no one as I went to my bower. The stables and the courtyard had been as empty as the town as I'd put Ebur in his stall. The servants, too, it seemed, knew of the townsfolk's pact.

I'd never felt so alone. Not since my parents had died. Not when Edmund had left. Now, there was emptiness within me, deep as a water well, numbness in my fingers and feet as though I had been in a cold place for a long time.

Around my bare body I pulled the blanket scratch tight. Still trembling, a leaf in a gusty wind.

The stable smell. A comfort.

I'd done what Leofric had dared me to do. No joy, no sense of triumph. No vindication mine. Not now.

Leofric. A strange dullness in my brain. I might never see him again. Never feel his hands discovering me or explore those river-deep eyes.

Our marriage would be over now.

He would return to Mercia. To Elfreda, perhaps.

Nothing left. I didn't even have the ruby ring he'd given me as my *morgengifu.* In this bower he'd vanquished. No longer even a white mark on my finger where it had been, though I rubbed the place again and again. My anxious fingers went there now, round and round, as though by some witchery my troth brand would re-appear.

Soon it would be as though my marriage had never happened.

My ride would be forgotten.

But I would never forget Leofric.

From the trunk I pulled the garland Aine had placed on my head on my wedding morn, unwrapped it from a piece of embroidery. The flowers and leaves were curled and dry.

Petals of day's eyes. The flower that opened to welcome the morn. *For new beginnings.* Wheat. *For fertility.* Clover. *For wealth.*

One berry.

For true love.

Crowned, I'd gone to meet him. Vows in the church of God. Vows in the sacredness of the bower. Husband. Wife. He'd disgraced me and I'd publicly defied him. No chance of happiness for us now. Too many suspicions, too many betrayals, too many doubts. The marriage I'd hoped for, the marriage I'd dreamed of, without knowing I dreamed at all, would never be. No equal with whom to govern. No ally to stand beside. No children to inherit. No lover in the night. Our marriage weave had been shredded, torn apart by our own hands. By no needlecraft could it ever be mended.

I'd gone too far. So had he.

Clambering to my feet, with care I laid the garland on the table by the window. On the wooden top beside it lay my knife, the one I usually carried, tucked in my belt. Aine hadn't given it to me before we set out. There'd been no need.

From its leather sheath I drew it and ran my finger over the amber hawk-eye on the handle. Along the edge.

Sharp.

I stared into the polished silver above the table. My pale reflection stared at me.

I'd changed. I saw it in the lines of my face. Perhaps no one else would discern it. Part of me had died on my ride through Coventry.

Over. My marriage was over. Never would I desire another man's eyes or hands on me. Never would I desire to touch another man. No arms would hold me as I cried out in my sleep, no lips seek mine in the dawn. No man would ever take Leofric's place in my bed, in my bower. My maidenhood had been my gift to him alone.

A widow, a nun. A convent, a tower.

These were places to mourn, to hide, for those as heartbroken as I. But I would have to carry on and rule Coventry.

Alone.

The blanket fell from my shoulders as I raised the knife.

In my trembling fingers I seized a lock of hair.

My crowning glory. My strength. My shield.

My hair fell like a shock of cut wheat as I began to hack with the blade.

The bower door crashed open.

Leofric wrenched the knife from my hand and stabbed it into the table.

Seizing the blanket from where it lay crumpled on the floor, he wrapped it around my naked body.

As if in a dream, I watched as in a swift movement he knelt. Reached for my hands, encased them in his.

"Godiva, forgive me."

My heart beat so fast I thought it would escape from my chest like a lark aimed for the sky. I struggled for breath, for words.

"You're asking for my forgiveness, my lord?"

"That I've brought you to this. I should never have made such a dare." Face agonized, he hauled to his feet. Pacing over to the window, his spine stiffened as he appeared to struggle to control his emotions.

Finally he swung around. A muscle worked in his cheek. "My only hope is that you can find it in your heart to listen to me. My anger . . . my pride . . . my stubbornness drove me to it. And—I didn't believe you would do it."

"I had to ride. I had no choice."

"I've never known a woman such as you." His tone became hoarse. "Your courage, your faith—I didn't think it possible. Aethelflaed, Wealtheow—your name will surely be greater than theirs."

Fripwebba.

Peace weaver.

I was one of them, now.

The blanket swept across the rushes as I went and stood beside him.

"I'm not so brave." I ventured a smile. "You once told me courage is only known after the battle is done, do you remember? I wasn't sure my courage would hold. Last night I spoke in anger but it had cooled by morning. On my ride I didn't even have it to keep me warm."

"How can you smile?" His glance swept from my hair to my bare feet. "Is it possible you've found it in your heart not to hate me?"

Didn't he realize?

"Last night I didn't sleep," he said. "I came and stood by your bower door."

I'd known.

"At dawn this morning, I determined to make sure I was there to watch over you as you rode."

My heart leapt. "You saw what happened."

"It's something I'll never forget. How your people love you! I watched as they went into their houses, and locked their doors. There's never been a lady loved as you are by her people, Godiva. I doubt there ever will be again. Can you forgive me?"

"For your terrible dare?"

"No." Leofric shook his head. "Because I've just used you as bait."

"Bait." The word thudded onto the rush-strewn floor between us.

"There's been an assassination plot against you, Godiva."

"What kind of plot?" My stomach roiled. Edmund had warned me of that, too, at the monastery.

"Let me start at the beginning." Leofric began to pace the room, the rushes crushing beneath his boots. "You know I met your father, Lord Radulf, at the Witan."

"Yes. I remember." So long ago. My father had mentioned Leofric then. Admired how he'd won his lands in Mercia.

"While we were at the Council your father took me into his confidence."

My father hadn't confided in me. For a moment, I felt hurt. But he must have had his reasons.

"What did he tell you?" I asked.

"For some time Lord Radulf had been afraid there was a traitor in Coventry."

"A traitor?" Edmund had believed that, too. "Who?"

"I'll come to that." He exhaled heavily. "Your father told me of his suspicions. He wasn't entirely sure of the traitor's identity, he had a few clues, but he'd become convinced there was someone amongst his people in league with the Danes. That's why I came to Coventry. Lord Radulf had asked for my help."

I recalled my puzzlement at Leofric's words when he first rode up on his great black horse. *Then I'm too late*, he'd muttered, as if to himself. It made sense now.

"When I discovered your father had been killed by the Danes, and your mother, too, I was determined to stay with you in the Middle Lands. I'd promised your father I would help him, and I'd failed. I vowed as a Saxon not to forsake his daughter."

"So that's why you stayed in Coventry." My heart lurched. "I thought you desired my lands."

"I know that's what you thought. But there was more to it than that. I was determined to discover the Saxon traitor who had betrayed your father and your mother, too. With my bodyguard, we began to gather intelligence. My suspicions were growing, yet we could find no solid proof of the traitor's identity. To accuse him, I needed more."

Those private conversations with Acwell. Conversations that always ended when I came near.

"Then news came from the north. That's why my younger brother Godwin traveled from Mercia. It wasn't safe to send a messenger, too much was at stake. Godwin told me that one of Thurkill's men had been captured by Saxon forces. He'd been part of the ambush that killed your parents. The Danish warrior had started to talk, so I went to Mercia to question him further. I had to be sure my suspicions were correct."

Anxiously I pleated the blanket. "Were your suspicions founded?"

"So it seemed. Eventually I got the information I needed. But the word of a paid Danish warrior wasn't sufficient. I still needed more proof. So I came back to Coventry as fast as I could. I didn't like to leave you alone."

"You were so angry with me."

"Angry? I was furious you'd left the safety of Coventry. By the time I returned from Mercia, I realized how danger had increased around you. I was running out of time to stop the traitor. When you started speaking of the penitent's ride, I seized the opportunity. And I knew the traitor would seize it, too."

Beneath the blanket a sweat of terror coated my naked skin. "That's what you meant by saying I was bait."

Curtly he nodded. "When you vowed to ride in front of all the townspeople, I knew it was my chance to bring the traitor into the open, to draw him out. How could he resist? You were alone. Undefended. *Naked*."

My body shook. I'd thought my honor in peril, not my life.

"It was a gamble." His lips whitened. "But we had to flush him out."

"You were in the town?"

"Inside a house on the main street."

"In the home of one of my people." I clutched my stomach, sickened. One of my own people had been plotting against me. Surely it wasn't possible. Then it came to me, in a flash of knowledge.

The house next to the tavern. A movement had caught my attention, a chink of light from behind a shutter. I had thought I imagined it. "It was Tomas the tanner's house, wasn't it?"

Leofric's jaw set. "Yes."

"Tomas is the traitor?" I'd never trusted him, always lurking, with his feaberry eyes always stuck on me, licking his lips.

He didn't reply.

"Tell me!"

Leofric came and stood in front of me. An odd expression in his river-deep eyes. Pity? Compassion? A message I refused to read.

Hell-dread came over me, icy cold, from where I could not say. "Tell me."

"Tomas the tanner wasn't alone." He hesitated. I'd never seen Leofric hesitate.

"*Tell me.*"

"Someone else was with him."

A numb circle to form the word. "Who?"

"I'm sorry, Godiva."

Now my voice was an owl screech. "*Who?*"

Leofric lifted his head. In his eyes I read the name, before he spoke.

"Edmund."

He caught me in time, the heat of his fingers searing through the woolen blanket to my bare skin as I collapsed onto the bench by the fire.

"Edmund betrayed me." A statement or a question? Not Edmund, my friend, my playmate. Not the orphaned boy my parents had fostered and made part of our family.

Not *Edmund.*

From childhood I'd loved him.

From childhood I'd believed he loved me.

A gory icicle found my heart.

"Godiva." Leofric moved in front of me. "For you, I didn't want it to be so. But it's the truth, I swear."

I tried to focus. "Edmund was in Tomas the tanner's house?"

"They were in league together and have been for some time. Do you remember how Thurkill the Tall knew exactly where to find us on the field for the battle of Coventry? It wasn't by chance."

"And Thurkill's ambush of my parents." *Moder. Fader.* "Not . . ."

"Yes. That, too."

Blood scald. Edmund, rushing into the hall, grey-faced, disheveled. *"Your parents have been killed . . ."*

"He lied to me."

"He lied to everyone."

Edmund.

"You were in his sights. He was in Tomas the tanner's house, at the window with his arrow trained on you. I got there just in time."

The best shot in the Middle Lands.

He made his own arrows.

Elm wood. Iron-tipped.

"Tomas the tanner was lying on the floor out cold. He'd outlived his usefulness it seems."

"Tomas is dead?"

"No. He was bleeding badly from his head but he's almost regained consciousness. He can be questioned later."

Corpse cold beneath the blanket. "And Edmund?"

Leofric paused. An expression too quick to make out flared across his face. "He's under guard here at the hall. In one of the grain storerooms."

The blanket clutched around my numb body I lurched to my feet. "I must see Edmund."

27

The barking cur . . .
——Tennyson [1842]: *Godiva*

Acwell stood outside the storeroom next to the kitchen. From the plant yard beyond floated the scent of lavender and rosemary, warming in the afternoon sun. It seemed incongruous I'd ever played there with Edmund, lain on the grass, made chains of day's eyes. Now he was under guard.

An unyielding rock, Acwell crossed his arms and moved his bulk in front of me.

"I can't let you in, my lady."

"Lord Leofric has given permission."

In the bower I'd told Leofric I needed to be alone with Edmund. He'd fallen silent, arms folded, as if holding himself in check. He'd hesitated, then bowed low. Left me to slip on the nearest garment.

"As you will, my lady." Acwell opened the door. It creaked open.

"Thank you," I said faintly. My legs were slow to move.

Naked

Inside the empty storeroom I could smell the wheat and barley that had been kept there during the winter. But there was no grain now, just the bare dirt floor, a few broken husks. No window but through the ajar door enough light to see. In the corner, a tall man in a grey tunic had his back to me.

He swung around. I bit down my gasp.

This was Edmund. This skeletal-faced stranger, his grey eyes empty in their sockets as they raked over me with cold detachment. His arm was in a sling, his face bruised. Leofric hadn't told me he'd been injured.

"You're hurt. What happened?" My words were instinctive. So were my movements, my rush across the room to tend my friend's wound.

With a snarl he drew back. "You can thank your husband for that. Ask him what happened. He broke my arm along with my bow."

Edmund's arrow.

Trained on me.

To the safety of the doorway I edged away.

"Why, Edmund?" A shred, a shard, a splinter. "Why did you do it? Why did you betray me?"

A mockery of a laugh cracked across his tight face.

His smile had been like lightning.

"Why do you think, Godiva?" The venom in his voice became toxic in my veins. He spoke my name in a putrid gush as if he loathed it. "For money. For power. For land. How do you think it was for me always watching you? So spoilt and petted. The precious heiress of the Middle Lands. The fine Lady of Coventry."

In horror I choked. Words splintered on my tongue.

This was Edmund. This was my friend.

Blindfolded, I'd been. Our hands gripped tight.

I reached for my braid but my hair was still hanging loose. From my clammy forehead I pushed the chopped strands away. "Have you always hated me?"

For an instant I didn't see the mercenary he'd become. For an instant I saw the orphan I'd befriended so long ago.

Then the boy was gone.

"My estate in the Angle Lands was greater by far than yours." More black bile. Spilled. "My family far richer, more powerful. Yet all I heard, day in, day out. The Middle Lands. Coventry, Coventry, Coventry."

How had I not seen this? His affection, feigned. His kisses a violence of hatred. Not desire. "And did you hate my parents, too?"

A savage shrug. "There are always casualties in any war."

"My family wasn't at war with you." Lips funeral numb. "My parents took you in, fostered you, treated you as a son and you betrayed them. We fed you, clothed you, housed you when you had nowhere else to go."

"And never let me forget it." He slammed the words back at me so hard I ricocheted. "For years I was treated as a slave, not a son. Like a kicked dog. Thrown a few scraps."

"That's not how you were treated! My parents loved you." Sweat dripped down my spine. Drops thick as blood. "And you killed them."

He snorted. "I led them to where Thurkill waited. That's all."

Talons scraped across my skin.

Moder.

Fader.

"You led them to their death."

"*Nidstang.*" Edmund swore.

The foul Danish curse.

More hideous knowledge cracked through my brain.

"You speak Danish." Something else I hadn't known.

"I learnt it when I was young."

Hideous understanding dawned. So when Thurkill had me slaughter-bound and gagged, ready to . . .

"It was you I heard talking to Thurkill the Tall. Outside the hut."

Another chilling shrug. "We needed a hostage."

As if Thurkill's dead fingers were on me I clutched my tunic at the breast.

"I was following my orders." Edmund's tone became cutting. Sliced. "The Middle Lands for the Danes. I'd made a vow to King Canute."

Edmund. The *huscarl*.

My heart sank. "What about your vows as a Saxon, Edmund? To the Middle Lands? My father made you a *cniht*, a knight."

"*Cniht* to the Middle Lands. Did you really think that was enough for me? How you expected me to bow and scrape. I'm a nobleman, born to rule, not serve. I'd have made a better lord of the Middle Lands than your father. If you'd agreed to marry me none of this would have been necessary."

A hate-knife. Twisted in my soul. Had I cost my parents their lives? Would they still be alive if I'd said yes to Edmund? "The Middle Lands were my inheritance. Even if we'd married I'd have governed these lands. Not you."

Another rictus laugh. "Did you think I'd let a *woman* rule over me? You'd have been in your place soon enough. Beneath me. Yes." His hiss snaked across the floor. "I would have taught you who was lord. Thurkill and I, together we planned it. I let him have you first as part of our bargain. But then you'd have been all mine."

My legs threatened to shatter. I staggered against the door frame.

"You were always meant to be mine. But you took your time

deciding whether to marry me, didn't you? And your father was beginning to get suspicious. He might have stopped you marrying me even if you'd finally said yes. I guessed Lord Radulf wasn't coming back from the Witan to give his blessing to our marriage and I was growing tired of courting you. Did you think a few longing sighs or a kiss kept me satisfied? There's been many a girl in my bed whose lips weren't so tight." His gaze licked my body. "But I'd have soon loosened those lips of yours."

I stared, aghast.

Malice gleamed silver. "How I played with your vanity, like a cat's paw to a mouse. Oh, the speeches you lapped up. How I admired you. You wanted to be admired, didn't you? Women are all the same. Like your friend Beolinda."

He spat on the floor.

"I had her, you know. She gave you away soon enough with my tongue inside her."

Another axe-blow. Blunt. Out of nowhere.

One more betrayal I hadn't been prepared for.

Pretty, frivolous, Beolinda. Fun. Flirty. Foolish.

She'd slept in my bower. Eaten at our table. I'd supped at her table, slept in her bower, too. While she'd handed over information to Edmund.

"So that's how you found out I was at the monastery."

"You've never been able to see what's going on around you. Always so idealistic, thinking everyone adored you, while she's been helping me all along. She put the *huscarl* sword in the stables, in Ebur's stall."

Letting go of the door frame, I almost doubled over as pain gutted me. Beolinda, who'd come to Coventry to witness my wedding to Leofric. She'd been my attendant, stood at my side, her arms full of flowers.

"At their hall. That is where you've been hiding all along. With Beolinda."

Where has Edmund gone? Her lashes fluttering wide.

"I've had other missions."

My hand blade fisted. "The *huscarl* sword was yours."

"Of course it was mine. I thought you'd work it out, but you didn't." He smiled thinly. "How well my sword served its double-edged purpose. It laid the way for your suspicions and a warning for Leofric. He knew what it meant."

Danger. Leofric had known it for a death threat aimed at me.

"So when I put the sword in the stables again—"

"Beolinda retrieved it and gave it back to me."

"You could have killed me that night at the monastery. Why didn't you?"

"I couldn't be sure your nurse wasn't hidden behind a blackberry bush. She's always out at night, the old witch. She'd have raised the alarm. Anyway, I hadn't decided then if I'd marry you once I'd gotten Leofric out of the way. It was easier to let the Middle Lands come to me through you. They're annoyingly loyal to you, your people."

"I trusted you, Edmund." Whispered words. Fragments.

"More fool you and your Saxon pride," he sneered. "I was glad I hadn't killed you at the monastery. The real opportunity came later on. How you played into my hands!"

"The ride." I shivered as though once more on Ebur's saddle, alone, a perfect mark for assassination. If anyone's arrow would have found its target, it would have been Edmund's.

That evil laugh again. "There'd have been civil war between the Middle Lands and Mercia once word got out you'd been killed on the ride your husband had so ungallantly sent you on. The beautiful and saintly Lady Godiva, struck down naked on her horse!"

War between the Middle Lands and Mercia. Two Saxon strong-holds torn apart instead of united. A gift for the Danes to divide and conquer.

My people. Slaughtered. Enslaved. A reign of terror.

"So you'd have blamed Leofric."

"Suspicion of him would have been enough. I'd have been able to get the Middle Lands under my control and probably Mercia, too. No one would have listened to a man who offered up his brother for power and then his wife."

Those rumors planted as rotten seeds in my brain. Why had I believed them? "Leofric loved his brother Northman. He never betrayed him to the Danes. That's a disgusting lie!"

Again he shrugged. "You'll never know."

"I do know." I said fiercely. "I know Leofric."

"Leofric of Mercia." Another spit. "It was so obvious you'd fallen for him. Ready to spread your legs for the great Saxon earl. He's a fool just as you. Canute asked Leofric to join the *huscarls*. He refused."

"You're the fool, Edmund." I let his coarse insults wash over me. "The *huscarls* are nothing but paid assassins."

His face darkened.

"What did Canute promise you? If you delivered the Middle Lands to the Danes?"

"My own lands restored in the east." His mouth turned child-ish, petulant. "They're under Danish control. I deserve to have what's mine."

"And you believed him? Canute was just having you do his dirty work."

"You don't know anything about Canute. He saw something in me, something your father never saw."

"Canute saw a traitor," I hissed.

"He saw a Saxon who would do what needed to be done. The Danes are here to stay. Fighting them is futile. It's all right for you to be so idealistic, so conceited about the Saxon way with your land and money behind you."

"Surely you know me better than that. I'd be true to the Saxon way if I had to live in the Forest of Arden for the rest of my days. I'd never surrender to the Danes."

"So haughty," he jeered. "*The Saxon way.*"

Edmund sprang.

Strangled my neck with my hair.

I screamed. "Leofric!"

He crashed into the storeroom, hauled Edmund off.

"Get her out of here!"

Leofric shouted at Acwell who'd followed hard behind. "Get her out!"

Aine was waiting for me in my bower, her dark eyes black as a raven's wing. Acwell had delivered me, pausing only while I retched in the latrine.

By the fire I shook and shivered, my hands wringing my neck. Still nauseated.

The hatred in Edmund's grey eyes.

So ruthless. Treacherous.

A Grendel. A demon-monster such as Beowulf had to fight.

I couldn't halt my twisting fingers.

Aine prised them off and thrust me a pottery cup full of a green liquid with leaves floating in it.

It smelt of mint but there were other herbs in it—I knew not what. It took the vile taste away.

"Your parents were betrayed by Edmund," Aine said.

Aine had always known everything. I could only nod.

Lifting her arms she muttered some words, a swirl, a summons, a curse that cracked around my head and filled the room with the stench of smolder.

"Aine!" The empty cup fell to the floor broken in pottery pieces. "What have you done?"

"What needed to be done," she muttered fiercely. "For your mother. For you."

"You've always suspected Edmund."

"From the moment he came here," Aine nodded. "So sly, he was, behind that smile. You were in danger, even as a child. Devious. Full of pride, envy, and hate. And you never saw it."

"I trusted him."

"You trusted the wrong man."

In shame I hung my head.

Into my hands she pressed a wooden trencher. A hunk of bread, some cold mutton. "Eat."

Hard to swallow. But I obeyed.

Slowly, strength crept into my limbs.

Aine brought a basin, washed my hands and face as if I were a child. A balm dabbed on the bruises on my neck. Witch-hazel and comfrey. All-heal. The mother of herbs.

Soothing.

When she'd finished she began to brush my hair.

"Lord Leofric is worth a hundred of Edmund." Her strokes were hard.

I winced. "I know that now."

"Some bindweed is poison. I tried to warn you."

"I know, Aine. I know."

With her mouth pursed she braided the ragged, short pieces into a kind of coronet. The remainder hung in waves. Free.

A memory came to me as her skillful fingers worked. "When you had a premonition, Aine. The night before my parents went away to the Witan. You said you saw a face. Was it Edmund's face you saw?"

"Not Edmund. I saw Lord Leofric."

Aine laid down the brush. "You must tell your husband of your feelings."

"I don't know if I can." What right did I have, now?

"You must." She tossed a log into the fire. "He comes."

Footsteps sounded outside the door.

A knock pounded.

So did my heart. "Come in."

Leofric opened the door.

Aine bowed and slipped away.

The bower filled with his presence as it always did when he entered. But he moved differently this time. The hard shell had gone as if tough armor had been removed.

His gaze searched my neck as if he touched it. Yet his fists stayed by his sides. "Are you all right?"

"Yes." Aine's treatment had been magic. There were barely any marks. On the outside at least.

Another searing search of my skin. Still no contact. Then a nod. "So now you've seen Edmund," he said.

As if for the first time.

"You were outside the storeroom door."

I'd known he was there.

"I thought you might need me. Even if you didn't want me." That stillness in him again. "It wasn't safe to leave you alone with him. But I understood you and Edmund had things to say to each other."

Such terrible things.

"I needed to hear him with my own ears, see him with my own eyes to believe it. I've been wrong about so much," I choked. "Edmund, Beolinda, Tomas the tanner. I didn't know I had such enemies."

"Those who have no enemies are not to be praised. Those who have no enemies have never stood up for what's right."

Everyone had their suspicions, except me. "But Edmund was my friend. At the monastery, when he showed me the *huscarl* sword, I didn't realize it was the same one that had been hidden in the stables. He told me . . ."

"He told you it was my sword," Leofric said quietly.

"Yes. He said . . . he said you'd betrayed your brother."

And my parents, too. But such evil slander could never be repeated.

Leofric's face became a granite mask.

I flew to his side. "Forgive me. I should never have listened to anyone saying such things of you, I . . ."

He held up his hand to halt my torrent of words.

When he spoke, his voice was so low I could hardly hear him.

"But I did betray my brother."

28

She took the tax away.
——Tennyson [1842]: *Godiva*

Leofric paced the bower like a caged beast.

"I don't understand. What do you mean you betrayed Northman?" Surely it was impossible.

"You know that Thurkill the Tall was in Mercia."

"When you four brothers were outlaws in Sherwood Forest."

"What he did to my people, to my lands and cities, was an abomination. We did all we could from Sherwood to fight him. But we were losing, badly."

Clench-jawed, the muscles of his neck stood out as he swallowed.

My own hands clenched, I braced myself. The ride. Edmund's betrayal. They'd sapped my strength. But I had to find more. For Leofric.

"Northman decided to cede defeat. I was furious. I believed that if we held out we would have been able to eventually gather enough forces to overthrow Thurkill. It was only a matter of time, if we had the will."

He paused.

"You had the will," I prompted.

"Yes. I would never have surrendered, never have made any concessions. Northman was losing heart. But not I."

"We call him Leo for his lion's heart." Godwin had revealed.

"Not everyone has the heart strength you do," I said.

"No." His mouth twisted. "I discovered that, when I found out the terms that Northman was going to make with the Danes. Northman would be returned to power, but Mercia would be under the Dane law. North refused to acknowledge that this would leave him a ruler in name only, a puppet of King Canute. Worse was the fact that our way of life and law, the Saxon way, would be lost."

"Surely that's what you were fighting for," I said with passion.

"You understand that." His mouth curled into a bitter smile. "To my shame, Northman did not."

The fire crackled as he tossed another log onto it. In silence, we watched the flames leap high.

"We fought," Leofric said at last, his face shadowed. "He had made arrangements to meet Thurkill in a ley not far from Sherwood. I refused to go. Northman begged me to accompany him, to ride out together, brothers in arms. But I would not. I didn't want peace with the Danes on such terms. I went deeper into the forest. Many of our men came with me, including Acwell, and Edwin and Godwin, though they were only boys."

Another leap of the flame before he could talk.

"It was a Danish trap," he said, anguished. "There was to be no truce. Northman was beheaded in a clearing by Thurkill's axe."

"This axe killed your brother." Thurkill had jeered.

"How is this your fault?"

"Don't you understand? If I had been there, if I had stood by him, ridden out with him as he begged me to, he would never have been killed. He wasn't just my brother, he was my lord. What good was my word as a Saxon, if I could not even obey our most valued principle, that a lord's command must be followed? No matter whether I agreed with Northman, I should have honored that."

His tortured tone made me wince. So heart sore. Grief- and guilt-stricken. There was no way of knowing if Leofric could have saved Northman or whether he too would have been killed. In his mind, it was his fault and his alone. But I had to draw out the bramble thorn that pained him, as if from Ebur's hoof. Only then could the pain be cured.

I had to bring healing to my husband's battle-scarred heart. If I could.

"Then what happened?"

"When I discovered what had happened to Northman, what the Danes had done, it was as if a fire burned within me. I had to avenge him. From deep within Sherwood, we used daring tactics we never had before, and they worked. Raid, ambushes, skirmishes, cutting off supplies, these became our mark, in preference to open battle. We wore them down. The power of Thurkill and his Danish forces began to lose its stranglehold, and it became clear that the men of Mercia would never submit willingly to Danish rule."

"So you won." Pride in him thrilled through me.

"Canute realized that the unrest and fighting in Mercia could go on for years. He arranged to meet with me, though I took no chances after what had happened to Northman. He offered to make me Earl of Mercia, if I would align with him. My condition was that we wouldn't buckle under the Dane law, but remain Saxon. He agreed.

We respected each other. I told you the story of the sycophants who surround him, who believed he could quell the waves. He despised such false flattery. He discerned I would never surrender. But I'll not blindly do his bidding. I'm no *huscarl*. I leave that to men like Edmund."

"There aren't many men like you."

"Now you're flattering me," he said wryly. "For the sake of Mercia, I was glad to have Canute's respect, but the truth was—I'd already lost respect for myself."

My voice as soft as a stroke of Ebur's mane. "You're too harsh on yourself. You were young. It was impossible to anticipate what happened to Northman."

"That's not what the rumormongers began to say. It was probably started by the Danes. Soon enough, the idea was abroad that I wanted power so much that I traded Northman's life for my earldom." He moved toward me. "But you've heard this already. And you believed it."

I bit my lip.

If only I could tell him I'd never experienced that moment of doubt at the Evesham monastery. That dreadful moment when I wondered if Edmund was telling me the truth, that Leofric was a *huscarl* who had played a hand in his own brother's assassination and the death of my parents. That seed of doubt had been planted in only seconds. Yet honesty forbade my denying its existence or the damage its tangled roots had done.

"It's all right." Leofric said gently. But he drew away ever so slightly. "I understand why you doubted me. I didn't show trust in you. Why should I have expected you to show trust in me?"

"I ought never to have doubted you. I'll always regret it."

"We'll both have our regrets. The two-sided sword belonged

to Edmund as you now know. The *huscarls* are double agents of a kind. The dual blade signifies that they believe themselves to serve both the Saxons and the Danes. But a dog can't serve two masters."

As I'd tried to love both Leofric and Edmund. Heart torn.

"At the monastery I saw Edmund with the *huscarl* sword." It had glinted in the moonlight, like his smile. "Even then I didn't suspect him."

"At the monastery. Ah, yes."

So Acwell had seen us. "You knew."

Leofric nodded.

"But why didn't you tell me your suspicions? Why didn't you trust me?"

He was on his feet. A stride away. His strategy to play for time. His back to me as he stared out of the window.

"I thought you were in love with Edmund," Leofric said. He spun around. "You've bared yourself. Now I must do the same."

Leofric's cloak billowed as he came and seized my hands. "I didn't come here to take your lands, Godiva. Coventry is indeed a jewel." His eyes as brilliant as a kingfisher's wing reflected on water. "But the jewel I sought was never Coventry."

The life in his eyes. In Leofric, who so carefully guarded his emotions.

"At the Witan your father spoke of you. He spoke of your beauty, your intelligence, your courage. He told me Coventry would one day belong to you, his daughter, and that he was prouder of leaving it to you than to any son."

I gulped back a sob.

"I also met Edmund at the Witan. He made it clear you'd long been intended for him, that yours was a match arranged when you were both children. He said he planned to marry you with Lord Radulf's blessing."

"That isn't true! I wasn't promised to him. It's my Saxon right as a noblewoman to choose my own husband."

"So you reminded me." One of his dry smiles. "When I went back to Mercia after the Witan I prepared to come to Coventry."

"You came to warn my father of Thurkill the Tall."

"And to stop Edmund. When I arrived here to hear that your parents had already been killed—I felt responsible. I'd come too late. I would have spared you any pain. But Thurkill's plans weren't my only reason for coming to Coventry. Thurkill the Tall at your borders. Edmund in your confidence. Menace all around you. I've been trying to protect you, but you haven't made it easy for me."

I tried to speak. No words.

"I'm a warrior. I don't lay down my arms easily." Leofric's tone grew husky. "I wanted to come and see the jewel of the Middle Lands for myself. But when I got here I realized how close Edmund was to you. I thought you aligned with him."

"You thought I was a *huscarl*?" How could he have thought such a thing?

"You're too much of a Saxon for that. I know that much about you. But I wasn't sure how much you might tell Edmund. You seemed very . . . attached to him."

Bindweed and hollen. It's dangerous.

My thoughts roamed back to when I'd discovered Leofric outside the stables after Edmund had asked me to go away with him. "I was never sure how much you knew."

"I knew your loyalty. And when you came home from the monastery—without your ring . . ."

His fist clenched my naked finger so hard I winced.

"I knew Edmund had been with you," he continued hoarsely. "Acwell informed me as soon as you came back from Evesham."

As I'd suspected.

"Leofric." I slipped my finger from his vicelike grip. "I don't know where the ring fell from my hand. We searched and searched. Believe me."

"I believed you found it unbearable to wear it, that you wanted Edmund all along. I thought you hated marrying me. You considered me too stern, too battle-scarred."

But I'd glimpsed the man beneath the battle-scars.

"We've been at cross purposes all this time. I thought you wanted to marry Elfreda."

Leofric's head reared. "Elfreda?"

"Godwin told me you intended to marry her."

"She was meant for Northman, never for me. We were close after he died," he conceded. "She and I both loved him; we shared the same loss. But she was a sister to me, nothing more."

"Godwin was full of her praises."

He startled me with a roar of laughter. "Of course Godwin was. He's been in love with her himself since he was a boy."

"I thought you were the one with regrets, that you were sorry you'd married me."

"I never regretted it for a single day. The pain of being near you, of making love to you, when your feelings didn't match mine. Intolerable." He gave another laugh; more hollow this time.

Then he sobered. "I, the great Saxon warrior, was afraid of laying myself bare. I knew you'd refuse to judge Edmund without evidence. So I went to Mercia to get more proof, but being away from you was even worse. When I journeyed back to Coventry to find you not here—it was the worst moment of my life. Coventry without you—

it wasn't to be borne. Then our argument over the tax. Your pledge to ride. I knew the risk I had to take."

He bowed his head.

A heart's breath.

He raised his river-blue gaze to merge with mine. "Better you ride naked and hate me forever than never ride again."

Hooves of wild horses. My heart thumped.

Courage.

He'd risked it all.

I had to risk it, too.

My courage wouldn't fail me, I prayed. No sinful pride to stay me. Not this time. Not now.

Into the depths of his eyes I dived.

"Leofric. While you were in Mercia, it was you I truly longed for. Each morning when I awoke, you were my first thought. Each night before I fell asleep, you were my last."

More courage.

Another wild beat.

Prancing. Dancing.

"I love you. Even as I rode through the street naked I loved you."

Across his face a sunrise burst. "Can this be true?"

"Didn't you realize? When you were gone . . . the days, the hours, the minutes passed so slowly. An eternity. I wanted you with me."

"And I wanted you. There's no other woman like you. When I watched you on your horse, cloaked only by your hair, never had I seen a woman more beautiful or more desirable. When you threw your arms to the sky, so strong, so brave, so free. And I used you as a lure."

My finger pressed his lips. "Hush. It's forgiven."

Disbelief. "How . . ."

"I need your forgiveness, too. I misjudged you."

Fripwebba.

Peace weaver.

"Forgiven." I vowed. "Today and forever."

"The jewel of Coventry. How could I have risked the people looking upon you?"

"They didn't look upon me. I'm still only yours to see."

His fingers tangled in my hair. "Your locks of mead saved you."

"You saved me."

With a twist, Leofric pulled me into his arms.

29

Unclad herself...
——Tennyson [1842]: *Godiva*

Leofric's lips found mine with a passion I never dreamed possible. The fire he'd ignited before became a mere candle flame. A white-hot blaze of bliss burned as his mouth came down on mine.

Returning his fierceness kiss for kiss, I ran my fingers through the mane of his beard, seeking more and more of him.

"*Godiva.*" He pushed my hair from my face. "From the moment I heard your name, you were always in my mind."

"It was the same for me when I heard your name. *Leofric.* Across time. Across place. It was my soul calling yours."

"I heard your soul call," he whispered. "I rode to Coventry to find you."

"But in the Forest of Arden. You walked away."

"Arden." A raw sigh. "I worshipped you in Arden."

As holy as a vow. He'd felt it, too.

Naked

"I thought you didn't want me. When I danced that night. Surely you knew I danced for you alone. And you left the hall." It had stung.

"Your whip. Your dance." He groaned. "My need to take you was too great. I wanted you, eagled on the high table."

Rippling desire followed his fingers as they pushed up the edge of my shift, trailing up my legs.

"After the honeymoon was over you didn't seem to desire me anymore," I murmured as molten heat filled my veins. "You'd done your duty."

"Duty." Beneath my shift his hand glided over the curves of my body. "You thought this was a duty."

"When you touched me in bed you never spoke to me. You didn't say a word."

"Not a word?"

Over my hips to cup my breasts, to torment their aching points. I bit my lip. "When I touched your naked body like this. You didn't guess what I wanted to say? I love you."

Down to my legs, between my thighs. I quivered. "And this. You didn't hear? I love you."

His fingers deep inside me. I could barely stand. "And this. When I touched you, tasted you. Sweet as mead. Sweet as honey. You didn't know? I love you."

The moan was mine now as he reached the place no other man had touched.

The body doesn't lie. Aine had told me.

The body hears.

The body knows.

And the body aches to sing.

Shuddering I fell against him. My legs, so long held strong, refused to hold me.

275

Onto the sheepskin. In front of the fire.

Leofric's hands in my hair. "From this day on, Coventry is yours alone. The love of your people is worth more than gold."

"You're Coventry to me," I whispered. "My land. My home."

I knelt.

Unbuckled.

Released.

Straining toward me. The scent of leather on his flesh.

My fingers caressing his skin. My lips a circle. My brand on him.

"*Godiva*." He groaned as I lifted my head.

"You'll never cut your hair again. Do you promise?"

"Yes."

"You'll dance for me. *Naked*."

"Yes."

"You'll stand on horseback. *Naked*."

"Yes."

"And you'll ride. *Naked*."

"Yes."

"Now."

My breath came shallow and fast.

My tunic.

Over my head.

A scarlet flash.

Gone.

My white shift.

My lashes fanned closed.

The scent of lavender.

Soft wings across my face.

Gone.

"Where is your belt?"

Naked

He found it. Seized it. Clasped it around my naked waist.

The metal burn on my skin. The molten heat. The beaked eagles below my navel, pointing to their target.

My hands. His clothes. Urgent. Tugging, tearing, untying.

His cloak. Vanished.

His tunic. Cast away.

All garments. Gone.

Territory revealed. Mapped by my kisses.

He pulled us down.

Speared me onto him.

And I rode.

Naked. Astride.

I rode.

Hard and fast.

I rode.

Into a frenzy. Into a lather.

I rode.

Into the fire blaze. My breasts tinted golden and rose.

Leofric's groan again, deeper this time, his mouth on their arrowed tips.

Arching my spine I tossed my hair into a mane. The tendrils chased down my back. In a surge of elation I lifted my arms into wings, my hair a banner unfurled.

I rode.

Until we became one.

"Godiva."

Reared up like a stallion he reached for me, rolled me under, to lay me gasping beneath him.

The belt ripped away.

"A daughter for Coventry. Tonight."

277

"A son for Mercia."

His lips.

My lips.

He was a river.

I drowned.

And drowned.

And drowned.

"Godiva."

Leofric's voice woke me.

I'd slept the sleep of the loved, the sheets scented with the secrets of our bodies.

My lashes fluttered open.

There he stood beside the bed, staring down at me. His blue eyes clear now, still and deep, a river after a storm.

He'd watched over me as I slept many times before, he'd admitted. As he would watch over me always.

"It's Edmund."

The linen clutched over my breasts, I sat up. The bower was warm, the fire still blazed. Leofric had added more than one log to it through the night as I watched the firelight caress his tanned skin.

"What is it?"

Leofric spared no mercy. It was not his way. "He's dead."

My head bowed.

Retribution. Swift.

"When did it happen?"

"During the night."

In the darkness. As I had slept.

Leofric's sword.

Acwell's axe.

Aine's curse.

His own hand.

Any of these may have killed Edmund. Any or none.

I would never ask.

I would never know.

"Leofric." I raised myself higher, my fingers winding the sheet. "I don't want this to come out."

Leofric heaved a sigh. "Loyalty?"

"Yes."

"You don't owe Edmund any loyalty, Godiva. Are you forgetting what he did to your parents? What he nearly did to you?"

But we'd grown up together, side by side. *Bindweed and hollen.*

"Loyalty to the boy," I said, "if not to the man."

And grief.

Grief for the boy. If not for the man.

He'd come to us more damaged than I'd ever guessed.

Leofric sighed again. "I wouldn't expect anything else of you."

My hands untwisted the linen. "How can it be done?"

"I'll think of something. My men will spread a tale. Much can be swallowed along with ale on a tavern bench."

"No one must know Edmund was a *huscarl.*"

"It's probably wise," Leofric admitted. "They're King Canute's secret force, after all. There's no point in angering him; it could cause trouble with the Danes. Trouble we don't need."

This was the earl speaking, the Saxon statesman. Who had won King Canute's respect.

"And what happened on the ride . . ."

Flint-fire blazed across his face. "Edmund's presence in Tomas the tanner's house won't be revealed. I can cover that, too, though he deserves a traitor's shame."

What had happened in Tomas the tanner's house?

"You can thank your husband for that. Ask him what happened. He broke my arm along with my bow." Edmund had spat at me.

I would never ask.

I would never know.

"Will Tomas stay quiet?" I wondered.

"Some men's silence is easily bought. Tomas the tanner is one of them, I expect."

Leofric wrapped a tendril of my hair around his finger. "It will be as you wish. No one will ever know."

30

Boring a little auger-hole in fear,
Peep'd——
*——*Tennyson [1842]: *Godiva*

Wilbert and Walburgha were waiting in the hall. Wilbert appeared shy but Walburgha had her usual, bright expression.

"Wilbert! Walburgha!"

My heart wanted to burst with gratitude as I held out my hands. At my time of need they hadn't forsaken me.

"How can I ever thank you for what you've done? I'm so grateful to all the townsfolk of Coventry."

Walburgha came forward, beaming. "As if we would look upon you, Lady Godiva. Not you. Never."

Tears smarted at her loyal words.

The people of Coventry.

My people. The right people.

They'd come at my bidding. To where Leofric and I stood by the dais, his wolfhounds beside us.

So I could hear what had happened.

So I could hear what was said in the town.

"But how did it come about? How did it happen that everyone went into their houses as I rode by?"

"Well, my lady," Walburgha grew cozy as she embarked on her story. "We weren't in the manor hall when you said you were going to do the ride through the main street, but we soon heard about it, didn't we, Wilbert?"

Wilbert nodded. "We soon heard about it."

"Yes, we heard about it," she carried on as if Wilbert hadn't spoken, "and we said: 'What's this? Our Lady Godiva to do the penitent's ride? That can't be. As if she's ever done anything wrong in her life to do a penitent's ride!'"

"Then we found out why you were doing it, my lady," Wilbert put in.

"That's right," Walburgha continued without seeming to take a breath. "We heard what you'd said in the hall. What Lord Leofric said. What a thing to ask of you! Not right, I said to myself, and to Wilbert, didn't I, Wilbert. 'Not right,' I said."

"That's right, Walburgha, not right, you did say that."

"Yes indeed. What a thing to ask a lady like you to do." She cast Lord Leofric a reproachful stare. "To ride through the streets in your all for nothing at your husband's bidding! Naked!"

So this was what would be said of my husband. When I was as much at fault. If only I had trusted Leofric instead of Edmund.

No! I refused to let my husband be maligned. I opened my mouth. To reveal the naked truth.

Leofric was a hero. He'd saved my life.

His hand clamped on my arm. A shake of his head.

My mouth closed.

"So I said, didn't I, Wilbert, get everyone in the town together quick." Her color mottled, Walburgha went on. "We haven't got much time. So we all got together in the tavern and I said: 'we're not having this.'"

"She did, she did," Wilbert intoned.

Walburgha threw Lord Leofric another hostile glance. The wolf-hound barked. She ignored it. "Don't know what they do up in Mercia, but here in Coventry, in the Middle Lands, we don't have Saxon ladies ride through the streets with no clothes on for all to see. Oh no. So then we decided not one of the townsfolk would watch you as you did ride."

What they'd done still both humbled and amazed me.

"I never imagined you'd do that for me."

"Well, my lady, what else could we do? Some said they would just stand on the street and try not to watch you, but I said, no, that wasn't good enough. We had to go into our houses and shut the doors. If you were going to do the ride for us, it was the least we could do for you. We love you, my lady, as we loved your parents before you, Lord Radulf and Lady Morwen, may their souls rest in peace."

Tears welled again at my parents' names.

"And let's not forget what you did for poor Wilbert on the battlefield. Would have had his throat cut by a Dane, wouldn't you, Wilbert, if it wasn't for the Lady Godiva?"

"Slit from ear to ear, I expect, if you hadn't come along and fought that Dane, my lady. From ear to ear."

"That's right," said Walburgha. "We know how much we owe you, my lady, and we're not the only ones. There's many others in the town who feel just the same. We all agreed on it. As it started to get near twelve o'clock, when you said you would ride, we all went inside our houses. Whole place closed up, tight as a drum. Heard your horse, as you went by though, didn't we, Wilbert?"

Wilbert mumbled a reply.

"I said: 'that's Lady Godiva's horse.' We waited until well after the time you had gone, just in case, and then we all came out."

"Thank you."

"No need for thanks, no need at all. Couldn't do naught else, could we?"

Tutting toward Leofric.

"It's to our shame that a Coventry man did try to see you," Wilbert said.

Instinctively, my hands flew to clutch my braid. Had the news got out? Had Leofric's men done their work on the mead-bench?

"Who was it?" I managed to ask.

"Tomas the tanner," Wilbert replied. "He swore he wouldn't, along with the rest of us. But he looked out his window as you passed by. Of all the men of Coventry, he was the only one."

I released my braid. Exhaled.

"To think of it, my lady!" Walburgha cried. "He tried to peep! That Tom! That peeping Tom! But he got what he deserved," she added with relish.

"Peeping Tom? What happened?"

"It's the strangest tale," Leofric said. To my amazement I realized he'd been trying to hold back a smile during the telling of Walburgha's story. There was the slight crease in his cheek I'd noticed before, as though a dimple of laughter had once lived there. "This man, Tomas tanner, was the only one not to keep to the vow your people of Coventry made."

"The shame of it!" Walburgha interjected.

"He, too, went into his house, like the other townsfolk, I understand." Leofric continued. "But he didn't look away as you passed. Instead, he tried to look on upon you."

"Oh! When I passed Tomas the tanner's house, I had the oddest feeling that there was someone looking. I wasn't sure."

The crease in Leofric's cheek disappeared as his hand went to his hilt. "He tried to see you from his window."

Gently I placed my hand on his arm, saw his hammer fist uncurl.

"Sly, that Tom. But he got his comeuppance!" Walburgha spoke with great satisfaction.

Tomas the tanner had been in Edmund's pay for some time, it had been revealed. Those feaberry eyes, always watching. Spying.

"Hand of God," inserted Wilbert dolefully.

"Hand of God?" Bewildered now, I turned from one to the other.

"There's more to tell," Leofric said. "When Tomas tried to peep as you rode past, he was blinded."

"Blinded!"

"Cursed, he was! Cursed!" exclaimed Walburgha.

"That's right. He's blind. Can't see a thing," Wilbert confirmed.

"A piece of sharp wood, I think, from a hole he made," Leofric explained.

"Poor Tomas! Blind!" But it could have been worse for him. Edmund had no more use for Tomas the tanner, Leofric had said. Lying in his house, bleeding. At least he was alive.

"Poor Tomas? After what he did? How can you say that, my lady? You always were so good and kind, I suppose. But I don't feel sorry for him." Walburgha waggled her finger. "Not at all."

"Some of the folk in the town are wondering if you are going to punish him for having tried to look upon you," Wilbert put in.

"No, no!" I exclaimed. "God's justice has been done. I won't punish him more than an eye for an eye."

Walburgha pursed her mouth and sucked noisily through her teeth. "Suppose that's the right thing to do. Suppose so."

"An eye for an eye, that's what the Bible stories say, Lady Godiva." A worried expression came over Wilbert's face. "There's something else we want to ask. The tax, Lord Leofric. Can you tell us? There are many in the town and the farms that are still worried about getting through the hungry month. The grain is running out. Is the tax still to be set at the same amount as Mercia's? So much higher than ours here in the Middle Lands? "

"We'll starve if it is!" Walburgha put in dramatically.

"There will be no one who starves in Coventry, as long as Lady Godiva lives," Leofric said. "The tax is lifted. It will be as Lady Godiva promised."

We had discussed it. But in the future, we would make our laws together, for the good of Mercia and the Middle Lands. Leofric and I stood together now. My lands were his lands. His lands were mine. I would care for Leofric's people as I did for my own. Our wealth, our stores, would be shared. No child would starve in the Middle Lands. Or in Mercia.

"Is that for certain? The tax is no more?" Undaunted, Walburgha faced Leofric squarely, her hands on her hips, and her chin stuck out.

The crease deepened in his cheek. "We should have sent you into battle against Thurkill the Tall, Walburgha. You're quite a weapon."

I smiled. "You have Lord Leofric's word and mine."

Walburgha gave a nod, though she still looked suspicious.

Wilbert stepped forward, his hand outstretched. "There's more, my lady. We believe this is yours."

The ruby glistened cherry red in the sunlight.

Naked

"My ring! I thought it lost forever. Where did you get it, Wilbert?"

"From the man who stole it from you. Tomas the tanner."

"Tomas?" He had been near me, I recalled, in the crush of townspeople in the hall. "It must have been at the *althing*."

"It seems he picked it up," Leofric said blandly.

His tone made me look at him sharply. Had Tomas the tanner had it? Or had Edmund?

"What will you do to punish Tomas?" Walburgha asked with relish. "Will you have him face the Saxon law for theft?"

By our law he would lose a limb. *No.* "This man has been already been avenged, by God."

Once more Walburgha appeared disappointed. "Well he got what he deserved, I suppose. We told him not to look upon you. We're proud of you in Coventry, my lady, and of what you did for us. We'll be telling our children and our children's children for many years to come."

Leofric smiled. My heart leapt again as I slipped the ring onto my finger.

It would be fitted this time.

"Aye, we'll always remember it." Wilbert bowed. "Never will it be forgotten: Lady Godiva's ride."

Light glinted through the bower window. Dawn had come, rose gold on the rushes, gilding the walls, hallowing us where we lay.

Leofric chuckled. The rumble of his laugh was still new to me. I would hear it more, I vowed. See the dent deepen in his cheek. Laughter would cast out grief in our home. There would be feasting, singing, dancing. Family. Friends.

Hall-joy would reign once more.

"What is it, my lord?"

We had been awake all night. The languor that is better than sleep contented me as I nestled beside him.

"It's what Wilbert said to us. I think he may be right. I doubt your naked ride for the people of Coventry will ever be forgotten. It will probably be spoken of in a thousand years."

"In a thousand years? That isn't possible."

"Your fame will grow, as will mine of a different kind. You'll be the heroine of the tale, as you deserve to be." He stroked my hair. "I'll be the villain, so ignoble, so cruel to his wife."

"There's still time," I said, "For us to set the story straight."

"It's as it must be. The cloth is woven, not to be unraveled. For the sake of peace."

"Perhaps the truth will come out one day." Rolling over, I rested my chin on his chest and gazed up at him, at the line of his jaw, the curve of his mouth. The beard was gone now to reveal the face I loved. "Even if it takes a thousand years."

Leofric smiled down at me. "Is that so, my Lady Godiva?"

"Truth is like love," I said. "It always triumphs in the end."

Epilogue

And built herself an everlasting name.
——Tennyson [1842]: *Godiva*

"How did you know, Aine?"

"I just knew, my lady." She snapped off a sprig of wintergreen. "Now no more questions. You need to get plenty of rest."

I sat in pale sunshine in the plant yard. I felt more in tune with the Yuletide season than ever before.

Here so many times I had sat dreaming, hoping, and wondering. *Leofric.*

My mind roved to when I first met him, when he had ridden into Coventry alone on Wyrd, his black stallion.

Wyrd. *Fate.* That is what it had been. In my recollection I could picture every movement—the lift of his helmet in a single, easy movement, and that first piercing glance, making me shiver.

Aine had been right, after all. The body doesn't lie. It sings the heart's song, even when the mind doesn't know the gleeman's verse.

Clouds floated in the blue sky like wisps of spun wool. True love wasn't what I expected it to be. I knew now true love could withstand anger, disappointment, and misunderstanding. The best sort of love came when forgiveness had already been granted.

"May I ask you just one more question, Aine?"

"Of course, my lady." Wiping her brow, she laid down her basket.

"Did you suspect that Lord Leofric had feelings for me?"

"Suspect?" Aine gave a kind of guffaw. "I didn't suspect anything. I knew it. It was only the pair of you who didn't know how you felt about each other. Obvious to everyone else. There is none so blind as those who are in love but those around them see exactly what is going on."

I smiled. "I knew how I felt, but I wasn't sure how he felt."

"Your love is deep. When love is that deep and that strong, the cost of telling it is greater. The risk of it not being requited can seem too hard to bear."

"That's how it seemed to me," I confessed.

"I knew it. I knew how much you loved him, right from the start, perhaps even before you did. And I could see what his feelings for you were, plain as day. After you'd lost your parents, the risk of loving and not receiving love in return might have seemed too much. But loving the way you and Lord Leofric love each other—it's what makes life worthwhile, in the end. Your mother would rejoice to see you. Here's Lord Leofric now, my lady."

My heart leapt as he strode into the plant yard. Would it always be that way? Would I always know that skip of joy when he came to me?

He placed his hand on my belly. "How is our warrior daughter today?"

"Very active, my lord," I laughed. "So active I think it's a son."

He laughed, too. "If so active, then it's our daughter for certain."

Leaning down, he kissed me lightly on the lips, with a passion that had not altered in my pregnancy. "In Coventry, there'll be great rejoicing, no matter whether a boy or a girl."

Son or daughter.

"Now come. It's time."

"You've been so secretive! There is no forcing you to reveal anything once you've set your mind to it."

"Ah, my stubbornness! My famous fault. I hope it will be worthwhile, in this case."

Headstrong. Willful. Defiant. I had a few faults of my own. "Won't you tell me where we're going?"

Leofric chuckled. "It isn't far. Come."

In the courtyard, Leofric and one of the serving boys helped me onto Ebur's broad back. Fur-clad, instead of astride, I sat with my legs on one side.

Side-saddled. But only for a while. Soon I would be back in my leathers. To ride to Arden. With Leofric.

Clucking like a hen with a chick, Aine stood near. "My lady is safe up there?"

"Lady Godiva will come to no harm," Leofric replied.

Holding Ebur's reins with one hand, I settled the other protectively on my rounded belly. "All is well, Aine."

Leofric took the reins. "I'll lead you."

We set off at a gentle pace, out of the manor grounds and into the main street of Coventry. I gave a cry of pleasure. The streets were lined with the townsfolk, holding greenery and calling my name.

"God's greeting, my lady!"

"Blessings to our lord and lady!"

At the end of the main street, outside the church we came to a halt.

Tethering Ebur to the lych-gate, I slid off and into Leofric's waiting arms.

For a moment he held me.

"Close your eyes."

"Leofric . . ." But I obeyed.

His arms a cloak, my lids shut tight, my feet followed the well-trod pilgrimage to the church. They knew the way.

"Open them now." We were at the end of the church path, in front of the wooden door. On the step was a large stone, pale, square, smooth.

"What is it?"

Leofric's cheek creased. Deep. "You can't tell?"

My braid flew as I turned my head from side to side.

"It's a foundation stone."

Realization started to dawn.

"Have you guessed? We're building a new stone church for Coventry, just as your parents always dreamed of."

Brother Aefic came up, beaming. "The Lord Leofric has been most generous. You know of course, my child, of our custom to bring a holy relic for each church or abbey we build."

I nodded.

"That's why we were unable to begin sooner," Leofric explained. "Brother Aefic sent to Rome for this relic of Mary, the mother of Jesus."

The monk unwrapped a hammered, silver box from a piece of fine-spun wool. "It is said that this was a lock of her hair."

Leofric touched my braids. "The same color as yours."

Naked

"This is a fitting relic, my lady, for you have acted as a mother to all your people." Brother Aefic bowed to me.

Lady. Loaf giver. My sacred task.

"This church will be known as St. Mary's," Leofric said.

Honor to the great mother. And to my mother. She had honored St. Mary, too. "It's the perfect name."

"Lord Leofric has also dedicated more lands to us so our monastery at Evesham will grow and one day be a fine abbey." Brother Aefic rubbed his hands together.

My fingers trembled as I put them to my cheeks. My ruby ring glowed. For a moment I was overcome. "This is what my parents always dreamed for Coventry."

"I could have built you a hall made of stone, a castle fit for a queen," Leofric said. "And one day, I will. But first, I knew I had to build this church. Well I know your happiness comes from the happiness of your people."

"So dreams do come true," I whispered.

"They do." Leofric placed his hands on my rounded belly. "You're my dream, Godiva."

Coventry, Engla-lond, 1024 *AD.*

Hail Elfreda,

God's greetings to you, dearest sister, and to our brother Godwin. Writing these words fills my heart with joy for now you are wed we are sisters indeed. How I wish we could have traveled to Mercia to witness your troth, and the occasion of such great happiness and celebration. May you find with Godwin all the happiness Leofric and I share together. Our happiness is doubled now, for at last, after many prayers, I have given birth to a son, whom we have called Elfgar. In thanksgiving, to the new stone church of St. Mary's we have built in Coventry I have bestowed a silver necklace Leofric gifted me in honor of Our Lady, mother of us all. I was afeared he would not like me doing so, but Leofric has said I can give all my jewels to the church if I have a mind to, so joyous is he at our son's arrival.

In not too long, when the seasons change, we will travel to see you. When I am able, I have vowed to bring our child north to Mercia, to see the might of its great cities, and to breathe the air of his ancestors in the forests of Sherwood. Yet it seems right that our babe was born in my home, here in the Middle Lands. The land of my people, the land of my cyn. Now, and always, the land of my love.

Godiva of Coventry

Godiva

Alfred, Lord Tennyson [1842]

I waited for the train at Coventry;
I hung with grooms and porters on the bridge,
To watch the three tall spires; and there I shaped
The city's ancient legend into this:

Not only we, the latest seed of Time,
New men, that in the flying of a wheel
Cry down the past, not only we, that prate
Of rights and wrongs, have loved the people well,
And loathed to see them overtax'd; but she
Did more, and underwent, and overcame,
The woman of a thousand summers back,
Godiva, wife to that grim Earl, who ruled
In Coventry: for when he laid a tax
Upon his town, and all the mothers brought
Their children, clamoring, "If we pay, we starve!"
She sought her lord, and found him, where he strode
About the hall, among his dogs, alone,
His beard a foot before him and his hair
A yard behind. She told him of their tears,
And pray'd him, "If they pay this tax, they starve."
Whereat he stared, replying, half-amazed,
"You would not let your little finger ache
For such as these?"—"But I would die," said she.
He laugh'd, and swore by Peter and by Paul;

Then fillip'd at the diamond in her ear;
"Oh ay, ay, ay, you talk!"—"Alas!" she said,
"But prove me what I would not do."
And from a heart as rough as Esau's hand,
He answer'd, "Ride you naked thro' the town,
And I repeal it;" and nodding, as in scorn,
He parted, with great strides among his dogs.

So left alone, the passions of her mind,
As winds from all the compass shift and blow,
Made war upon each other for an hour,
Till pity won. She sent a herald forth,
And bade him cry, with sound of trumpet, all
The hard condition; but that she would loose
The people: therefore, as they loved her well,
From then till noon no foot should pace the street,
No eye look down, she passing; but that all
Should keep within, door shut, and window barr'd.

Then fled she to her inmost bower, and there
Unclasp'd the wedded eagles of her belt,
The grim Earl's gift; but ever at a breath
She linger'd, looking like a summer moon
Half-dipt in cloud: anon she shook her head,
And shower'd the rippled ringlets to her knee;
Unclad herself in haste; adown the stair
Stole on; and, like a creeping sunbeam, slid
From pillar unto pillar, until she reach'd
The Gateway, there she found her palfrey trapt
In purple blazon'd with armorial gold.

Naked

Then she rode forth, clothed on with chastity:
The deep air listen'd round her as she rode,
And all the low wind hardly breathed for fear.
The little wide-mouth'd heads upon the spout
    Had cunning eyes to see: the barking cur
Made her cheek flame; her palfrey's foot-fall shot
Light horrors thro' her pulses; the blind walls
Were full of chinks and holes; and overhead
Fantastic gables, crowding, stared: but she
Not less thro' all bore up, till, last, she saw
The white-flower'd elder-thicket from the field,
Gleam thro' the Gothic archway in the wall.

Then she rode back, clothed on with chastity;
And one low churl, compact of thankless earth,
The fatal byword of all years to come,
    Boring a little auger-hole in fear,
Peep'd—but his eyes, before they had their will,
    Were shrivel'd into darkness in his head,
And dropt before him. So the Powers, who wait
    On noble deeds, cancell'd a sense misused;
And she, that knew not, pass'd: and all at once,
With twelve great shocks of sound, the shameless noon
Was clash'd and hammer'd from a hundred towers,
    One after one: but even then she gain'd
Her bower; whence reissuing, robed and crown'd,
    To meet her lord, she took the tax away
    And built herself an everlasting name.

Acknowledgments

My thanks to editor, Brenda Copeland, for giving me a publishing home in the United States; to assistant editor, Laura Chasen, for her calm efficiency; and to everyone at St. Martin's Press in the Flatiron Building (surely the most magical building in New York). To my wise and wonderful U.S. agent, Joelle Delbourgo, I know just how lucky I am to have you. Jenny Schwartz, my critique partner, a woman of integrity who knows how to spot a villain—this book would never have been finished without you. The Wordwrights group, Janet Woods, Deb Bennetto, Karen Saayman, Anne Summers, and Carol Hoggart, who saw the manuscript in various stages of undress, thank you for your feedback, even when it was tough love. Thanks to historical fiction author, Michelle Diener, who generously shared her publishing knowledge; Romance Writers of Australia and the Hearts'n'Wined gang in Western Australia, who support each other's

Acknowledgments

work with affection. Pamela Weatherill, dear friend and social media queen bee of the buzz, my love and thanks. Tracey Stephens, for her research assistance and good cheer. Marina Gillam Geldsetzer and Anne Symes in England, Pearl Proud, Josephine Griffiths, Yonna Sunderland, and Lekkie Hopkins in Australia, your friendship got me through the threadbare patches. My gratitude to Vesma, who keeps the home fires burning and makes my writing life possible. Within my large extended family (too numerous to mention!) special appreciation to my sister, Catherine Marinceu, for her Web site help; my niece, Madeleine Lester, for social media advice; and my nephews, Lachlan and Jeremy, who encouraged me through the final draft and advised me to "watch the cricket" and "eat peanut butter sandwiches" when I was done. Finally, my love to those who lived with Godiva and Leofric wandering around the house, my daughter, Jessica, who bears a startling resemblance to the girl on the cover; and my husband, James, my own English hero: I was poor, and had only my dreams . . . you didn't just tread softly; you laid down your cloak.

Attributions

In this novel I have utilized an idiosyncratic poetic translation of *Beowulf*, lines 1–11, by Cheryl Hazama (2007, California State University) available at http://www.csun.edu/~ceh24682/beowulf.html.

My thanks to Professor Scott Kleinman at California State University for his advice regarding this translation. He points out that "Awesome Earl" in line six corresponds to "egsode eorl" in the original, and "egsode" is a verb (literally, "awed"). For my purposes, "awesome" proved irresistible. Thank you, Cheryl Hazama. My thanks also to my fellow author, Carol Hoggart, for delving among dusty library shelves to find other versions.

I have included two Anglo-Saxon riddles, numbers 25 and 54 from the *Exeter Book of Riddles* (still hilarious after a millennium). The translations from Old English were kindly provided by Dr. Megan Cavell and Dr. Matthias Ammon. If you enjoyed these riddles do visit their "Riddle Ages" Web site at http://theriddleages.wordpress.com/.

Further Reading

Over the centuries, there have been many versions of the Godiva legend (but that's another story). I have utilized both primary and secondary historical sources. From my shelves, *inter alia*, I highly recommend:

Donoghue, Daniel. (2003). *Lady Godiva: A Literary History of the Legend*. Oxford: Blackwell. An inspiring nonfiction sourcebook about Godiva including where to see paintings and sculptures.

Giles, J.A. (Trans.) (1849). *Roger of Wendover's Flowers of History, Comprising the history of England from the descent of the Saxons to A.D. 1235; formerly ascribed to Matthew Paris*. London: Bohn's Antiquarian Library. A medieval source of the Godiva tale. [e-version].

Heaney, Seamus. (1999). *Beowulf*. London: Faber. An award-winning translation of the ancient poem.

Lacey, Robert, and Danziger, Danny. (1999). *The Year 1000: What Life Was Like in the First Millennium*. London and New York: Little, Brown and Company. An accessible month-by-month guide to the Anglo-Saxon year.

Swanton, Michael. (Ed. and Trans.) (1996). *The Anglo-Saxon Chronicle*. London: J.M. Dent. The old text that is central to our knowledge of English history.

- Historical Godiva http://www.octavia.net/books/godgyfu/historicalgodiva.htm
- Coventry and Warwickshire http://www.visitcoventryandwarwickshire.co.uk/
- Historic Coventry http://www.historiccoventry.co.uk/
- Godiva Sisters/Tours http://www.godivainspires.co.uk/